Uncharted

Desires

by

Leatrus Iversen

Editor: Joy Hammond Nelson
Graphic Designer: Brittani Williams at www.tspubcreative.com

ISBN-10: 069231587X
ISBN-13: 978-0692315873

Table of Contents

ACKNOWLEDGMENTS

I would like to give all praise and glory to the Lord above for giving me the wisdom and talent to finish this novel. I thank Him for the gift of creativity and for the virtue of patience.

I would like to thank my mother Anne Iversen for encouraging me to be the strong woman I am today.

I would like to thank my children Uniqua and Don for putting up with my mood swings and countless hours of working on this project. Everything I do, I do for you. I love you guys so much.

I would like to thank my sister Author Inger Iversen for her love and support throughout my journey. You have truly been my inspiration and I love you dearly.

I would like to give a special thanks to Author Davian Clifton for his encouragement, motivation, and support during the writing of this novel. You believed in me when I didn't believe in myself. I thank you.

Special thanks to Joy Hammond Nelson and Author Brittani Williams and to the many different authors that showed me support along my journey.

CHAPTER ONE

Lydia laid in bed staring at her alarm clock. *It's almost six,* she thought. She focused her attention to the ceiling fan whirling around wishing he would hurry up.

"I'm almost there baby…Almost…YEAH!" he yelled out as his body shivered then collapsed beside her trying to catch his breath. "I love you babes," Jackson sighed quietly.

"Love you too," Lydia replied as she rolled her eyes. She hated when her boyfriend spent the night. He always wanted morning sex and all she wanted was to sleep until the menacing sound of the alarm clock jolted her awake.

"I'm gonna take a quick shower and go babe, I've got to meet Earl and Tommy at the gym by seven." He looked at her and gently kissed her on the forehead then went into the bathroom. Jackson adored Lydia. They met three years earlier at the café that was located just outside of her job. He loved how sweet and innocent she appeared to be. She wasn't like the other females he had dated in the past. They were very demanding and extremely vocal. Jackson loved the fact that Lydia allowed him to be the man in the relationship; he enjoyed making all the decisions and she wouldn't voice her opinion at all. She would meekly go along with whatever he decided for them to do and he loved that. After she heard the shower going, she jumped up and ran into the half bath located off the kitchen. She aggressively grabbed for the white tea and lilac scented soap and her washcloth and began to wash up. Jackson's smell bothered her, she hated for it to linger on her skin after they made love.

She knew she loved Jackson, they had been together for three years, but their mundane relationship was taking a toll on her. She was bored out of her mind. With Jackson, it was always the same meals, the same television shows, and the same sexual positions. Whenever she bought up something new, he would shoot down the idea or they would get into a heated argument. Eventually, she just gave up and kept her mouth shut, just the way Jackson liked it. Her whole life was predictable. She wanted more but how to achieve that was the real dilemma.

There's gotta be more than this, Lydia thought as she slipped her robe back on and went to start the coffee.

Lydia usually took a cab to the collection agency where she worked but today her neighbor and good friend Francesca gave her a ride. "I saw Jackson leave girl," Francesca said with a devilish grin. "No wonder you look so radiant this morning!" she snickered slapping Lydia's leg.

"Yeah I'm ready to start my day," Lydia responded nonchalantly.

Francesca didn't know that Lydia's "radiant" look was the result of her vigorously scrubbing her face after her morning session with Jackson. Lydia Morrell was a natural Latina beauty; her makeup was always perfect, what little she wore and she dressed very conservatively and rarely wore heels. She felt that at 5'7" she had more than enough height for her 130-pound frame. Her long brown wavy hair fell just past her shoulders and her honey brown eyes always seemed to draw attention.

"I am so tired of this place!" she complained as she swung open the glass door that separated her from the outside world. She walked down the long brightly lit hallway. "I feel like I'm walking the green mile."

She rounded the corner to her cubicle, sat down, and put her purse in the usual spot, the bottom file-cabinet drawer. She was glad the night cleaning lady didn't disturb her desk. She logged into her computer and the usual message popped up, "Good Morning Lydia Morrell." She put on her headset, pushed enter on the keyboard and began her work as a collector for American Express.

"Good morning Ms. Morrell!" Michael sang very loudly. "I took the liberty of bringing you your chai tea…thank you Michael," he said before Lydia could say it.

"Michael, what do you do every morning that keeps you in a great mood all day?" she inquired.

Michael was 6'2", lean, tan, and very clean-shaven. His hair was cut short on the sides and back and a little spikey on the top. His light brown hair supported his blond highlights perfectly. His pants were always creased and dress shirt starched and pressed. His cologne wafted over the cubicles like a soft spring breeze. Michael was filled with charisma.

"I probably do the same thing you do in the morning that gives you that glow," Michael grinned. "I get a good workout with some morning wood!" Michael laughed. "You know Robert won't let me out the front door until he has his way with me honey."

Lydia laughed at Michael's comment. She would love to have some morning wood that sent her to work skipping but what she was getting just sent her to work tired and frustrated. She thanked him for the tea and Michael glided down the hall to his cubicle. The morning went by quickly and it was almost time for lunch. Lydia generally ate her lunch at her desk while she listened to the office gossip. Apparently, the head director of the Visa collection project was sleeping with one of the married collectors from the First Premier Bank project and now she was pregnant.

Lydia thought that wasn't the kind of excitement she wanted in her life but it was interesting. She could hear Michael telling Shirley, another American Express collector, about his hot and raunchy night with Robert. Michael didn't mind telling people about his sex life. Apparently last night's adventure included warming massage oil and a twelve-inch toy. The conversation made Lydia cringe a little. Shirley slowly bit into her sandwich and eagerly listened.

"Another lonely lunch Lydia?" Katrina smirked, "I just had lunch at the new bistro down the street compliments of the chef. He really has a thing for me.

Anyway enjoy your...uh...Lean Cuisine." Katrina rolled her eyes, gave Lydia a dismissive wave, and walked off.

Katrina Stewart was 5'6", curvy and statuesque with chin length naturally curly red hair. She dressed everyday as if she was going out on a night on the town. She wore all the latest fashions, designer jewelry, and very expensive perfume. She flirted with most of the men in the office. She actually had the audacity to flirt with Jackson one day when he came to pick up Lydia after work.

God I can't stand her but I would give anything to be like her, Lydia pondered.

As she fell into a daydream, someone placed a piece of paper on her desk and quickly walked away. She was in a full daydream and didn't have time to look up to see who it was. She looked at the memo. COME ONE; COME ALL TO THE COMPANY'S NEW YEARS EVE PARTY! Lydia stared at the paper as if it smelled offensive. *That time of year again? Great,* she thought as she threw her finished lunch away and went back to work.

Home. The only real safe haven in Lydia's life was her small one bedroom, one and a half bath apartment. She decorated the plain white walls with pictures of brightly colored flowers, landscape scenes of places far away and exotic birds. She had an ordinary cream colored leather living room set complete with two glass end tables and a glass coffee table and a cozy dark cherry wood dining room set just big enough for two. She loved her hardwood floors even though they were very worn and uninviting.

Her bedroom consisted of a full sized bed draped in a black and white flowered down comforter and several black and white tasseled decorative pillows. A simple white painted nightstand and dresser kept the small dim room company. She had a small green sitting chair with a high back that sat in front of her bedroom window. She agreed that it was out of place but she loved her chair. She found it outside one day by the trash and decided to shampoo the upholstery and claim it as hers. She would sit in her chair curled up under her favorite blanket and read or watch the people at the park that was located across the street. It was her favorite piece of furniture.

"I need a hot bath," she noted before she pulled back the purple and pink flowered shower curtain and shuddered. Melted soap and pubic hair lined the bottom of the tub. "Ugh!" she shouted as she reached for the bleach cleaner and sponge. She really hated when Jackson took a shower in her bathroom. She tossed the full bar of soap in the trash and proceeded to scrub the tub with all her might. She rinsed the pubes down until she was satisfied they were all gone. She ran a tub of water, poured in her favorite lavender vanilla bubble bath, and eased down to let her muscles and body relax. Lydia ran her fingers over her arms and up her neck. She rubbed her breasts and gently squeezed her nipples.

She thought about Katrina and how her breasts filled her blouse. With that thought, her nipples stood even more erect. She slid her hands underneath the water and down her thighs, gently caressing her inner thigh. She gently touched her vagina and thought that maybe she should shave in case Jackson showed up unannounced, which he was known to do. She decided against it and slowly separated her lips and began to do what she did almost every night—masturbate to her own vivid sexual thoughts.

After her bath, she made a simple garden salad and a cup of chai tea for dinner. She drifted off in thought with each bite; the sound of the neighbors arguing broke her out of her spell. She looked at the clock; it read eleven p.m. If Jackson hadn't shown up by now then he wasn't coming. "Thank God" she said aloud, she could actually sleep until six a.m. without the worry of him fondling her while she slept. Deep down she felt bad for having such ill feelings towards the man she loved but her frustration and boredom with their relationship was beginning to consume her. Lydia climbed into bed and smiled, she was content with sleeping alone tonight. She pulled the covers over her head and drifted off with random thoughts still lingering in her mind.

CHAPTER TWO

Everyone in the office was excited about the New Year's Eve party except Lydia. Mr. Frasier, her short balding supervisor, was walking around handing out vouchers for two free drinks at the party. "Lydia," his deep voice boomed, "here is your voucher hun!" Lydia looked at it as if it was toxic and slid in into her desk. "You are coming aren't you?"

Lydia looked uncomfortable. "I don't know, I...I haven't decided." She knew she had no intention on attending the party but Mr. Frasier looked so disappointed.

"Lydia we will have door prizes, raffles and great music and food! You have to attend! Also, it's the awards ceremony. You never know, your name may be called!" With that, he waddled down the long hallway. Lydia headed home deep in her thoughts.

Maybe I will go, she thought. She would get Francesca to help her go shopping. She debated if she would ask Jackson to accompany her, she really didn't know if she wanted him to be there especially if Katrina would be in attendance.

Lydia let herself into her quaint apartment. "Why is the light on in my room?" She grabbed her mace out of her purse and carefully headed towards her bedroom. As she peeked in, there lay Jackson naked.

"You're an hour late! You're usually here by 5:15, what happened?" Jackson had already stood up and was approaching Lydia. She wanted to tell him to leave, that she wasn't interested in having the same boring sex with him, but she couldn't do it.

"I worked overtime Jackson," she frowned as she pushed past him to go into the bathroom.

"Well get washed up because I've got something for you," Jackson smirked. "I've been thinking about this all day!" Jackson stood in the doorway of the bathroom stroking his hard six-inch member. Lydia wanted to run and hide but there was nothing she could do. She washed up and reluctantly climbed into bed. Jackson did his usual move and climbed on top with very little foreplay. Lydia lay there very unsatisfied. She thought that maybe she should say something; maybe she should try to spice things up.

"Jackson," she whispered, "suck on my breasts baby." Jackson slowed his pace and looked down confused.

"Huh?" he asked.

"Please suck on my breasts," she repeated. Jackson hesitated but did as he was asked. He wasn't sure how he felt about Lydia giving him directions. She closed her eyes and concentrated on the sensation of her nipples growing hard in his mouth. The wetness of his tongue circling her nipples gave her goose bumps. She felt somewhat in control but she longed for more. Lydia pushed him away and instructed him to lie down on the bed.

"Lydia what has gotten into you?" She mounted on his hard dick, tightened her vaginal muscles, and closed her eyes. She tilted her head back and lost herself in the motion and the feeling. Lydia ground her hips and leaned forward so she could feel the friction of her swollen clit up against Jackson's pubic hair. She almost came instantly which she rarely did with Jackson. She was so lost in the sensation that she didn't hear Jackson talking to her.

"Lydia! ENOUGH!" Jackson literally pushed her to the side. She looked as if she were in a daze, as if she was completely unaware of what was happening. He scrambled to collect his clothes and put them on. "I don't know what the hell has gotten into you! What was that all about? I didn't need your help, I had everything under control!"

Lydia sat on the edge of the bed with tears filling her eyes. She felt a wave of hotness take over her body; she was furious. "I just wanted to try something different...new...EXCITING! I'm tired of the same old thing every time we have sex Jackson!" Lydia was almost screaming. "It's boring and I'm never satisfied! Sex with you is awful!" Finally, tears began to stream down her cheeks.

Jackson looked puzzled and in shock. He glared at her as if she were a complete stranger. Jackson always thought their sex life was great. He always managed to make her orgasm...well at least he thought. He started to wonder how many times she had faked it. His ego and pride was definitely bruised. She wasn't sure if he was going to console her or walk out. He picked up his keys, frowned at her, and walked out.

"Jackson please don't leave. Please don't leave me." She heard the front door slam loudly. Lydia laid in bed sobbing until she finally fell asleep.

****

"Girl this dress is you!" Francesca held up a strapless glittery red sequined dress. Lydia pretended to shield her eyes as if the dress was blinding her. Francesca was a very outgoing and cheerful woman. At 5'5" 215 pounds, she was confident and sexy. She loved her curves and voluptuous breasts. She adored her hips, thighs, and even her poochy stomach. She embraced her body and walked with a love me or leave me alone persona. Lydia envied her. "Just look girl, this will accentuate your breasts and make your ass stand out!" Francesca smiled from ear to ear.

"Frannie, look at me…. and look at that dress. Come on now." Lydia chuckled as she looked at the electric garment. Francesca sighed and tossed the dress back on the rack. The ladies looked and searched until the perfect dress caught Lydia's eye. It was black with spaghetti straps, fell just above the knee, and it came with a wrap. "This is it!"

Francesca frowned, "But girl it's so plain."

Lydia tuned out Frannie's opinion. She paid the $110 eagerly and left the store very happy. Francesca helped her with her makeup; she looked fantastic. Lydia hailed a cab and started towards the New Year's Eve party.

She thought about Jackson, she hadn't heard from him in four days. She contemplated calling him but she couldn't bring herself to go through with it. Was she glad to be rid of Jackson? She knew she loved him but longed for something different, exciting. As the cab stopped in front of the office building, Lydia felt the anxiety fill her chest. She paid for the ride and stepped out onto the sidewalk.

She looked around and felt compelled to run. "No," she said out loud. "I'm going in, have a couple of drinks, then go home."

Lydia walked into the banquet room. The music was so loud and there were several couples on the dance floor. Waitresses and servers scurried about; people laughed and talked loudly. Lydia quickly looked for an empty seat and got comfortable. She didn't plan to move until it was time to go.

"May I get you something to drink?" the young waitress gave her a quick smile.

"Umm...oh may I have a Cosmopolitan?" The waitress grinned and hurried off.

Lydia was not a drinker but from the racy novels she read, she knew a "Cosmo" was a ladies drink, very flirty and seductive. Lydia looked around the room. She saw Michael dressed in a black suit with a metallic red shirt and red-patent leather shoes, dancing seductively with his lover Robert. She admired Michael's charisma; she wished she could be outgoing and bold like him. She saw Katrina surrounded by a group of men. They seemed hypnotized by her charm...or maybe it was her low cut green sweater and her black mini skirt. She seemed to be floating on air in her six-inch rhinestone studded stilettos.

Lydia frowned and shook her head at the sight of Mr. Frasier and Eileen Goldman, his secretary dancing together. Mr. Frasier was almost sixty and Eileen was in her early thirties but you could tell there was an attraction between the two. Shirley stood near the buffet table emptying her plate as soon as she filled it. Shirley was in her mid-fifties, short and chubby. She always wore the same five outfits just on different days of the week. She made her way over to Lydia with a plate full of party wings and mozzarella sticks.

"Lydia sweetie, I'm so surprised to see you here! You look beautiful." Shirley's voice sent chills up her spine.

"Thanks. I decided to attend for a few minutes, I'm not staying long," Lydia looked uncomfortable. She stared at Shirley as she bit into the chicken wing then licked her fingers. She really wanted to leave but she looked at her watch and realized she had only been there for forty-five minutes. Lydia watched the crowd and noticed a very handsome man standing near one of the exits. She didn't recognize him. He was very tall, muscular, clean-shaven, and extremely attractive. She loved his black curly hair and his delicious looking mocha colored skin. He seemed to look about the crowd as if he was looking for someone. Lydia thought that perhaps he was the date of one of the employees. She found herself staring at the handsome stranger.

She imagined what he must be like in bed. He looked so strong and in control. She felt her panties getting damp as her breath quickened. Her nipples were hard and showing through her black dress. She felt her hands getting sweaty as she imagined lying naked next to this gorgeous stranger. She was so deep in thought she didn't notice that Michael was talking to her.

"Ms. Thang! Hello?" Michael teased. "Where did you drift off to?"

Lydia was fidgeting around in her seat; she was so embarrassed. She decided it was time to leave. She didn't want to bring New Years in with her coworkers, she wanted to be home...alone. As she left out to hail a cab, she caught a glimpse of the handsome stranger leaning against the wall. As she got into the cab, she mustered up enough courage to look over at him. As the cab drove off, they locked eyes then the handsome stranger licked his lips and winked at her. Lydia caught her breath and quickly looked away. When she turned around to see him again, he was gone.

CHAPTER THREE

The month of January was very trying for Lydia. She realized Jackson and she were officially over when she saw him kissing a beautiful blonde outside of what used to be their favorite cafe. Francesca was moving back to Virginia at the end of the month so Lydia would have no one to talk to anymore.

The only thing she had to take her mind off her dull life was work, and that wasn't any better. Lydia answered call after call, listening to the sob stories of the customers. They were too far in debt to make a payment or the charges were fraudulent, or they just refused to pay and hung up in Lydia's ear. She could hear Michael laughing and socializing with the clients, that's probably why he always met his quota for the most phone pays every month. She thought maybe if she became friendlier with the clients, she could accomplish the same results.

As Lydia was getting ready for lunch her phone line at her desk rang. *Probably another client calling to make a payment,* she thought.

"Thank you for calling American Express, this is Lydia, how may I help you?"

There was no answer but she could hear breathing.

"Hello?" she asked again.

"Is this Lydia Morrell?" the deep voice inquired. Lydia was confused; she never gave out her last name to the clients. "Is this Lydia Morrell?" the voice sounded intense as he asked again.

"Yes this is she; may I ask who is calling?" The line went silent again. Lydia wanted to disconnect the call but her curiosity would not let her.

"I want you to go to 704 W. 34th Street at 8 p.m. tonight. Come alone and wear that sexy black dress that you wore at the New Year's Eve party. 704 W. 34th street," and with that, the line went dead.

Lydia sat like a statue glaring at the phone. She was in complete shock. Was it the mystery man from the party? Lydia quickly jotted down the address and went to open the file cabinet where she kept her purse, and there on top of her bag was one long stemmed crimson red rose. She picked it up and attached was a note that read 704 W. 34th Street. Lydia dropped the rose on the desk like it was poisonous. She felt scared yet intrigued all at the same time.

"This is crazy; I can't go meet a complete stranger at an unknown address!"

Lydia's common sense told her to stay home but her heart and sense of adventure encouraged her to go. Lydia glanced at the clock, her lunch break was almost over, but that was ok. Lydia hungered for something else and she decided she was going to give into the temptation.

****

The night air was crisp, almost sharp. Lydia pulled her leather coat closer around her. She stared at the tall gray brick building. It was covered with several dark windows; bold black numbers marked the outside of the main door. Lydia considered running but she couldn't move. She looked up and down the long sidewalk; it was almost as if she were the only one on the street. Lydia rang the buzzer, a woman answered, "Yes?"

Lydia stumbled over her words, "Umm…yes I was supposed to be here tonight at eight, and I'm not sure who to ask for."

The buzzer chimed. "Take the elevator to the fourteenth floor." Lydia opened the door and walked in. The smell of lavender filled her nostrils; she adored the smell of lavender. As she deeply inhaled, she walked to the shiny stainless steel elevator doors. She silently rode the elevator to the fourteenth floor as instructed. She was torn by her thoughts; she couldn't believe she was there to meet a complete stranger. With each passing ding of the elevator passing floor after floor, she grew more and more anxious. Finally, the doors opened and there he stood…the handsome stranger from the New Year's Eve party.

"Hello Lydia Morrell," his voice washed over her like a calming beach breeze. "Let's go," he said as he winked at her and held his hand out.

Lydia was shaking. She took his hand and clumsily walked beside him. The hallway was cloaked in plain white paint; the carpet was a dark matted gray...the typical office

building décor. There were several blank, black doors that
were unmarked.

Lydia began to shake her head, "I think I need to
go, I've changed my mind." She stared at the stranger's
face. He bore no emotions at all. He slowly looked at her
and finally smiled, that made her feel a little more at ease.
He gently kissed Lydia's hand, it made her tingle all over,
and she could feel the moistness in the seat of her black
lace panties. Her nipples stiffened underneath her bra.
"What is your name?"

"Gregory," he said without looking at her. They
turned the corner and there they stood in front of a lone
door at the end of a dark hallway. Gregory breathed heavily
up and down Lydia's neck, which was one of her weak
spots. She swayed back and forth as if she were intoxicated.
Gregory pulled her close and nibbled her ear lobe; Lydia
moaned in delight, her heart was racing. He softly kissed
her lips and gently whispered in her ear, "Are you ready for
a good time?"

Gregory took her hand tightly in his and led her
through the door. The aroma of lavender and vanilla
scented candles assaulted her senses. The room was dimly
lit and draped in crimson and cream sheer draperies; the
cream-colored carpet was so plush that Lydia's heels began
to sink deep into it. Women and men relaxed on the velvet
animal printed sofas and sectionals. Some were clothed;
some were not. Lydia's eyes were as big as golf balls. She
could not believe what she was seeing. There were couples
intertwined, rubbing, and fondling on the sofas.

The smell and sound of sex filled the room. She felt
herself beginning to get hot...and bothered. She struggled

to catch her breath and sweat beaded on her forehead. Gregory led her to the elaborate glass top bar that made its home in the corner of the room. "Champagne for the lady, it's a special night," Gregory stared at her as if he wanted to devour every inch of her body.

"What is this place?" Lydia questioned as two naked ladies walked by laughing and kissing.

"It's whatever you want it to be. The gateway to sexual pleasure and happiness, where there are no inhibitions. A place where you can explore yourself and others with no regrets."

Gregory downed the champagne in one long gulp without taking his eyes off her. Lydia sipped her drink and surveyed the dimly lit room. Everyone seemed so carefree and happy. Couples fondling hungrily at each other, men with hard members lay draped on the sectionals stroking themselves inviting women or men to keep them company. Women were sucking and feeling the breasts of other eager women, inserting their fingers into each other's saturated tight holes. Lydia's head began to spin. She used to feel guilty, almost dirty for watching adult movies and now here she stood in a true-life orgy. She felt her clit begin to ache and throb immensely…the moistness between her legs was hot and sticky.

She looked over at Gregory then straight down to his swollen member. She was speechless but outrageously turned on. Gregory slid the bartender a piece of paper then beckoned to Lydia. He pulled her close, their eyes locking. She struggled to breathe; the smell of his cologne was intoxicating. His cocoa brown eyes seemed to look deep within her soul.

"Are you ready? Are you ready to allow me to bring out a side of you that you've never met, never experienced?"

She wanted to speak but she could not, her legs grew weak as she leaned on Gregory for support. All she could do was nod her head yes.

"Come with me."

She took his hand and deeply exhaled. Gregory took Lydia to a secluded room not too far from the main lobby. He turned on the light and she let out a gasp. The room was magnificent! The walls were painted the most beautiful hue of violet; silver draperies covered the three windows in the room. The carpet was crisp white and very thick. A large glistening crystal chandelier hung from the middle of the ceiling. Lydia glanced over to the bed. The beautiful bed, a king sized bed with a brass headboard and footboard. It was covered with a sexy lavender and silver silk comforter and numerous throw pillows. The room was filled with various arrangements of rose bouquets; the smell was amazing. There was champagne chilling and soft music playing from the speakers mounted on the corners of the wall. The wall in front of the bed was lined with crystal clear mirrors. Gregory walked up behind Lydia and firmly gripped her hips. He gently kissed up and down her neck; she felt she would faint.

"I have to leave for a few moments but I want you to get comfortable. There is a surprise for you in the bathroom. Please enjoy yourself; I will be back in a few." He turned her around, grabbed a handful of her long brown hair, and pulled her head back. He licked up her neck until he reached her mouth and parted her lips with his tongue.

Gregory kissed her so aggressively, so passionately that she could barely breathe.

He left and Lydia looked around the room once again. She poured herself another glass of champagne and drank it straight down, and then she poured herself another. She wasn't much of a drinker but she needed something to calm her nerves.

She couldn't believe how beautiful the room was...she also couldn't believe that she was in it. Lydia opened the bathroom door and was blown away! She was in heaven! The bathroom was decorated in silver and white. Shiny silver fixtures gleamed against the crisp white porcelain sinks. The shiny white granite countertops glistened with flecks of silver throughout. There were several bouquets of deep purple roses all over. A large glass shower stall was neatly tucked in the corner. Several showerheads of different sizes lined the white tile walls and a large waterfall showerhead was at the top. Then there was the Jacuzzi tub with vanilla scented candles that lined the perimeter. There were several assortments of bubble bath and scented oils at hand. Lydia slipped off her heels.

"Oh wow the floor is heated!" She walked across the floor in sheer delight. She decided to run herself a hot bath, she felt so comfortable in the strange place. Who was Gregory? Why was he interested in someone like her? What was this place? Anxiety started to wash over Lydia. As much as she wanted to experience the man, her mind was urging her to leave.

"No, I'm going to stay and keep my phone close just in case." Lydia poured the rose scented oil into the steamy water. She took a purple rose out of the vase and careful pulled the petals apart and laid them on top of the sudsy water. Lydia undressed and slowly lowered her body into the deep tub. She glanced at the clock and realized it was already nine thirty.

"I have to leave by midnight," she said to herself. The hot water seemed to relax every muscle in her body. She wondered when Gregory would return. He was so mysterious, so handsome. She thought about all the things that she would love to do to him. Lydia knew she was not that experienced when it came to sex, but her imagination took her on wild erotic adventures.

She started to rub her breasts, squeeze, and flick her nipples. Her vaginal walls began to contract. The more she flicked her hard nipples the more aroused she became. She slid one hand down to her wet sweet spot and slowly fingered herself while her other hand continued to tease her nipple. Her low moans quietly filled the room. She took her finger and put the tip of it flatly on her swollen clit. The overwhelming sensation made her jerk. She rotated her finger clockwise while feverishly stroking her nipple. Lydia began to sweat, her body jerked and contracted. She cried out in pleasure.

"Gregory," she moaned, her finger moved faster and faster on her wet bud. "YES Gregory…YES…YES…Papi! Ahhhh!"

Lydia released her hot sticky cum into the rose scented water. She struggled to catch her breath; a wicked grin came across her face as she imagined it was Gregory between her thighs instead of her fingers.

"Oh Gregory," she moaned again.

"That was sexy as hell," a deep voice from behind her whispered. Lydia jumped and turned around. There stood Gregory in the doorway rubbing himself and he had seen the entire episode.

"Oh my God Gregory!" Lydia went to get out of the tub but he insisted that she stay put.

"It's okay, there's nothing to be ashamed of. You are beautiful and watching you pleasure yourself was such a turn on." Lydia could feel the blood rushing to her face as she blushed, she felt so embarrassed.

Gregory stepped out of the room and came back with a platter of assorted fruit. He turned on the hot water to freshen up her bath then sat on the side of the Jacuzzi and picked up a plump red strawberry from the silver platter. She looked at him with curiosity. He dipped the strawberry in her glass of champagne and slowly brought it to her lips. He circled the tip of the berry around her lips then parted her lips with the luscious fruit. Lydia closed her eyes and gently took a bite; the sweet nectar trickled down her chin. Gregory leaned in and licked the juice from her chin. He fed her green grapes, ripe pieces of mango, juicy pineapple, and sweet kiwi fruit. He slowly kissed her, tasting the sweet cocktail of juice on the inside of her mouth with his tongue. She began to shiver a little bit as her bath water began to cool.

"Your bath water is getting cold. Get out and get dressed and meet me in the bedroom," he stood and left to give her privacy.

Lydia stood up and got out of the tub. She removed the plush white towel from the heated towel warmer. *Wow this is the life,* she thought. She couldn't wait to have sex with Gregory. She needed it, she craved it, and her body ached for it. After three years with Jackson, she needed sexual healing and Gregory was just the man to rescue her.

I don't know why I'm getting dressed just to have to get undressed again, Lydia thought then laughed to herself. She dressed and stepped in the bedroom. Gregory looked at her with passionate eyes, "Are you ready to go?"

"Go where?" Lydia asked surprised.

"Well…home. This is the end of our evening."

Lydia blinked hard with disappointment. "I'm confused, I thought tonight was going to be...special. I thought we were going to be together." She felt a lump form in her throat, she was upset that the night was ending and she wasn't going to be with him…she almost felt betrayed.

Gregory walked over to her and grabbed both of her hands. "Have you ever seen such a beautiful room? Have you ever had a man feed you fruit and pamper you?" She shook her head no. "Then tonight was special and it was just for you."

She smiled at Gregory because he was right. She had never experienced that kind of ecstasy before. Lydia slowly gathered her coat and purse and walked to the door. She followed him down the long narrow hallway; they went a totally different way than when they had entered. When he opened the large gray door, they were outside in front of the building. A cab sat at the curb.

"Did you enjoy yourself?" he motioned for her to walk through the door.

"Yes I did but I'm still confused. I thought there would be more."

"I plan to see you again. Soon." He kissed her goodbye and helped her in the cab.

Lydia rode home almost in tears. She wanted much more from the evening. She was happy for the attention she received but her body wanted more. She tried to pay for the cab ride when she got home but the driver informed her it had already been paid. She walked up to her apartment and unlocked the door. The smell of roses drifted through the air. She flicked on the lights and to her surprise; her living room was filled with vases of red roses. Lydia leaned against the door and smiled. She looked around at all the beautiful arrangements and then a feeling of panic overwhelmed her. How did he know where she lived?

CHAPTER FOUR

Lydia was a complete mess the next morning at work. She couldn't focus. She missed phone calls, messed up paperwork; she even let a potential phone pay slip through her fingers. She felt hung over. What was that place she went to last night? How many people knew about it? Who was Gregory exactly? Her head was pounding; she couldn't stop thinking. The everyday noise of the workplace seemed to aggravate her even more. She wondered if she went back to that building after work could she get in. It seemed easy enough. She would just ring the buzzer and ask for Gregory. The thought of seeing him again made her wiggle in her seat. The warm sensation took over her body. She felt goose bumps form on her arms and moistness fill her crotch. She closed her eyes and breathed deeply.

Lydia was missing calls left and right but she didn't care. She slowly started to grind her hips as she sat in her office chair. She still remembered the way Gregory smelled, the touch of his hand on her hips. She felt sweat slide down the side of her temple. The more she rotated her hips the hotter she became…she could feel that familiar sensation becoming more and more intense. She grabbed on her thighs grabbing the material of her skirt in her fist, she was so close to cumming.

"Oh my God, Lydia! Are you ok? Do you need an ambulance?" a voice shouted.

Lydia jumped out of her sex-induced trance and looked around. Michael stood glaring at her as if she were dying.

"Lydia, answer me! I'm going to call 911!" Michael pulled out his cell phone.

"No, I'm fine Michael!" she tried to catch her breath as she wiped the sweat from her forehead, "I just need to go to the restroom."

Lydia pulled off her headset and hurried down the hall to the ladies room. She locked herself in the stall and sat on the toilet seat. She held her head in her hands.

"What is wrong with me? At work Lydia? Really? And Michael saw you!" It's a good thing that Michael was gay and had no clue what she was doing. Lydia stood up, removed her cream soaked panties, and tossed them in the trash. She washed her hands and splashed water onto her face. She straightened herself up and went back to her cubicle. Michael interrogated her, asking question after annoying question. She reassured him that she was fine and that it must've been something she ate at breakfast that made her feel ill. She wasn't sure if Michael was buying her story but at least he left her alone.

Lydia hurried to the leave the building promptly at five pm. She hailed a cab and went straight to 704 W. 34th Street. She stepped out of the cab and took a deep breath.

People walked past her in their own private worlds as she stood staring at the building. She cautiously walked up and rang the buzzer, no answer. She rang the buzzer twice this time, still no answer. She peered through the glass doors. The only light she could see was the light from the exit sign at the end of the hall.

"This is a huge building and it's only five thirty, someone has to still be here." She rang the buzzer three or four times in a row. Anxiety took over her body. She began to sweat and she felt tears fill her eyes.

"Excuse me miss, but this building is vacant."

Lydia turned around and looked impatiently at the elderly woman.

"No it is not. I was just here last night visiting a friend."

She shook her head as soon as the words left her mouth. "Sweetie, I work in the flower shop across the street," she pointed behind her. "This here building has been empty for three months. I think the owner is trying to sell it but he wants way too much if you ask me."

The lady continued to ramble on as Lydia stood lifeless looking at the plain gray building. She kept replaying "empty for three months," over and over in her head. She knew she was there last night. She saw the naked bodies and people having sex. She still remembered the taste of the champagne on her lips, the smell of Gregory's cologne, the violet and silver bedroom, the bath, the fruit, EVERYTHING! She began crying and the elderly lady abruptly stopped talking and looked at her in silence.

Lydia excused herself and waved down a cab. She finally arrived home and flung herself on the bed. How could she be so foolish to allow herself to get so worked up over a complete stranger? Was she so desperate for attention and excitement that she would allow herself to be manipulated by Gregory? Lydia got up, toasted half a bagel, and ate two bites. She didn't really have an appetite. She showered instead of taking her usual bath. She sat on the edge of the bed and stared out of the window at the night sky. She knew she would never get a good night's sleep. She called Francesca but got the answering machine.

She debated calling Jackson but the thought of him in bed with his new blonde changed her mind. She lay back on the bed and closed her eyes. For a split second, she drifted off but a hard knock on the door interrupted her nap. She sat up and blinked to focus on the clock. "Nine thirty? Who in the world?" She grabbed her robe and her aluminum bat and stepped lightly towards the door.

"Yes?" she said firmly.

"Delivery for Lydia Morrell."

She left the chain on the door and cracked it open. "What?" she asked in disbelief.

"Yeah I got a delivery for Lydia Morrell, is that you or what?" the man asked rudely.

"Yes, that's me," she opened the door and signed for the package. She placed the gold box with the red ribbon onto the dining room table. The box itself was beautiful. She carefully opened it not having a clue what to expect. Inside was a pair of pink fuzzy handcuffs and a black silk scarf. She pulled the items out of the gold box and laughed. She looked around the room in embarrassment even though she was the only one in the room. She looked at the items and immediately started having naughty thoughts. She imagined Gregory cuffing her hands and having his way with her. The vision excited her.

Lydia went to replace the items in the box and noticed a gold envelope inside. She opened it: "The Wilson Hotel, 514 E. 17th Street, March 1st 11 pm. Go to room 615, enter, and await further instructions." Lydia read the message again out loud. She picked up her cell phone and typed in the address in her GPS. It was thirty-five minutes away and located in a bad area of town. She sat down at the table; her mind was racing. Was it Gregory? Of course...it had to be. March 1st was two days away.

"I have two days to decide," she pondered. Lydia had two days to decide if it would be the biggest adventure or biggest mistake of her life.

****

Gregory lay in bed looking at the blank TV screen. He listened to the birds chirp, the cars driving by, the trash truck picking up the city cans and the faint snore of the woman next to him. He watched her chest rise up and down, the way her eyes moved under her eyelids as she dreamed. Her long black hair was a tangled mess. She looked so peaceful but he wanted her gone. He slid out of bed and walked into the bathroom.

Goose bumps covered his naked body as his bare feet hit the cold tile floor. He stared at the image looking back at him in the mirror; his dark curly hair was unruly.

He rubbed his hands over his face and looked at himself again. He looked around the bathroom at his black toilet and bidet, the shower stall with the black and white checked tile and his two black pedestal sinks. He wish he had heated bathroom floors but in due time that wish would become a reality. He put on his robe and went back into the bedroom. He looked at the woman in his bed again, she looked comfortable...too comfortable.

Gregory frowned, "Sasha. Sasha!"

The woman stretched and yawned, "Why the fuck are you yelling?" Sasha sat up on the side of the bed with the sheet wrapped around her; she gazed at him like he was crazy.

"Time for you to go, I got shit to do today." Gregory crossed the room and opened the blinds.

Sasha shielded her eyes from the blinding sun. "Damn Greg, what's wrong with you lately? This is the second time you've rushed me out the door early in the morning." She snatched her pink thong off the floor, put it on, and rolled her eyes.

"This isn't a bed and breakfast; you got what you paid for so you need to leave. Besides if Renee knew I was doing side work she'd kill me."

Sasha stood up with just her thong covering her, walked over to the dresser, and pulled her wallet out of her purse. She tossed ten crisp one hundred dollar bills onto the dresser. She picked up her dress, went into the bathroom, and slammed the door. Gregory picked up his cell phone, six missed calls, and two messages. One of the missed calls was from Renee, Greg's employer.

"I'm not calling that bitch back yet." He tossed the phone down on the bed and sat down beside it. Sasha came out of the bathroom and gave him a dismissive glance.

"So are we still on for next weekend?" she asked.

"I'll call you ok?" Greg said with an attitude.

Sasha stormed out and slammed the glass front door behind her. He lay back on the bed, he was so unhappy. That was not the life he wanted for himself, but the money was so easy. It would be much better if he could pocket all the money for himself. He thought about Lydia, how innocent and shy she was. It was easy to romance her. He knew it wouldn't take much to make her fall head over heels for him. He thought about how she was a natural beauty. He hadn't seen her completely naked yet but he could only imagine how beautiful her naked body must look. He could feel himself getting aroused at the thought of bending her over.

"Shake it off man, get it together," he said aloud. He had to make sure everything was perfect for Lydia when he saw her again. Everything had to go right and exactly as planned. March 1st was a crucial part of his plan and everything had to go smoothly, no room for errors.

CHAPTER FIVE

Lydia decided to go shopping after work on Friday. She wanted to wear something sexy for Gregory. She thought back to the last time she bought lingerie. She was so excited to rush home and model the black and red lace ensemble for Jackson. She waited for him to come home while she sat seductively on the bed. Jackson came in and literally ripped the garments off her, and gave it to her hard from behind, no compliment or foreplay. Sixty dollars completely wasted and ruined. Lydia shook her head and came back from her daydream. Gregory would never do that to her. He was gentle and romantic, charming and mysterious. She knew he would appreciate her efforts.

Lydia looked through the rows of sexy lingerie and nighties. She wanted something different from whom she really was, plain and boring. Lydia wondered what kind of lover he would be. *Is he gentle? Rough? Does he like to make love or is he a freak?* It didn't matter to her, she wanted him badly, and she already decided that she would be any kind of lover he wanted her to be. She decided to purchase a matching black lace satin panty and bra set with a matching garter belt. She also purchased two different fragrances. Lydia checked her messages when she arrived home. She was so happy that Francesca finally called her back; she immediately dialed her number.

"Hey girl, I miss you!" Francesca sang into the phone.

Lydia giggled, "I miss you too. It's so boring here without you." She looked at the pink and gray bag from the lingerie shop, "I don't have anyone to help me shop or to gossip with."

"I know hun; I miss our coffee dates, our shopping trips, and our late night veg outs! Eating all those damn veggies late at night used to give me gas girl!" They both rang out in laughter. The ladies caught up on their gossip and work lives.

"Have you spoken to Jackson?" Francesca quietly asked.

Lydia bit her lip, "No things are over, and there's no need for us to talk to each other."

"Yeah I guess you're right. Please tell me you're dating? Please tell me you're not sitting in that lonely ass apartment like a hermit!"

Lydia wanted to tell Francesca all about Gregory but she knew her best friend would never understand. She would ask her if she were crazy, she would judge her for her poor decision. No way could she tell her she was getting involved with a complete stranger.

"No I'm not dating Frannie. I'm concentrating on myself and work and getting over Jackson."

The ladies talked for another hour then said their goodbyes. She took her bath and lay in bed. She usually wore pajamas in a futile attempt to keep Jackson from pawing at her, but she didn't have that concern anymore.

That night she decided to sleep nude, the crisp cool sheet felt good against her freshly cleaned skin. The next night was all she could think about. She could not believe a sexy man wanted her and that she was willing to give herself to him. She wanted to know everything about him and she intended to ask him any and everything she could think of.

Lydia dosed off feeling excited and anxious at the same time. She knew she was insane for wanting to be with him but her curiosity would not let her think clearly.

****

Gregory walked into Renee's office early Saturday morning. He did not feel like dressing up like he usually did so he wore black sweatpants, an orange and black muscle shirt, and his black Jordans. He really did not feel like dealing with her, he couldn't stand her stuck up ass but she was the one who paid him so there was no way around it. Renee sat at her large mahogany wood desk staring at her computer screen when Gregory walked in. He plopped down in the chair in front of her desk and chugged his bottle of water.

"So what's going on Renee? What's up?"

Renee blinked and focused her green contacted eyes on Gregory. She stared at him then began to speak. "You're not bringing much business in these days G. I mean in the past three months, you've had several leads but only a couple of ladies came through."

Gregory hated when she called him "G" and he definitely hated when she got on his case as if he were a child. At thirty-two years old, Gregory was quite capable of handling his business. He didn't need a fake bitch telling him what he had and hadn't done.

"What do you want me to do?" Greg snapped.

"I can't make them give it up! Shit!" Gregory stood up and looked out of the window.

Renee swirled her high back leather desk chair around to face him. She brushed her long red and blonde wavy weave away from her face. "Look I'm not trying to give you a hard time; I'm just trying to put some money in your pocket. You have got the skills, the looks, and the talent." Renee looked Gregory up and down. She always thought that Greg was so damn fine. His skin was flawless and he always dressed nice, even when he was in his workout gear. She loved how his chest bulged underneath his shirt and she was dying to run her long manicured nails through his thick dark curly hair. "I know you can do this G, you've done it before."

Gregory soaked in everything Renee was saying. He knew she was correct, he did have everything necessary to get the work, he was just tired of sharing the profits with her. She wasn't the one dicking down those lonely desperate females every night. He thought back to the time he had a "date" with a woman that was old enough to be his mother. After he wined and dined her then fucked her senseless, he went into the bathroom and vomited until he was dizzy. That was the kind of thing he was getting tired of.

Renee had no idea that Gregory got plenty of business that he was taking for himself. Yes, he brought a few clients to her but mostly he considered himself an independent contractor and he was working for himself. It was only a matter of time before he left her high and dry. Renee went to the printer and handed him a sheet of paper.

"Here is your lead sheet for next week. That new gym around the corner is a prime location. I made sure you got first dibs on it. Hey whatever happened to that chick from the collection place?"

Gregory continued to stare out of the window, "I'm still working on it, but I don't think she's a good potential client. She doesn't have much to offer. Besides I doubt I could get her to budge." Greg knew exactly what he was doing. He had no intention on sharing Lydia with Renee. She was going to be his cash cow and he wanted her all to himself.

Gregory went home and switched on his sixty-inch flat screen to the sports channel. He looked out of the sliding glass door at his beautiful beach view. The crashing waves seemed to play a soothing song that put his mind at rest. He looked around his den in disgust. He took out his special furniture brush and gently stroked his black microfiber sofa and loveseat, putting even lines on them. He looked at the glass coffee table and frowned. He saw the water ring that Sasha had left on the glass the night before. He grabbed his Windex wipes and wiped down the coffee table, then the glass end tables. He cleaned the sliding glass door and the glass front door. He looked around in satisfaction. He hated bringing certain women to his house; they had no class and did not know how to treat his things.

He remembered when he bought one woman home and she put her dirty bare feet up on his furniture. He promptly told her to get her ass up and leave. If her feet were that filthy, there was no telling what her pussy was like. There's was no way he was going to screw her, rubber or not.

Gregory went into the kitchen, poured a large glass of almond milk, and drank it straight down. He walked into his room and stripped out of his clothes. He looked at his naked body in the full-length mirror and flexed his arms and chest. He squinted his eyes and looked closely at his crotch, "Damn I gotta shave before tonight," he said as he stroked his cock. He hated hair down there; it was disgusting. He thought about the plans he had for Lydia that night, it would definitely be the beginning of a beautiful relationship. Gregory chuckled under his breath as he went into the bathroom and turned on the shower.

CHAPTER SIX

Lydia awoke to the sound of birds chirping outside her window. She turned over and stared out of the window, a smile spread across her face. The sun was shining and the sky was clear. *A beautiful Saturday,* she thought. She had several errands to run and she wanted to get them done early. She jumped out of bed so she could start her morning coffee. She shivered as she walked in the kitchen; she had forgotten she slept naked.

She went to get her robe but then quickly changed her mind. Walking around her apartment naked felt freeing, natural. She opened the fridge to get the cream and giggled as goose bumps took over her body. She made a cup of coffee and went back to her room for her robe. She went back into her quaint little living room and flipped on the television.

There was breaking news regarding a woman who discovered her husband of fifteen years had been cheating and she shot him to death then called 911 on herself. They showed a picture of the woman at a church picnic two years ago. The woman looked so happy, so full of life. Her hair was neatly in place and she had on a very nice sundress and sandals. Lydia thought that she did not look like a woman who could murder someone. She looked so normal.

Lydia shook her head while she sipped her coffee and continued to listen to the broadcast. Apparently, the woman followed her husband to a local motel and caught him having sex with another local woman. The couple did not lock the door and his wife let herself in while carrying the .22 caliber gun that her husband bought her for protection.

Wow, how ironic, Lydia thought. The camera panned towards the grief stricken lady being led away in handcuffs. Her makeup mixed with tears streamed down her face, her head hung low. The woman that was sleeping with her husband stood wrapped in a sheet and sobbing by a police car. The entire scene was sad and dreadful. Lydia felt sorry for the wife but thought she was dumb for sacrificing her freedom over a man, especially a cheating man.

She looked over at the dining room table at the gold box. She wondered what Gregory was doing. She wished she had his phone number so she could hear his seductive voice. She made a mental note to ask him for it tonight. Lydia showered and slipped on a pair of jeans, a plain black t-shirt, and her black flats with the silver rhinestones. She pulled her long wavy hair up into a ponytail. Her plan was to walk down the street to the corner produce store but her cell phone rang before she reached the door.

"Lydia, I am so sorry to bother you honey on your day off but Mr. Clifford called and he wants to pay off his ten thousand dollar balance but he will only do the transaction with you! PLEASE PLEASE PLEASE can you come in for a few minutes? He's going to call back in about an hour!"

Lydia sighed and looked at the clock, "Michael its noon and I have things to do. You can't convince him to call back Monday?"

"Mr. Frasier wants this phone pay done today! It's ten thousand dollars girl, you have to get down here!"

Lydia sighed and reluctantly agreed. She arrived at work and waited for Mr. Clifford to call. Katrina looked Lydia up and down. Lydia tried to ignore her but her rudeness made her cringe.

"I guess you were planning on spending your Saturday inside," Katrina said looking at her choice of outfit. Lydia sat staring at the phone on her desk trying to ignore her. Katrina snickered under her breath," I mean why else would you have that on?" Lydia glared at her with disgust. She wanted to get up and slap her across the face as hard as she could. Katrina sensed that she was getting under her skin. "What does a person like you do on Saturday night?" Katrina glanced over at Michael who was now standing in between the ladies cubicles. Michael looked at her and shook his head.

"People like me? What does that mean exactly Katrina?" Lydia swirled her chair around to face her.

"Come on girl, don't make me say it."

Lydia looked up at Michael who now had an apologetic look on his face. Lydia gave Katrina a blank look.

"You know," Katrina batted her eyes, "someone ordinary, and someone who doesn't have friends or a man. Someone boring and who dresses…like that!" Katrina pointed up and down at Lydia's outfit. Katrina burst out laughing and leaned back in her desk chair.

Lydia stood up out of her seat and started to walk towards Katrina, she was so busy laughing that she did not see Lydia coming towards her. Michael grabbed her by the wrist and pulled her back to her seat. Katrina jumped and looked at her stunned.

"Oh bitch I know you weren't coming for me!" Katrina jumped out of her seat and Lydia followed suit.

Michael begged and pleaded as he stood in between the two women. "Please stop this nonsense! Come on ladies, we are better than this! This is childish!"

Just as Michael thought he would have to referee the catfight, Lydia's desk phone rang. The loud ringing shook both the ladies out of their violent rage.

"You're lucky bitch!" Katrina said as she stormed off.

Lydia rolled her eyes and answered the phone, "Thank you for calling American Express, this is Lydia, how may I help you?"

****

"Damn this girl is always late!' Gregory looked at his watch; it was fifteen after six. The doorbell rang and he got up to answer the door.

"I know, I know! Don't start with the bullshit! I couldn't get a fucking cab!" Alexis came in, sat down, and brushed her short black bangs off her forehead. "Just look at my hair Greg! I just got it done this morning!"

"I can't tell," Greg said studying her short pixie cut. "I liked it better long anyway. That shit ain't sexy at all."

Alexis gave Greg the bird and continued rummaging through her large purse. "Do I still have to go outside to smoke? It's windy as hell out there!" Alexis had her cigarettes and lighter in hand.

"Hell yeah! I don't want my shit smelling like smoke. Why don't you just quit?" He despised the nasty habit of smoking. The way it made a woman's hair, clothes, hands smell, and although he couldn't prove it, he swore it affected the taste of the pussy too.

He watched as Alexis stepped out of the sliding glass door. He loved the way her ass looked in her tight fitted jeans, the way her breasts sat up in her low cut turquoise sweater. He hated when she wore those patented leather stripper heels, it made her look ridiculous, but that was part of her wardrobe where she worked, so he understood. Greg could feel his dick getting hard. He sat back on the love seat and started rubbing the raised form in his pants. He watched her as she smoked her cigarette, the way her full lips formed around it. He bit his bottom lip and stared at her ass. He needed to release.

Alexis came back in and smiled at him, "Damn baby, for real?" Alexis started to unbutton her jeans but Gregory stopped her.

"Nah Lex, I want that mouth."

Alexis looked disappointed but cooperated anyway. She knew exactly how he liked it, her on her knees in front of him, as if she were bowing down to him. She never understood why he never wanted to have sex with her; he always wanted head. He had never kissed her in the two years they had known each other. She was getting fed up but she didn't want to risk losing Gregory altogether so she kept quiet.

Gregory pulled out his ten-inch hard member and stroked it while he looked at her cherry red lips. He pulled her by the back of her head toward his dick. Alexis slowly licked the swollen head and Gregory flinched. She licked her wet tongue down one side and up the other then slid her mouth down the entire length of his cock. He tilted his head back in ecstasy. She did the same move again but that time when she slid her mouth down, Greg held her head in place. Alexis fought to bring her head back up but Greg held it in place until she began to slightly gag. He let go of her head and she came up gasping for air, her eyes were full of tears and mascara ran down her cheeks.

"Spit on it!" he said firmly.

Alexis did as she was told; he watched the saliva ease down his swollen dick. Alexis started in on him again, gripping her jaws up and down and sliding her tongue on the base. Gregory placed both hands on each side of her head so he could control her rhythm.

"Right there Lex, slow it up. Come all the way up to the head; suck it. SHIT!"

She moaned as her cheeks became tired and sore. He loved the feeling of his head touching the back of her throat. Greg moved her head slowly; he had to time it perfectly. He had the rhythm just right.

"Get ready Lex." As soon as he was about to release, he shoved her head down to make her deep throat, the thick hot cream shot down her throat as she gagged again. He let her head go and she fell back on the floor wiping tears from her eyes and wiping her mouth. Gregory sat looking at her while he caught his breath. Alexia never disappointed him in this area. She was a tough girl and she could take anything he threw at her. She always knew how to get him there. Alexis went into the bathroom to clean up. She came back with a washcloth and tossed it at him.

"Can I get a beer?" she asked with a slight attitude.

"Yeah and bring me one. Hurry up so we can talk business."

CHAPTER SEVEN

Lydia stood in front of her full-length mirror studying her body. She was pleased at how the new bra and panty set fit her, although she still wished she had more breasts to fill out the bra. She thought about Katrina's full breasts, how her cleavage seem to rise above the top of her bra perfectly.

"Bitch," she said out loud.

She sprayed on her new fragrance, Pink Sugar. She pulled her long brown hair on top of her head and let a few tendrils of hair surround her face. She did not want her hair to get in the way of the black scarf when Gregory put it on her. She slipped on her black stretch skirt and dark blue blouse with a v neckline. She loved the way her cleavage looked, so seductive and inviting. She slipped on her black opened toed heels, she hated wearing them, but she wanted to look her best for Gregory. She gave herself another look and smiled. She could not believe how pretty she looked; it was as if she was looking at a stranger. She put on her black leather waist length jacket, grabbed the gold box and her purse, and went outside to catch a cab.

She got inside and told the cab driver the address. "514 E. 17th Street," she said with a smile.

The driver looked at her through the rearview mirror. "The Wilson Hotel?" he said in disbelief.

"Yes! Is there a problem?" Lydia said with an attitude.

"Hey if you're cool, I'm cool," he laughed and switched on the meter.

They rode in complete silence, which was fine with her. She daydreamed about what Gregory had planned. She was wondered why they did not rendezvous at the lavender and silver room again. She glanced at the gold box sitting beside her. She was dying with curiosity. Lydia looked out of the cab window and realized she was in a different world. Women dressed in next to nothing paraded the streets beckoning drivers to pull over and talk to them. Men gambled on the corners, two men were fighting. Lydia caught a glimpse of the driver peeking at her in the mirror, "You ok mami? You cool?" The cab driver knew the area was nothing she was used to.

"I'm…I'm ok. Are we almost there?" She couldn't understand why Gregory would want to meet in that part of town. Vacant rundown buildings decorated the street. Beer bottles and trash lay on the grass and sidewalks. The cab pulled up to the Wilson Hotel and Lydia could not believe what she was seeing. A run down building with a flashing sign that read The ilson Hoel. People cluttered the outside of the hotel talking laughing and drinking. There was a pool that was green with algae and floating leaves. The driver looked at Lydia again through the rearview mirror, "Your stop mami, it's forty dollars even."

She gave the driver forty-three dollars and cautiously stepped out of the cab. Her mind was racing with random thoughts. Her pulse quickened, she was terrified. She walked into the breezeway to the elevator. The smell of funk and urine overwhelmed her. She looked around anxiously while she waited. Several men were staring her up and down while some of the prostitutes looked like they really wanted to hurt her. The door finally opened and she stepped in and pushed six. She looked around the urine-scented elevator. There was a pool of red liquid on the floor in the corner; Lydia quickly moved to the other side. Anxiety started to take over her entire body; she felt lightheaded and wobbly in her six-inch heels. She felt like she did when she was meeting Gregory for the first time at the large gray building. The elevator door opened and she stepped out into a long walkway, which was still outside. A row of several green numbered doors lined the walkway.

She slowly started walking and looking around at the beat up establishment. Some people sat in their rooms with the door open, television blaring. A few people leaned against the wall smoking cigarettes and blunts. They all looked at her oddly; she was definitely out of place. She kept walking looking at the numbers on the doors, 609... 611.... 613.... 615.

Lydia looked at the door. It wasn't too late for her to get out of there and go back to what she was familiar with, her boring job, her small apartment, no friends, and nonexistent love life. Lydia took a deep breath and gently knocked. No answer. She remembered the note said to let herself in. She put her hand on the doorknob, took another deep breath, and opened the door. Lydia walked in and locked the door behind her. She looked around the hotel room; it was basic. A king sized bed with a standard flowered bedspread like most hotels had. A small round wooden table with two chairs sat in the corner. An out of date 32-inch television sat on a long dresser but there was a DVD player on top of it, it seemed out of place. There was a small kitchenette with a small stove, microwave and economy sized refrigerator.

Lydia took off her jacket and laid it on the bed. She sat for a few minutes still looking around the room. She thought she heard the sound of water running. She looked towards the bathroom door; it was closed. She didn't know whether to run or investigate. What if it was Gregory? Lydia kept looking at the door, she wanted to get up and knock or open it, but she was paralyzed with fear. Lydia stood up and put on her jacket. She was almost to the room door when the bathroom door opened. Steam billowed out of the small bathroom and a voice questioned, "Leaving so soon?"

Lydia stopped in mid step and slowly turned around. There in the bathroom door way stood a very attractive tall naked woman. She smiled at Lydia and raised her eyebrows as if she were waiting for an answer. Lydia gazed at the beautiful stranger from head to toe. She didn't seem real; she was too perfect.

"Oooh I am so sorry, I'm in the wrong room!" Lydia went to reach for the doorknob.

"No, you're good sweetie. You're looking for Gregory right?"

The mystery lady grabbed a towel and wrapped it snuggly around her. Lydia was still in a trance, confused as to what was happening. The woman walked over to the fridge and pulled out a beer and a miniature bottle of vodka. She watched Lydia's awkward body language as she unscrewed the top off the small bottle.

"You want a drink sweetie?"

Lydia shook her head no.

"Huh...ok." The woman drank the contents of the bottle in one swift gulp. She smiled as she wiped her mouth and let out a slight cough.

"Listen I'm here to meet Gregory. He sent me this box and instructions to meet him here," she looked at the woman with concern.

"I'm Alexis. I know why you're here. Greg sent me to keep you company until he got here. He got held up...at work," Alexis smirked. "So get comfy, it's all good baby."

Lydia shook her head, walked back over to the bed, and sat down. She kept staring at Alexis wondering why Gregory sent her to THEIR hotel room. As she studied Alexis' body, she wondered what it would be like to be intimate with another female. This was one of many of Lydia's secret fantasies. She often fantasized about being with Katrina even though she could not stand her. Alexis was tall and sexy, her legs went on forever. Her ass was firm and her stomach was tight like she worked out every day. Alexis walked over to her and handed her a plastic cup filled with rum and coke.

"Relax hun, here sip on this." Lydia took the cup and slowly sipped the beverage. Alexis sat very close to her; she leaned in and inhaled deeply, "That's nice. What perfume is that?"

"Pink Sugar," Lydia responded, still sipping her drink and fighting the urge to look down Alexis' towel.

"Smells really nice, very feminine," Alexis opened her beer and took a long drink. "Do you like my hair Lydia?" Alexis ran her hands through her short pixie cut. Honestly, Lydia did not care for it but she was not in the habit of being rude to strangers.

"It's very cute and playful" she responded as she continued to sip her drink. Lydia was feeling very warm and relaxed. She pulled off her jacket and tossed it on the chair next to the bed. She looked at Alexis and smirked. Alexis smiled back and offered her another drink and Lydia gladly accepted. She was still curious about Gregory and why he hadn't shown up yet. Alexis handed her the drink and she started to drink it immediately. She really didn't drink liquor except for mixed girly drinks but it was very good. Alexis downed another bottle of vodka and sat back beside Lydia.

"Your hair is so pretty. Can you let it down so I can really see it?"

Lydia looked bewildered at the question, "But I wore it up especially for Gregory and so it wouldn't get in the way." She thought about the silk scarf in the box.

Alexis licked her shiny red lips and stared at Lydia with a look of complete lust. "Sweetie you can put it back up whenever he gets here. Let me see all that pretty long hair." The potent beverage was taking control of Lydia's being. She liked the way Alexis called her sweetie; it made her feel pretty. She felt her nipples harden under her new bra as she struggled to catch her breath. She reached up and started pulling the decorative hairpins out of her hair. Her long dark brown shiny locks fell down around her face and onto her shoulders. She brushed a few stray strands from her face and looked timidly at Alexis.

"Oh my God, girl you are so fuckin sexy!" Alexis gently brushed Lydia's hair behind her ear. Lydia's heart was racing; she felt all the effects of the alcohol taking over. "So what's in the box?" Alexis glanced at the gold package on the bed.

Lydia reached over and opened it. She pulled out the pink fuzzy handcuffs and black silk scarf. "Gregory sent it to me and told me to bring them with me tonight."

Alexis winked at her and started laughing. She already knew what was in the box; actually, it was her idea. She took the handcuffs out of her hands. "Let's have some fun." Alexis leisurely removed her towel and tossed it on the floor. The two ladies eyes met in an awkward yet lustful way. The chemistry was definitely there, it filled the room like a thick fog. Alexis reached over, took Lydia's hand, and placed it on her breast. Lydia closed her eyes and took a deep breath. She could feel Alexis's nipple grow hard underneath her hand. Before she knew it, she was rubbing and kneading her firm breast and loving every minute of it. Alexis reached over and started to unbutton Lydia's blouse, staring her in the eyes the entire time. She looked at Lydia's black lace bra the leaned over and seductively kissed Lydia's neck right below her ear. Lydia felt the goose bumps rise on her flesh. She wanted Alexis. She wanted to kiss her deep, run her hands along her flesh, soak in the very essence of the woman but she kept questioning about Gregory.

"Alexis, what about Gregory?"

Alexis continued kissing down her neck until she reached her shoulder. "Sweetie he will be here when he gets here. He wanted us to meet and enjoy each other." She leaned in and gently kissed Lydia's lips. Lydia pulled away and looked down. She knew she wanted to experience this perfect stranger but she felt so unsure of herself. She did not know what to do, what to feel. Alexis lifted Lydia's face and gently kissed her again. That time Lydia allowed herself to give into the temptation. Alexis's mouth felt so good, so warm, so inviting. Lydia hungrily searched for Alexis tongue as they kissed deeply and heavily. Alexis broke the kiss and walked over to the mini fridge. She took out yet another bottle of vodka and downed it. She didn't offer Lydia another drink; she knew she had had enough.

"Get undressed sweetie," Alexis ordered while she studied Lydia's facial expression. She knew she wanted her and truth be told Alexis wanted her too and not just because she was being paid to do so. Alexis walked over to the dresser where the television sat and put her empty bottle by the fake plant. She watched Lydia take off her blouse then slide out of her skirt. Alexis could feel herself getting wet between her thighs. Lydia sat on the edge of the bed with her bra and panties on. Alexis walked over and kissed her neck, Lydia let out a low sigh. She kissed down the front of her neck to her cleavage.

The smell of the Pink Sugar fragrance was hypnotizing to Alexis. She reached around and unfastened Lydia's bra and eagerly snatched it off and flung it across the room. Alexis latched on to her nipple...sucking, slurping, and teasing it while rubbing and gently pinching the other nipple with her hand. She circled her hard gumdrop with her tongue causing Lydia to lean her head back and moan in delight. Lydia wanted to touch Alexis but she was frightened, it was all so new to her. Her mouth felt so good on her flesh, her hands felt so wonderful on her body. Alexis slowly leaned Lydia back on the bed. She gazed at Lydia's small breasts, her flat stomach.

Alexis was used to dealing with women with large fake breasts and women with made up faces and long extensions. That's all she was accustomed to seeing at the strip club where she was employed. When she started doing "side work "with Gregory, she started dealing with rich women that treated her as if she was the hired help, which oddly enough, in a way, she was. She was hired to help these women fulfill a fantasy that they were ashamed or afraid to admit...to be with another woman. She had done several threesomes with Gregory but she always felt cheap and unsatisfied afterwards.

She knew it was his job to please these women; she just hated the fact that he never pleasured her in the process. He only seemed to want oral sex from her. What was wrong with her? Her pussy was just as good, if not better, than those stuck up rich women. She hated feeling jealous...especially over a man that would never be hers.

She admired Lydia's natural beauty. It was a refreshing difference from what she normally worked with.

She got on her knees and slowly pulled Lydia's panties down to her ankles and then completely off. Alexis handcuffed Lydia's hands to the cheap wooden headboard. Lydia looked unsure of the situation but she didn't want Alexis to stop. Alexis slid down to Lydia's thighs and slowly separated them. She started kissing the inside of her thighs up to her stomach as Lydia began to tense up.

"Alexis, I think we should wait for…"

Alexis quickly quieted her by licking straight up her pink slit. Lydia let out a loud gasp; the feel of her tongue caught her completely off guard. Lydia could not remember the last time she had a wet tongue on her sweet spot. Jackson wasn't into oral sex so it had to have been over three years since she got to enjoy this stimulating treat. Alexis separated Lydia's wet lips until her swollen clit sat front and center. She slowly teased her with her tongue, circular motions then light and playful flicks. She slid her wet tongue down her creamy center and slid her tongue in and out. Lydia panted for air. She slowly rotated her hips to intensify the pleasure. Alexis planted her face deep into Lydia's wet spot and began to suck and lick the hold time holding her in place by her thighs. Lydia fought to wiggle away, the feeling was so intense.

"Aaahh! RIGHT THERE! YEAH…YEAH…!" Lydia let out an orgasmic cry as she bucked her hips against Alexis face. She eagerly sampled Lydia's sweet nectar; she licked her clean. Lydia lay there trying to catch her breath. She couldn't remember the last time she came so hard. Her muscles throbbed, her clit was still swollen and sensitive, but Alexis wasn't finished with her yet. She kissed her passionately, Lydia had never tasted herself before, and it turned her on immensely. She pulled the black scarf out of the box and tied it around Lydia's head, covering her eyes.

"Now just lie back and enjoy yourself. I got you." Alexis worked her way back down to her sweet spot. Lydia was spent from her last session but she definitely wanted more. The idea of the blindfold made her a little uncomfortable. She didn't like not being able to see Alexis's moves. Alexis put her finger in Lydia's mouth encouraging her to wet it then slid it into Lydia's wet hole. She began to stroke the soft spot deep inside her. She concentrated on sucking her swollen bud in a hard fast rhythm, then licking it. Lydia began to squirm and rotate her hips, bringing her butt off the bed to meet Alexis's mouth even more.

Alexis continued stroking her G spot with her middle finger and licking her clit. Lydia yelled out in passion, begging her to stop but Alexis didn't let up. The more Lydia begged and pleaded the more turned on Alexis became. She loved the feeling of being in control. She wanted to control Lydia's body and make it do what she wanted it to.

Lydia could feel tears build up in her eyes. The feeling was like none other she had ever felt. She trembled and shook as if she were having a mild seizure...then an overwhelming sensation took over her body, she never felt that way before. She tried to focus on what was happening but her senses were on overload.

"Alexis, stop! PLEASE STOP!"

Alexis knew exactly what was happening as she held Lydia in place and fingered her vigorously. She knew she was close and then it happened. A gush of warm clear liquid spewed from Lydia's swollen wet pussy. She yelled out and tried to sit up but the handcuffs kept her in place. She couldn't believe what was happening. Alexis, the comforter and the floor were soaked. Alexis smiled widely and grabbed the towel off the floor. She laughed and wiped her face. She took the blindfold off Lydia's face, her eyeliner and mascara was smeared. Lydia was in total shock and outrageously tired. Alexis took the handcuffs off Lydia's wrist.

"Did you enjoy that that doll?"

"Yes, I cannot believe…I am so sorry!"

Alexis let out another laugh, "It's cool sweetie. I'm glad I made you feel good. You did exactly what I wanted you to do. Oh…by the way, He's not coming."

Lydia sat up and shook her head," But you said he was!" Lydia felt betrayed by the both of them.

"He wanted me to give you a sexual experience you've never had. He wanted you to let your guard down and enjoy yourself…with me."

Lydia gave Alexis a weak smile," I better get ready to go."

Lydia gathered her things and went into the bathroom. She was confused by the entire situation. How dare Gregory do this to her. What kind of games was he playing? Alexis leaned back on the bed and twirled the handcuffs around on her finger. She was getting tired of being Gregory's sidekick in these sexual adventures even if it did put a few hundred extra dollars in her pocket. She looked towards the fake plant on the dresser making sure the small red light was still on. She put up her middle finger and mouthed the words, "Fuck you," then got up and turned the camera off.

CHAPTER EIGHT

Renee Mitchell was the owner/CEO of Premier Escorts. She started the business six years ago with her best friend Erica Curlew. Erica had since fallen in love with one of the escorts, gotten married, and left the business. Renee knew she was more than capable of holding the business down alone. She just needed to make sure that she hired the most attractive sexy eligible men she could, and so far, she had done just that.

She had seven gentlemen working under her, including Gregory Summit. Each gentleman was required to help bring in clients and she did some scouting as well. They were paid a percentage of what each client paid for their dates. Dates ranged from one hundred dollars to as high as five thousand, depending on the needs and wants of the client. Tipping and gifts were prohibited but she knew some of her employees accepted them anyway. Some of her employees had other regular nine to five jobs and some used the escort service as their primary source of income.

Renee looked through the new client roster for the past two weeks. Most of the men brought in five to six new clients bi weekly. They would meet these women at gyms, spas, or country clubs. After they would "date" these women, they would in turn tell their friends then they would call in to make an appointment with these eligible bachelors. Some women called looking for dates for black tie affairs, some were just looking for companionship, and others just wanted sex with no strings attached...the more charming the gentleman, the more return phone calls the women would make.

Once sex became involved, if the escort really put it on them, they would call repeatedly to set up additional dates. Side work was a definite no no! Renee considered it stealing and she would not tolerate it. She made each man sign a "contract" stating that they understood the rules and if they were broken here would be serious consequences, and not through a court of law.

The last man that was caught doing "side work" was found in an alley, bloodied, and badly beaten. The police questioned him about the attack but he would not cooperate. Renee looked at Gregory's client sheet.

"What is this shit? Three women?" She typed his name into the computer. It showed that in the last two weeks, Greg had only been on four dates. Renee sat back in her chair. Something was not adding up. She knew he liked the finer things in life...the nice condo, the car, the clothes. How was he making all it happen off such little money? She decided she would have a talk with him on Monday morning. She didn't want to jump to conclusions but she knew she had to get an explanation and soon. Renee stared out of her office window at the busy city street; she ran her fingers through her now jet-black and midnight blue wavy weave.

She thought back to fifteen years ago, the lowest point of her life. She was working at a fast food restaurant barely making ends meet. She needed extra income to cover her rent, electricity, and food. She took a job at Papa Mack's strip club on 39th and Washington. She despised dancing every night so to ease her anxiety she would smoke a blunt and drink all night. Erica also worked at the club and the two became close friends and supported each other through their nightly shifts.

One night Renee got off earlier than usual and started towards the bus stop. The two ladies usually rode the same bus home together every night, but Erica had hit the jackpot with a major spender and wanted to stay to milk him dry of all his cash. Renee's feet were throbbing and she was exhausted but she managed to make $230 in tips, at least the lights would stay on for another month and she could eat. She stood waiting at the desolate bus stop, almost asleep on her feet when she felt a sharp blow on the back of her head. She stumbled and tried to catch herself from falling but she hit the ground face first. She felt herself being dragged. She fought to turn over but her assailant had a tight grip on her ankles.

She could feel the cement below her ripping her clothes and flesh. She screamed as loudly as she could but it was two a.m. and no one was around the lonely bus stop. The assailant held her face against the ground, hiked up her mini skirt, and had his way with her. The combination of Renee's tears and dirt muddied her face as she lied there helpless and in intense pain. Luckily, the mystery man ejaculated quickly, took her purse, and ran off into the night.

Renee lay on the ground lifeless until she was sure he was gone. She stood up and brushed the dirt off her face with her hand. She couldn't believe she was raped, but then again, yes, she could. What did she expect? Her life was one disaster after the next. The man had taken her purse so she had no money, no way to get home.

She was not going back to the club looking a hot beat up mess so she took a deep breath and walked the four miles home...broke...tired...ashamed...and bloodied. Renee brought herself out of her trance and blinked back her stinging tears. She was a businesswoman now, those bitter memories were in the past, and there was no need to think of them...ever. She did know that she would never be taken advantage of again; she would never allow herself to feel vulnerable. She would protect herself by any means necessary.

****

Lydia sat at her dining room table drinking her third cup of coffee for the morning. What happened last night? She let out a deep sigh. She would be lying if she said she didn't enjoy being with a woman. Alexis was beautiful and amazing, she definitely knew her way around Lydia's body, but where was Gregory? She was so confused, so frustrated. She wanted answers but she had no way to contact him. She still hadn't experienced him and she longed and ached for him.

Lydia spent the rest of her day organizing and cleaning her apartment. She made her groceries for the week, did her laundry, and watched television. She did anything she could think of to keep her mind off him. Before she knew it, the day had passed and it was six p.m.

She had no desire to go to work tomorrow, especially if she had to deal with Katrina. She had fifty hours of vacation time just sitting on the books. Maybe she would go visit Francesca in Virginia. She needed some time away from the madness and emotions she was feeling. All she knew is that she wanted to experience the magic she felt the first night they spent together.

Lydia got up the next morning and prepared for work. She wanted to call out sick but then she would just stay home angry and confused over Gregory. She gathered her things and went outside for a cab. The cab driver talked to her the entire ride and she was definitely not in the mood for small talk. She walked through the double glass doors and down the long narrow brightly lit hallway. She turned the corner and walked up to her cubicle and stopped dead in her tracks.

"What in the world?" On Lydia's desk was a giant white teddy bear holding a red heart that said, "I'm beary sorry," and a vase with twelve long stemmed red roses. Lydia was beyond speechless!

"Girlfriend! Who are they from?" Michael leaned in to smell the flowers.

"Oh, um, just a friend," Lydia smiled at her gifts. Katrina sat in her cubicle looking in silence. The look of jealousy was all over her face and Lydia loved it! Lydia rubbed the stuffed bear's fur and smelled the fragrant roses, the entire time keeping her eyes on Katrina. She felt empowered, important, and in control. Katrina got up and left her cubicle, rolling her eyes as she walked away.

Michael and Lydia giggled like little girls. Honestly, she was very excited about her gifts but she was still very unsatisfied. She wanted HIM! She wanted to smell his intoxicating scent and taste his sweet juicy lips. She did not understand why he didn't show up Saturday night but she couldn't deny that she enjoyed Alexis. Lydia sat back in her chair and let her mind wander. Alexis had taken her to a place she had never been before. She couldn't believe how great she made her feel…she actually made her squirt! That was something that Lydia only saw in the adult movies she sometimes watched.

Alexis. A strange feeling overwhelmed Lydia, a feeling of worry and jealousy. Who was Alexis to Gregory? Why did he send her to the room? How well did they know each other and had they slept together? She felt herself getting angry. Her common sense told her that she barely knew Gregory and she had no claim to him but her heart and feelings told her something different. He was the change she needed. She could not believe she actually missed him. Lydia forced herself to calm down and continued through her workday as usual.

She ate lunch at her desk and listened to the office gossip. She planned on going home, making a grilled chicken salad, and watching TV. She desperately wanted to talk to Gregory or at least talk to Alexis so she could get his phone number, but she had no way of reaching either party.

Five o'clock came; it was time to head home. She decided to leave the bear and flowers on her desk; she didn't feel like toting them home in the cab. She grabbed her purse out of the bottom file cabinet drawer, and put on her sweater. She logged out of her computer and started to leave.

She unlocked the door to her apartment and went inside, "I need a cat, dog, something to welcome me home every evening." She stripped out of her pinstriped pants, white blouse, underclothes, and threw on her black pajama shorts and grey tank top. She felt her nipples grow hard as she walked over to the fridge for a bottle of water. She hated how cold her hardwood floors were but she refused to cover them in tacky throw rugs. She lied down on the sofa and stared at the ceiling. She thought about Saturday night and instantly became aroused.

Although she enjoyed Alexis, she was definitely missing something…dick. The thought of him stroking her made her hot and moist. She slid her hand down her shorts and began rubbing her protruding clit.

"Se siente tan bein," she moaned as she pleasured herself. She was lost in her sexual pleasure when a loud knock interrupted her thoughts. She wasn't expecting anyone. GREGORY! She jumped up and straightened up her clothes. She finger combed her hair from her face and headed for the door. She could feel her heart racing, anxiety building. She could not wait to see him so she could hug him and kiss him deeply.

Lydia smiled as she opened the door and her expression quickly changed. She frowned and asked firmly, "WHAT ARE YOU DOING HERE?"

CHAPTER NINE

"Damn chica! That's how you welcome your big bro?" Anthony stepped through the door carrying a backpack and a large black duffel bag. Lydia could not believe it! She had not seen Anthony in about six months and she was happy with that. She slammed the door and watched him open her fridge and help himself to a beer.

"This is all you got?" He stared at the bottle, "This some girly shit. You don't have anything stronger?" Anthony plopped down on the sofa and looked at his sister.

"Ant, why are you here?" Lydia was frustrated beyond words.

"Look sis, I just need a few days to crash, I...I got nowhere else to go."

Anthony sat down and put his bottle on the table. Anthony Morrell was 6'3" with a golden honey complexion. His arms and chest were built and muscular, his biceps were large and cut with precision. He kept his hair cut in a dark Caesar and his goatee was always neatly trimmed. The man definitely took pride in his appearance.

But Anthony had a dark side that Lydia was all too familiar with.

Growing up in the Morrell household was an everyday challenge. Their father, George Morrell was a severe alcoholic and gambler. He would get paid on Friday morning and be broke by Saturday night. There were many nights Lydia and her brother went to bed hungry. Their mother, Sophia, had a part time job cleaning office buildings three nights a week and it was barely enough to pay any of the household bills, but it did put minimal food in the house.

George often came home from his job as a city garbage man in a foul mood. He would sit at the kitchen table pouring shot after shot of whiskey and yell at their mother because he was tired of Spanish rice with every meal. It was the most inexpensive side she could buy so therefore they had it almost every night. He would yell at the children and call them "burdens" and "worthless."

Lydia would always remain quiet and take the tongue-lashing but Anthony would lash out. He would argue with his father and call him names; sometimes it would escalate into a physical confrontation. Sophia would always try to dissolve the arguments before that happened but most of the time she failed.

When Anthony was fifteen, he skipped school and came home early. He knew his mother and father would be at work so he could smoke his weed in peace. He walked into the house and heard moaning coming from his parents' bedroom. He slowly opened the door and saw his mother in bed with a strange man. His mother was face down; ass up, and the man had a tight grip on her hips. He furiously pounded her. "Amas a esta polla?" the foul stranger kept asking. Hearing his mother moan in delight as the man roughly penetrated her was more than he could stand.

Anthony slowly backed out of the room and ran out the front door. When he returned home at dinnertime, his mother was putting together plates of beans and rice, Carne Guisada (stewed beef), roasted chicken, and fried plantains.

"Mama! Look at all the food!" eleven-year-old Lydia exclaimed. "How did we get so much to eat?"

Sophia looked lovingly into her baby girl's face, "God has blessed us baby."

Lydia hugged her mother tightly around her waist. Anthony began to grow angry with his mother.

"How…EXACTLY were we blessed to be able to afford this food huh? Where did the money come from MAMA?"

Sophia could see the familiar look of anger in her son's eyes; it was the same look she saw every day in her husband's eyes. "Ant, I got a raise at work sweetie. Isn't that great?" Sophia could feel the lie she just told forming a lump in her throat. She was tired of struggling, she was tired of her and the children going to bed hungry, she was tired of her loveless marriage. She saw the way some of the men in the office buildings she cleaned looked at her. She knew they had money and did not mind spending it on any and everything they wanted, which included her.

Anthony knew his mother was lying, he knew exactly how she earned the extra money. He felt his temper growing…all he could see was the strange man handling his mother. Before he could lash out at her, his father came in drunk and loud.

"Bitch I'm hungry! Where's my damn plate?"

Lydia crouched behind her mother as Anthony stared with both fist clenched. Sophia took a deep breath, made George's plate, and placed it in front of him. He looked at the plate of delicious food and began quietly eating. The rest of the family sat at the table and ate in silence. Anthony shot hateful looks from across the table at his mother. He knew things were bad but he could not believe that his own mother would stoop so low to sleep with a complete stranger...to him, she was now a whore.

That day Anthony lost all respect for her. In the weeks and months to come, there were more lavish meals, new clothes, shoes for the children, and she always made sure beer and whiskey were in abundance in the home. Sophia's appearance changed. She dyed the gray out of her long black hair and wore it down more often, she was happier. Their father continued to drink and gamble away his check but Sophia never said another word about it, she had things under control.

By the time, Lydia was fifteen, her brother had moved out of the family home. She missed him but not the constant arguing and disrespect he showed their mother. Shortly after Anthony left, so did her father. He left Friday morning for work as he usually did and Lydia did not expect to see him again until Saturday evening after he drank and gambled most of his check away. When Sunday afternoon arrived, Lydia's mother began cooking dinner. Lydia stared out the window anxiously awaiting his return.

Although her father was mean and insensitive, she loved him greatly.

"Mom, have you heard from Papi?" Lydia was more than worried.

"No baby. I'm sure he is fine. He will be home soon. Please, come and eat."

Lydia ate dinner and shortly after went to bed. She felt alone and sad. Besides her family, she did not have any friends to talk to. She did not have a boyfriend. She was extremely curious about sex. She would listen to the girls in the locker room after P.E. about their sexual experiences. The girls used phrases like "he ate me out" or "blowjob." Lydia was confused and didn't know what they meant. She would love to have a boyfriend but no one paid her any attention.

Three months went by and George Morrell had not returned home. Lydia's mother carried on day to day as if nothing were wrong. She went to work, cooked dinner, and took care of the house. Lydia was glad her mother had found a way to take care of the house but she was not pleased with the way she went about it. Lydia lied in bed several nights listening to her mother entertain her gentlemen friends. Whenever she would ask about her father, her mother would say he would come home when he was ready. That answer never satisfied Lydia and it made her angry that her mother did not seem to care about her husband's whereabouts.

Sophia began to have male friends over during the week and always on weekends. She would watch her mother brush her hair and apply makeup. She started wearing more seductive and revealing clothes…and drinking. Her mother never drank!

By then, Lydia was seventeen and a senior in high school. She had blossomed into a beautiful young woman. She had her father's smile and her mother's eyes. Her golden complexion was flawless. The girls at school envied her but Lydia never noticed. Lydia looked forward to chatting with her brother on the phone every Saturday.

Anthony was living with some friends on the other side of town and was working part time at the shipyard, the other time he spent selling weed. He would give his sister a few dollars to buy herself something nice. Lydia never told her brother about their mother's gentlemen friends. She knew it would anger him but for some reason she figured he already knew.

"Lydia, I'm going out shopping for a couple of hours. I will buy you something nice ok?"

She smiled at her mother and said goodbye. She loved when the house was quiet and she loved being alone. She curled up on the sofa with her new book and began reading. Fifteen minutes later, a knock on the door startled her. Frustrated, she got up to see who it was.

"Hey beautiful, Sophie home?"

Lydia looked at the man standing in front of her. He was a tall, very clean-shaven white man with wavy light brown hair. His eyes were a piercing hazel color and he had a wonderful smile. He wore a very fancy charcoal gray suit with shiny black leather shoes, and he smelled fantastic.

"Um, no she's not in. She should be back soon, I think." She stumbled over her words.

"May I come in and wait? She's expecting me." The stranger flashed a wide smile.

She knew it wasn't smart but she let him in. As he walked past, she closed her eyes, and inhaled his cologne. The gentleman sat down and looked around the room.

"I am Jeffrey, a friend of Sophie's from work. You are?"

"I'm Lydia, her daughter."

Jeffrey looked at her and let out a chuckle. "She never mentioned a daughter. You look like her. How old are you?"

Lydia sat down on the sofa across from him, "Seventeen."

Jeffrey tilted his head and stared at her. He couldn't believe how beautiful she was. He could feel himself getting aroused. He would much rather be with her than her mother. They shared small talk about school, her grades, and the weather. She offered him something to drink, he accepted. When she handed him the bottled water, he grabbed her hand and pulled her down beside him on the loveseat. He brushed her hair away from her face. Lydia wanted to speak but nothing would come out. He leaned in and kissed her on the lips. He kissed her again and slowly separated her lips with his tongue. Lydia had never been kissed before.

She didn't know what to do. She felt confused, frightened, and turn on all at the same time. Jeffrey pulled her by her shoulders closer to him. He explored her mouth with his tongue and rubbed her arms. Lydia loved the new feeling she was experiencing. She felt a tingling between her thighs. Jeffrey could sense that she was enjoying what was happening. He slowly slid his hand up her t-shirt onto her breast and squeezed her hard nipple, Lydia let out a gasp.

He pulled her shirt up and began hungrily licking and sucking her breasts; he pulled them together and licked the nipples at the same time. Lydia moaned and squirmed around in ecstasy. He took her hand and laid it on the bulge that had formed in his suit pants. Lydia had never actually touched a penis before; she was in shock. He reached up her shorts to feel her sweet spot, it was hairy and very wet, Lydia tried to push his hand away but he slid a finger in and she let out a timid cry.

"Lydia, are you a virgin?"

She nodded her head yes with a look of embarrassment in her eyes.

Jeffrey caressed her face, "I won't hurt you. I just want to make you feel good. You're so beautiful, so sexy."

Those words resounded repeatedly in her head. She wanted someone to think she was beautiful and sexy. She longed to feel loved and desired. He leaned her back on the loveseat and pulled her shorts down. He took a condom from his pocket and pulled his pants and underwear down. Lydia's mouth opened as she stared at his long hard dick. She was scared.

Jeffrey filled his hand with spit and gently rubbed it all over her pink slit. He massaged her clit and she could feel the heat rising between her thighs. She wanted him so bad she was unsure of herself; she didn't know what to expect. He lowered himself down on top of her. He warned her it would hurt a little but not for long. He slowly slid his swollen head into her tight hole. She closed her eyes and tightened her face. She felt a burning sensation, almost like she were stretching or tearing. Jeffrey continued to ease his dick into her.

When was all the way in he started stroking her. He began stroking her harder, faster, going deep into her virgin pussy. They were both moaning; Lydia was grabbing onto the sofa cushion. Tears ran down her face, it hurt but felt so great at the same time. Jeffrey kissed her up and down her neck and whispered in her ear telling her that she felt great.

She began to panic, "Oh no! I think I'm peeing!"

Jeffrey became even more excited and began stroking slower but deeper. "No baby, you're cumming. Relax and enjoy it."

Lydia closed her eyes and let the intense wave of orgasms wash over her. Her body jerked and twitched. She tried to control herself but the feeling was overwhelming. She couldn't believe she was losing her virginity to such a gorgeous man. He continued to stroke her and rub her clit and suck her nipples; eventually she came again.

"Fuck me!" Jeffrey yelled out as he filled the condom with his hot cum.

He pulled out of her and asked her where the bathroom was. She pointed down the hall. As he disappeared, she sat up. She could still feel the stinging and burning between her thighs. She looked down and was in shock to see blood all over the beige love seat cushion.

Lydia jumped up, went into the kitchen, and grabbed paper towels. She wiped between her thighs and pulled her shorts back on. She grabbed a dishcloth, put dish soap on it, wet it, ran back to the love seat, and started scrubbing until only a faint red stain was left. Jeffrey came out of the bathroom looking as if nothing had just happened between them.

"Well beautiful, I gotta go. You were great." He tossed a folded fifty-dollar bill at her. "Look if your mom asks, I wasn't here ok? Hopefully we can hook up again."

He winked at her then let himself out. Lydia looked at the money lying on top of the bloodstained cushion and began to cry.

CHAPTER TEN

"Go harder! Come on! That's all you got? Pump it boy!"

Gregory hated working out with Brent; he was always such an asshole when it came to working out in the weight room. Gregory dropped the fifty-pound weight and wiped his face.

"Good workout today man," Brent huffed.

"This body doesn't happen on accident you know." Greg kissed his biceps.

Brent shook his head at Greg and began to admire himself in the gym mirror. He was also employed at Premier Escorts but he only worked there in the evenings. During the day, he worked security at the high-rise office building downtown. Brent wasn't quite as handsome as Gregory but what he lacked in appearance he made up for in his charming good old boy personality and rock hard six foot chiseled body. His bright red close cut hair and shining blue eyes were always a topic of conversation with the ladies, not to mention his deep country accent.

"So when is Renee throwing the next party?" Gregory asked as he wiped off the weight bench.

"I believe it's this weekend man and I've already got the perfect date. Man, this woman is fine as hell...and rich! She caught her wealthy husband cheating and took him for everything he had...and she don't mind spending some on Big B!" Brent bust out laughing, the people in the gym looked in their direction.

Gregory laughed at Brent's remark and looked around the gym. "Yeah I got some fresh meat I'm working on too. She's not the baddest but I know she can really hook a brother up."

Brent frowned at him and shook his head. "Hook you up how?" he asked.

Gregory looked around cautiously and started to explain. "Dude, listen. This chick is a gold mine! She's so sweet," Gregory smirked sarcastically. "She so sweet and easy. She's looking for that sexual high and I'm gonna make sure I keep her high as gas!"

Brent took a long a long gulp from his water bottle. "I still don't get it."

Gregory continued, "She works at the collection agency collecting for American Express. Only major businesses and wealthy people usually get those. And there are no limits on those things! By the time they catch on to what's going on it will be too late and my name won't be in it at all."

Brent stared at him in deep thought. He stared so long that Gregory became uncomfortable. "So...you're gonna try to get her to give you credit card numbers? Man get the fuck outta here!" Brent broke out into his hearty country laugh again.

"Man shut the hell up!" Gregory felt himself getting mad. He knew it was the perfect hustle and he didn't care what Brent, with his country bama ass, thought.

"She can't be that sex crazed and naïve that she would do something that risky...or illegal?"

Gregory gave Brent a sideways look. "This chick is sprung dude and I haven't even put the monster on her yet!"

Brent shook his head and smirked, "Are you going to fuck her soon?"

"Yes that's the next move. I may take her to the next party, get a private room, and do damage."

"She's going to pay the thousand dollar registration fee?"

"Hell no! She doesn't know what I do fool! If I bring her, I got that covered."

"You're playing a dangerous game brotha. You're playing with this girl's emotions and you fucking Renee over doing this side work shit." Brent looked at the clock, "I gotta go man. Be careful, that's all I'm saying."

The two men gave each other a pound and Brent left. Gregory sat on the weight bench looking at himself in the mirror. He heard everything that Brent said but he was still determined to carry on with his plan. Lydia was an easy target. She was gullible, naïve, easily persuaded...and best of all desperate. He had arranged for Alexis to turn her out and make her burn with even more sexual desire. She could have easily told Alexis no and left but she didn't. She stayed and enjoyed every lick and tease and the best thing was he had it all on DVD, collateral. He wanted to have control over her. He planned to unleash all his tricks on her that weekend and seal the deal by giving her the best night of her life.

Gregory went home and showered. He had a meeting with Renee that he was not looking forward to. He was supposed to see her Monday but blew her off. Gregory dried off and walked out of the bathroom naked. His mocha brown body was smooth and silky, and not a strand of hair anywhere. He always shaved everything from his neck down, including his toes. He absolutely hated body hair. He decided to watch the video of Alexis and Lydia again before he got dressed. He lay on the bed and turned on the DVD player and TV. He watched Lydia's facial expressions intensely. He loved the look of passion on her face. He watched Alexis slide her tongue in and out of Lydia's sweet pussy. Gregory's manhood started to swell and jump. The head began to throb. He continued to watch as Lydia wiggled and squirmed while Alexis planted her face deep into her snatch. The way Lydia moaned and cried out excited him. His dick continued to jerk and throb but he kept his hands down beside him.

He continued to watch the video and talk to the TV, "Yeah...eat that shit Lex! Make that bitch cum again!" Gregory began to breathe harder, he started sweating, the feeling was intense, but not once did he stroke his swollen wood. He grabbed onto the sheets and started to growl. When Lydia started to squirt all over Alexis, he couldn't hold it in anymore. Hot semen squirted out of his engorged member like a geyser. He let it fall where it may, never once touching himself. It excited him that he had control of his body, that he could make himself nut without having to jerk off. He caught his breath and wiped his forehead.

"Damn now I gotta shower again."

He wasn't looking forward to seeing Renee because he already knew what she wanted. He had to get his lie together before he got to her office.

CHAPTER ELEVEN

Alexis sat in her beat up Honda Accord looking at the envelope of money. Two hundred dollars. That's all she meant to Gregory, two hundred dollars. She wouldn't have slept with Lydia if it weren't for him asking her to do so. She felt the hot tears build up in her eyes but she quickly blinked them away so she wouldn't mess up her makeup. Why couldn't he see that she was the one for him?

She was so tired of doing side jobs for and with him and not being able to get his full attention. She fantasized about them starting their own escort service and bringing in big money. He could tell Renee to kiss his ass and she could give the deuces to the wack ass club where she worked. But now she had a new obstacle in her way, that Latina bitch. Gregory was dead set on keeping her around until he milked her dry, which meant no time for her. Alexis glanced over at the tacky looking strip joint; she hated working at Papa Mack's. It was old and outdated.

The red leather upholstered chairs and booths had rips and tears. The beige carpet, at least it was supposed to be beige, was covered in all types of stains and cigarette burns. She was convinced that some of the liquor bottles were older than her. The dressing room smelled like mold, ass, piss, and sweaty lady parts. The thought made her nauseous. She knew Gregory was special the night she met him in the club. He looked so good in his black dress pants and dark gray dress shirt. He looked so wonderfully delicious that he looked completely out of place in Papa Mack's.

All the dancers watched him as he walked through the place. She watched the way he moved as if he owned the club. She was instantly aroused by his presence. She waited until all the other strippers tried their hand at giving him a lap dance but he just turned them away. Alexis watched him sip his drink as she walked over to the bar.

"Missy, what's that guy right there drinking?"

Missy glanced over at the table, "Oh Crown Royal on the rocks."

Alexis smiled, "Give me another one."

Missy fixed a fresh drink. Alexis pulled ten ones from her G-string and paid for the drink. She took a deep breath and swayed her thick hips over towards his table. She sat the freshly made beverage in front of him, "I thought you could use another."

Gregory looked at the tall sexy woman and smiled. "Thanks sexy. You know how to take care of a man huh?"

Alexis licked her pouty lips and leaned in closer, "In many more ways than one sweetheart."

Gregory rubbed his chin and studied Alexis' body. He instantly fell in love with her thick hips and fat ass. She looked about 5'10" but that was because of the stripper heels she had on. At the time, Alexis had a mid-length jet-black bob with a china bang. He thought the hairstyle was very sexy on her. They talked for a few more minutes and Gregory wrote his number on a napkin and handed it to her.

She was overjoyed but played it cool. She thanked him, folded the napkin, and slid it into her bra. As she turned to leave, he playfully slapped her on her butt. She winked at him and walked away. She knew she had him or at least she thought she did. Alexis blinked back tears again. She stuffed the envelope into her oversized red purse and went to start her shift.

****

"What's up man? Renee in her office?" Gregory asked Kevin, another escort. He went to knock on her door but hesitated. Honestly, he did need the job; the money he made was great. It allowed him to live comfortably, and let's face facts…he loved the sex. But every once in a while he came across a hustle he couldn't let pass. That one woman that had money and didn't mind spending it solely on him. The key? You had to make them want to give you their money or material items. That way when you cut them off it couldn't be considered a loan.

The black Corvette he was driving was a "gift" from a fifty-year-old woman he used to date. He was caught off guard when he arrived at her house and the car was sitting in the driveway with a big red bow. She told him that it would be registered in his name and she had already paid the insurance for a full year. Gregory fucked the shit out of her to show his appreciation. Two weeks later, he stopped taking her calls. He decided he was going to be sweet and turn the charm on with Renee. He had to keep her mind at ease so she wouldn't get suspicious.

"What's up Miss Mitchell?" Gregory smiled widely at his boss as he sat down in the chair in front of her desk.

"Damn G, what happened to you yesterday? I waited for you all day!" Renee had her hand on her hip and stood in her ghetto girl stance.

"Girl I was ripping and running all day, but I'm here now sexy. What's up?" He studied her with a lusty look. He licked his lips and looked her up and down.

Renee felt herself getting warm; Gregory turned her on. She wanted him but it was business and not personal.

"G, what's up with your stats? I mean two dates in a week? What...you part time now? Be real...what's up?"

Gregory rubbed his face and let out a sigh. He looked at Renee as if he were about to cry. Renee sat on the edge of her desk waiting for him to speak. "I've been going through some things lately," he cleared his throat and continued to speak, "You know down there." Greg almost wanted to laugh at the lie he just told. Renee gave him a turned-up mouth look indicating she didn't believe him.

"So what you caught something? Please tell me that ain't it!"

"Hell nah! Nothing like that! I'm just having a hard time keeping it up. Man, I got shit on my mind and my focus is off. That's all."

He looked at Renee hoping she was buying his far-fetched excuse. He never had any problem with "the monster" getting erect. He could stay hard for hours at a time. He mastered the skill of cumming and immediately regaining his erection and it drove the ladies absolutely crazy! He would sex them swollen until they begged for mercy. He loved being in control. He got off on making women submit to his dick, it made him feel powerful.

Renee gave him a sympathetic smile. She walked over to him and rubbed his shoulders. "I know baby, you just need to relax...loosen up a little."

Gregory despised her touching him. He had no attraction at all to Renee. She was so fake. Her breasts...her nails...her hair. He thought she looked ridiculous with her hot pink and black weave. Nicki Minaj looked better with those hairstyles than she did. Renee walked back to her desk and sat on it in front of him. She had on a very small tight red skirt and she didn't mind him knowing she had no panties on.

"Let me relax you and take your mind off things."

Gregory shook his head no. "I'm good Renee, plus this ain't good for business." He did not want to go there with Renee. The thought of being with her made him sick to his stomach and he began to sweat.

Renee walked over and slid his hand up her short skirt. She was dripping wet and ready. He wanted to push her away but he knew she held all the cards. He couldn't lose his job, not yet. He slowly slid a finger inside her wet spot and rubbed her clit with his thumb. She put a hand on his shoulder to keep her balance; she was swaying as if she was intoxicated. Even though he didn't want her, his dick began to grow larger and longer. Renee pulled away and pulled her skirt around her waist. Gregory knew there was no way out of this and he had to deliver if he wanted his job.

"You got rubbers?" he asked hoping she would say no.

She walked over to her purse and tossed the gold wrapper to him. He dropped his pants and boxer briefs and slid on the rubber. He twirled her around and bent her over her mahogany desk. He knew Renee was a freak so that's how he was going to treat her. Greg put his hand on the back of her neck and slid hard inside of her. Renee just softly grunted as if the roughness didn't faze her. Gregory gave it to her deep and hard; he was digging in her hole with everything he had yet all she did was lightly moan and curse.

Oh, this bitch wanna be tough? he thought to himself. He continued to stroke her wet pussy hard while filling his hand with spit. He gently rubbed it on her asshole then began fingering it with his thumb.

"Shit G!" she called out. She began to tense at the touch of his thumb in her back door. Renee was not prepared for what happened next. Gregory slid out of her front and forcibly into her ass. Renee let out a yell and grabbed onto the desk.

"Greg! G! Damn…Wait!"

Her pleas didn't faze him at all. He kept stroking her back door hard and slapping her ass. She reached back and pushed him in an attempt to slow his rhythm but Gregory slapped her hands away each time. He grabbed a handful of her hair as he continued to punish her; he knew for a fact that would piss her off.

"Let go of my fuckin hair G!" Renee moved her head back and forth.

"It's not even yours so shut up." Greg started laughing as he stroked her harder.

She continued to beg and scream but never said no or asked him to stop. He felt the sensation building up; damn it felt good. Right at the point of release, he snatched off the rubber and came all over her ass, her back, and her skirt. He didn't care where it landed; he wanted to disrespect her as much as possible. Gregory plopped down in the chair, his ten inches still dripping. Renee slowly stood up, cum dripping down her butt and the back of her thighs. She pulled her skirt down and slowly turned around to face him. He could tell she was in shock and in pain.

"What the fuck was that G?" Renee's red lipstick was smeared and black mascara ran down her face from the tears she shed during the session.

"Thank you sexy! That was just the sex therapy I needed!" Greg stood up, tucked himself back into his underwear, buttoned, and zipped his pants. "So we done here?"

"Yeah, we're done."

Gregory winked and walked out of her office with a smug grin on his face. He drove the entire way home blasting Jay Z and laughing aloud. He had just punished Renee and it felt great. His next move was to contact Lydia and set up a date for the weekend.

Renee slowly walked over to her chair and sat down carefully. Her ass was on fire. She stared off into space thinking about what had transpired. "That muthafucka thinks he's funny," she said aloud. She didn't care what G said, she didn't believe a word of it.

She went into her office bathroom to fix her ruined makeup job and check her loose tracks. She didn't know if she was more upset about the soreness of her ass or her three loose hair extensions. She glared at herself studying her redbone complexion. She knew one day she would get to sample some of his goods but she hated the way he manhandled her. That shit was uncalled for. She wet a paper towel and wiped the dried cum that had trickled down her thigh and leg. She knew she would need to soak in the tub that night to relieve the soreness. She was determined to find out what he was really up to and she didn't care what she had to do to find out.

CHAPTER TWELVE

Lydia sat at her desk staring at the computer screen. It had been a slow morning, which was good because she was not focused at all. She was mentally drained from agonizing over Gregory. Why was he taking so long to contact her? Had he lost interest? She felt like crying every second of the day. Her heart ached continuously. All she wanted was to feel his arms around her and taste his lips. Not having contact with him was driving her insane.

Then there was Anthony. She did not want him staying at her house. The presence of him made her ill. All he did was drink beer, watch television, and mess up her place. He would stay out late at night then come home making noise and interrupting her sleep.

He once came home at four in the morning and decided to boil some sausage. He fell asleep on the sofa and all the water boiled out and the food began to burn. Lydia was awakened by the loud screech of her smoke detector. It took her three days to air out her apartment and get rid of the smoke smell. She decided she would give him a few days then ask him to leave. She prayed he wouldn't get confrontational; he had such a short fuse.

She remembered when they were younger he beat up the neighbor's son because their dog got loose and defecated on their lawn. Anthony beat him bloody then shoved his face into the dog's shit. Any little thing could set him off. Although he'd never been violent towards her, she didn't put anything past him.

It was 4:45 and the phone lines had been slow all day. She had finished all her callbacks so now she was just riding the clock. She glanced over at Katrina filing her nails. She followed her long legs with her eyes and stopped at her thighs. She snapped herself out of her daydream, the last thing she needed was Katrina catching her admiring her body. She listened as Michael ranted on about how he was going to make Robert get on his knees and put in overtime tonight. Lydia couldn't help but shake her head and giggle. At 4:55, her desk phone rang. "Ugh!" She was tempted not to answer but it could be a potential phone payment.

"Thank you for calling American Express, this is Lydia, how may I help you?"

"Lydia? Hey girl."

Lydia froze in her seat. She was completely stunned and caught off guard.

"Lydia...it's Gregory. Are you there?"

She could barely get the words to come out. "Yes, how are you?"

"I'm good. Did you get your gifts?"

"Yes and thank you. That was very nice of you." She was dying to ask when she could see him again but she didn't want to sound too desperate…but at that point, she was.

"I would love to take you out to dinner. I need to see you. I miss you," Gregory said as he rolled his eyes.

"When?" She was smiling ear to ear.

"Soon, very soon."

Lydia was not satisfied with that answer. She wanted an exact day and time but she didn't want to push. "Ok Gregory. Um maybe we could exchange numbers so we can keep in contact."

There was a long pause; she thought he had hung up.

"Let's discuss it when we get together, ok?"

Lydia sighed and agreed.

"I'll talk to you soon," he said and with that, he hung up.

Lydia sat staring at the telephone. He wanted to take her to dinner, a date? She was so excited. That had to mean he was truly interested in her! She couldn't wait to get dressed up and share a meal with him. They could get better acquainted and she could ask him all the questions that she had in her mind. Lydia clocked out and went outside to catch a cab. These were the days she missed getting a ride from Jackson or Francesca.

She stood on the sidewalk watching the traffic go by. She often wondered where people were going, what their life was like. She wondered if they were happy, were they in love? If when they were home, were they lonely...like her? Lydia was deep in thought when she heard someone call her name. She turned around and there he was…Gregory.

He had on a khaki dress pants with a sharp crease down the front, a black short sleeve button down shirt, and shiny black Stacey Adams. His shiny black curls sat perfectly on his head. She noticed a tattoo on his left arm peeking out from under his shirtsleeve but she couldn't quite make out the image. His mocha complexion was flawless and even. He wore black sunglasses, which made him look mysterious. He was perfection. Lydia was smiling so wide that her cheeks were hurting. She could not believe she was face to face with this sexy man again.

"Gregory what are you doing here?"

"I came to take you to dinner'" Gregory flashed his perfect smile at her. His teeth were so white and straight; they looked almost unreal.

"But you said soon, not today!"

"Right now is soon," he laughed. "So are you ready?"

Lydia looked down at her attire. She definitely picked a terrible day to dress down. She had on her plain black stretchy dress slacks, her white V-neck blouse, and her black flats with the bows on top. She had her hair up in a simple bun. She hadn't even worn earrings.

"Gregory, I'm...I'm not dressed for a night out. Maybe we can go back to my pla…." Lydia stopped in mid-sentence. She forgot about Anthony. There was no way she would take Gregory to her house.

Gregory took her hand and kissed it. "You look fine. Can we please go?"

She could tell he was getting impatient so she nodded her head ok. Gregory could have easily driven them to the restaurant in his Corvette but then Lydia would know what kind of vehicle he drove, possibly even his license plate number. He couldn't risk that. He hailed a cab and they rode six blocks to Aldinos Italian Restaurant.

The greeter seated them in a cozy booth near the back of the restaurant. Instead of sitting across from her, Gregory sat next to Lydia. She felt the butterflies fluttering in her stomach. She tried to keep calm but her nerves were getting the best of her, she couldn't sit still. She fidgeted around in her seat. Greg leaned over and gently pulled her close and kissed up and down her neck. She closed her eyes and felt herself getting lost in the moment as he kissed her cheek then gently pulled her face in his direction and kissed her lips. She felt her body begin to tingle as he began to kiss her harder, their tongues wrestling with each other. He sucked her bottom lip then began kissing her again. He pulled her hand underneath the table and placed it on the long hard object that had formed underneath her pants. Lydia moaned loudly, a little loudly than she should considering she that she was in a restaurant.

"Um may I get you something to drink?" the embarrassed waiter asked. Lydia jumped and quickly looked away.

Gregory laughed, "My bad man. Yeah, um bring us a bottle of Pinot Grigio please." The waiter smirked, nodded his head ok, and quickly walked away.

"Gregory I really missed you! What happened to you Saturday night?" Lydia didn't want to sound like a whiny child but she needed answers.

"I set Saturday night up for you...and Alexis. I wanted you to experience something new and exciting...get a little naughty." He flashed a devilish grin at her.

"Who is she to you?"

"She's just a friend, that's it. She likes to play...especially with the females so I set everything up. I knew she would treat you good." Greg looked around the restaurant checking out the two ladies sitting at a table near the front of the restaurant. He made a mental note to come back on another day; they looked like they could be potential clients.

"But why couldn't you have joined us? You sent me to be with a complete stranger. And besides, you didn't know if I would be comfortable...being with a woman, I was looking forward to being with you that night."

Gregory felt himself growing impatient; he couldn't stand a whiny crying female.

"Look, you had fun right? So, that's all that matters really. If you weren't comfortable being there with Alexis, you could have left...but you didn't did you?"

Lydia looked down at the table. She was beginning to feel uncomfortable because he was right. She could have left as soon as she realized that Alexis wanted to have sex with her but she did stay.

Besides, I have plans for us this weekend. Are you free?"

Lydia's demeanor quickly changed, "Of course! I would love that!"

The waiter bought their wine to the table, opened it, and poured them each a glass. The two toasted and drank in silence. Lydia ordered a large house salad without onions. She feared that if she ate anything heavy, she would be nauseous. Gregory ordered the shrimp Alfredo with extra shrimp, garlic bread, and a small house salad.

"Gregory, do you have a number that I can reach you? I would love to be able to call you and hear your voice."

He wiped his mouth with his cloth napkin and cleared his voice. He knew he had to answer the question carefully. He couldn't give her his number to reach him; he couldn't give her that much access to him. Gregory cleared his throat and rubbed her thigh.

"Baby, I would love too but right now I don't have a cell phone. I broke it and the company is sending me another one. Tell you what; as soon as I get it, I will call you with the number ok?"

Disappointment covered Lydia's face. She tried to smile through her sadness because she didn't want to ruin the evening.

Gregory sighed, "Do you have a cell phone number? I'll call you on that instead of calling you at work from now on."

Lydia smiled and quickly looked through her purse for a pen and piece of paper. She quickly jotted down her number and put it in his hand.

"I wanted to ask you, where do you work?"

Damn, he thought to himself. This bitch was asking too many questions. "I work overnight security at the high rise building downtown." Gregory thought about Brent since that was where he worked. Besides what were the odds, she would come looking for him during the early morning hours.

Lydia pictured him in his security uniform...she knew he looked so handsome. The waiter placed the check on the table, smiled, and walked away. The couple sat in silence as Gregory rubbed her arm and caressed her face. Lydia looked into his deep brown eyes. She didn't know how to feel about a man she barely knew. Her mind said to slow down, proceed with caution...but her heart and body wanted him as her own. She wanted to fall in love with him and him with her. She wanted to wake up beside this perfect person every morning. Her feelings and emotions were literally strangling her common sense. Gregory reached for his wallet to pay the bill. His wallet.

"SHIT!" he said aloud.

"What's the matter?" Lydia looked puzzled.

"My fuckin' wallet is gone! Damn it!"

Gregory stood up and began patting himself down. He couldn't believe his wallet was missing. Other patrons were beginning to look over at their table. Lydia began to feel flustered and embarrassed.

"Let me take care of it. Please sit down."

He looked around at the numerous eyes watching him. Lydia pulled out her wallet and he noticed several different credit cards. She pulled out her Visa and took care of the sixty-dollar tab. Once they got outside, he pulled her close and kissed her deeply while fondling her breasts. She moaned and held on to him tightly.

"Thank you baby, I am so embarrassed. Now I'm going to have to get a new license, credit cards...everything!"

Lydia was still in a daze from the kiss. "It's ok; I just hope everything works out."

Gregory smiled at her," I'm going to call you and give you the address to where our date will be. Can we get together Friday night?"

Lydia felt the warm tears begin to pool in her eyes, her bottom lip quivered. "How can I trust you Gregory? How do I know you will be there waiting for me?"

He pulled her close and kissed her hungrily...passionately. He began rubbing her sweetness through her pants. She wanted to look around to make sure no one was watching but she couldn't open her eyes. She was taken over by the fire that he was igniting inside of her.

"Listen to your heart Lydia. Trust me. I will be there." He pulled away and looked at her. He knew he had her right where he wanted her. He got a cab for her and she left for home. She wanted him to share a cab with her but he explained he had errands to run in preparation for Friday night. He watched the cab go around the corner then he walked back into the restaurant and headed towards the kitchen.

"What's up playa? You are definitely the man!"

Gregory smirked and shook his head, "Shut up Vic. My baby out back?"

"Yep, she's waiting on you."

He walked out to the back alley to his shiny black Corvette, his baby. He pulled his keys out of his pocket, hit the unlock button, and got in. He started her up and listened to the engine purr.

Everything was going as planned and he would completely have her sprung after Friday night. He was going to pull out every trick and position he could think of. He was going to make her fall so deep that she would do anything he asked…anything. He reached over to the glove box, took out his wallet, slid it into his back pocket, put the car in drive, and left the restaurant.

CHAPTER THIRTEEN

Anthony peeked out of the window for the third time in ten minutes. He was restless, uneasy, and paranoid. He had dodged these guys for four months; it was just a matter of time before they caught up with him. They had already killed Rico and Mike; he was the last piece of the puzzle. He looked over at the black duffel bag. All they had to do was drop the bag off at Cinnamon's house, which was Big Kendrick's girlfriend.

Big Kendrick was a well-known drug dealer on the east side. Anthony met him the last time he was locked up and Big Kendrick had promised him a job. Anthony thought it was the opportunity of a lifetime. Big Kendrick a.k.a. Big K got out before Anthony but he made sure he had an address to come find him.

Once Anthony hit the streets six months later, he went straight to the address on the paper that he held on to like it was gold. Big K gave him a job selling nicks and dimes, just to start him out. Soon Anthony had so many customers that he recruited his boys Rico and Mike to help him. Rico worked doing security at the parking garage downtown and Mike worked at a construction site. Both of those areas were perfect for selling their product.

Anthony got a job at the shipyard but after a while, he started messing up and he was let go but he still went back on occasion to make a few "deliveries." He was making decent money and he proved to Big K that he was trustworthy. Big K had called Anthony to the back room of his four-bedroom condo.

"What's good Ant?" Big K looked at him up and down as he lowered his 350-pound frame down on the foot of the bed.

"Nothin' Big K. Just trying to keep business booming for you."

Big K rubbed his chin and looked up at the ceiling. "Yeah Ant, you have been pulling your weight. I may have something for you to do for me. It's very important. Don't fuck it up."

Anthony snapped out of his daydream. Those words kept playing in his head like a broken record, "Don't fuck it up." He had done the complete opposite and now he was running for his life. He looked at the clock on the stove, 7:15.

"What the hell? Where is that girl?" He knew Lydia got off at five and was always home no later than five thirty. He called her on her cell and it went straight to voicemail. He called again, same thing. "Fuck!"

He peeked out the window again, his mind racing. What if Big K found out where he was and snatched her? He sat down at the dining room table and held his head in his hands. If anything happened to his baby sister he would kill whoever did it and he would definitely kill that fat ass Big K. Anthony dialed her number again, voicemail. He stared at the duffel bag and felt anger begin to overwhelm him. He was about to go out looking for her when he heard the doorknob begin to turn. He quickly grabbed the aluminum bat that Lydia kept by the front door and took his stance…just in case.

Lydia walked to her front door with the biggest smile on her face. Friday night was three days away and she was so excited. Finally, she would be with her Gregory. The very thought of him made her body tingle. She was determined to make him her man. She opened the door and jumped at the sight of Anthony standing by the door holding the aluminum bat.

"What is wrong with you Anthony? And why are you sweating?

"I...I was worried chica! Where the hell you been? I called your phone like a dozen times!" Lydia stood staring at her brother as if he was insane. She dug her phone out of her purse and realized it had died. She immediately began to worry that she missed a call from Gregory.

"My phone died that's why it didn't ring! Why are you so worked up?"

Anthony glanced over at the bag and back at his sister. "Nothing. Where were you?"

She tried not to smile as she thought about her evening. "I went to dinner after work." She walked over to the fridge; she could feel her brother's eyes following her. She took out the last beer and sat on the sofa. He sat on the loveseat across from her and looked at her suspiciously. She opened the beer and began to drink never looking at Anthony.

"Dinner huh? With who? One of your girlfriends from work?"

She looked at the TV screen pretending to watch whatever was on. She knew she had to answer carefully. Although she was a grown woman, he had a way of making her feel like a shy little girl.

"Yes Ant, I went out with a friend. Now I'm tired. I'm going to take a bath and get ready for bed." Lydia put her bottle in the trash and walked towards her room. Anthony jumped up and blocked her path. "Boy move!" she tried to push past him but he wouldn't budge.

"You got a man huh? Yeah, baby sis got a little boyfriend."

Lydia rolled her eyes, "I have a friend, not a boyfriend. Now move Anthony!" Lydia pushed past her brother and slammed the bedroom door.

"Yeah you got a man! I hope you aren't turning into a fuckin' whore like your mother! YOU HEAR ME?"

Lydia sat on the bed looking at the bedroom door…then she heard the front door slam. She quietly got up and cracked her bedroom door. She looked around and realized he had left. She couldn't understand why he was always so angry, just angry at the world. He had definitely inherited his temper and control issues from their father. She was grown and she did what she pleased. Nothing was going to stand her way of being with Gregory...not even Anthony.

She went out into the living room and started to straighten up. She put her throw pillows back on the sofa and threw away numerous beer bottles. She put his dirty clothes in the hall closet. She looked around for his duffel bag but he must have taken it with him. Lydia turned off the main lights and left the lamp by the front door on. She was about to go to bed when loud knocking on the front door made her jump.

"Yo Ant! Ant! Yo Ant, you here? You in there?"

Lydia stood by her bedroom door paralyzed with fear. She knew the kind of company that her brother kept and she was scared that one of them knew where she lived.

BANG BANG BANG BANG

"Yo Ant! Come on man, please… I need to talk to you!"

Lydia reached for her cell phone but forgot it was dead. "Please go away," she whispered to herself almost in tears. Lydia tiptoed to the door and peeked out of the peephole. The stranger had finally left. That was it! Anthony had to go! She couldn't have strange men wanting who knows what knocking on her door. He would have to leave by the end of the week.

Lydia couldn't sleep; her mind was full of thoughts. She laid in bed looking out the window at the starry sky. She thought back to the day she finally saw her daddy again. She was nineteen and had graduated from high school. She worked at the Discount Barn, which was a retail shop located just outside of the main mall in the city. She didn't love the job but it allowed her to make her own money and feel independent. Each payday she treated herself to a new outfit or a pair of earrings. She watched some of the girls her age as they shopped to see what the newest style was and what was in. She loved feeling pretty and attractive. She also loved sex.

She felt so ashamed and cheap after she slept with Jeffrey when she was seventeen, especially after he had paid her, but she couldn't deny how wonderful she felt during the experience. The way her body responded when Jeffrey touched and teased her was unreal. She longed to feel that feeling as much as possible. Lydia didn't have a boyfriend but plenty of men were interested in her. Some of the men she slept with were the same men that dated her mother. On occasion, they would hand her a few dollars afterwards but that was not the reason why Lydia let these men have their way with her. They made her feel special and beautiful; they made her feel wanted. Wanted? That was a new concept for her.

Her father never made her feel wanted or loved. He never told her she was beautiful, good, or smart. She used to long to sit on his lap and hug him around his neck. She wanted to sit and tell him about her day at school or about the bad dream, she had the night before, but instead she settled for being called stupid or lazy, burden, or mistake. She would always wake up early on Friday mornings to make sure she saw him before he left for work because she knew it wouldn't be until Saturday night when she saw him again.

Sometimes he would just look at her, other times he would offer a small smile. Although she did not understand why he didn't love her, she loved him with all her heart. He was her daddy.

Lydia left work at the Discount Barn in a hurry to get home. She knew her mother would be going out to the bar around nine and wouldn't be back until after midnight. That gave her plenty of time to have her date come over and get her itch scratched. That night's lover would be Ricky. Lydia met Ricky at the Discount Barn where they both worked; that is until Ricky was caught stealing merchandise out of the storeroom.

Now he worked at the convenience store that his uncle owned. He was two years older than she was and much more experienced. He taught her the art of oral sex. He was the first guy ever to put his mouth on her sweet spot. The way he flicked his tongue across her swollen clit made her cum almost instantly which sometimes made her upset because she wanted to make the feeling last forever. When he sucked on her bud and fingered her, she would cream all over his fingers. The thought of him made her wet. She was a virgin when it came to fellatio before she met him. She thought all she had to do was move her mouth up and down on it. She remembered the first time she tried it on Ricky.

"Uh Lydia? Hold up mami," Ricky moved her head away from his lap. "It's called SUCKING dick boo, you playing with this rock!" Lydia looked away embarrassed. She watched porn and thought she knew exactly what to do. It looked easy enough. "Look baby, just slide your mouth all the way down this dick, and suck on it, like a popsicle. I know you ate a popsicle before right?"

Lydia giggled at the silly question. She envisioned herself sucking and slurping a juicy red cherry popsicle. She looked at Ricky and gave him a lusty look. She started in on him, slowly sliding her wet mouth up and down his hard organ. She sucked and slurped. Ricky held her hair out of the way so he could see the show.

"Damn baby! Shit!"

Lydia was happy she was pleasing him; all she wanted was acceptance. She felt so sexy and desired. Ricky grabbed her hand and placed it on his six inches. He guided her hand up to the head and back down to the shaft. She caught on quickly. She worked him over, teasing his head with her hot mouth. Ricky leaned his head back and moaned obscenities. Although she was doing an excellent job, she wasn't aware of the signs of when a man was going to explode. Ricky moaned louder as his dick began to jerk and throb, he grabbed a handful of her hair as she continued to stroke and slurp and suck.

"Oh...I'm cumming! Lydia I'm cumming!"

Lydia was in her zone and didn't heed the warning. Before she knew it, hot semen filled her mouth and throat. She jumped up coughing, spitting, and gagging. Ricky bust out laughing, he was laughing so hard he was crying.

"Yo, I said I was cumming. Why you ain't move?"

"I...I didn't know!" Lydia ran to the bathroom to rinse out her mouth.

That was almost two months earlier and Lydia knew exactly what to do after that. She got home a little after nine and her mother had already left. She had told Ricky to come over around ten. Lydia hurried, showered, and changed into her short shorts and tank top. She went into the kitchen to grab a soda out of the fridge and heard a noise coming from the backyard. Someone was messing with the trashcans.

She grabbed the metal pipe that her mother kept propped behind the back door in the kitchen. She peeked out the curtain into the backyard but she couldn't see anything. She took a deep breath and held the cold pipe tightly in her hand.

She flipped on the outside light and flung the door open. "Who's there? Who's out there?" Lydia blinked her eyes to focus on the figure by the trashcans. He was eating a chicken leg that Lydia threw away the previous night. Her heart raced and tears built up in her eyes. She fought to catch her breath and she began to shake as she let the pipe fall from her hand. She tried to speak but all she could manage to get out was, "Daddy?"

The man looked down at his feet and swayed back and forth as if he were intoxicated. His once jet-black hair was now salt and pepper and wiry. His clothes were tattered and dirty. He wore flip-flops that were too big and his feet were dusty. He glanced up at Lydia then quickly looked down.

"Daddy? Where have you been? Why…why did you leave us?"

George mumbled under his breath but she couldn't understand what he was saying. She stepped down off the porch and slowly moved towards him...the closer she got the more pungent the smell from him became. George backed away from his daughter. He longed to do what he had never done...what he had always neglected to do...reach out and hug his daughter. He wanted to look at her but his shame wouldn't allow it.

"Dad...please...talk to me. Let me help you. I miss you so much. Come inside and let's talk."

He looked up at the house...the same house that he used to call home. This was the place that he carried his newly wed wife over the threshold, where they brought both of their kids after they were born. And now he was sneaking into the backyard to eat leftovers out of the trash.

"No. No. Nah...I...I can't go in there. Besides Sophia doesn't want to see me. I know she's moved on. I've seen her around town. She deserves better...always did."

Lydia felt her heart sink. She had never seen her father show remorse for anything. Was it possible that he had changed? "She's not home. We could sit and talk. I could fix you something to eat. Dad...I..."

"I ain't your daddy!" George's voice made Lydia jump and step back a few steps. "I ain't your daddy! I ain't...nobody. I ain't shit."

Lydia began to sob uncontrollably. George finally looked up at his daughter. He saw the pain and hurt in her deep brown eyes...the same hurt he saw in her face when she was a child and he would yell at her. He wanted to hold her and tell her it would be okay, but he knew it would just be a lie. George turned around to leave.

"Dad please don't go. Please don't leave me again. I love you!"

He continued to walk away and she could hear her father sobbing. Lydia watched as her father disappeared into the night. She went back into the house feeling broken and numb. Her father had rejected her yet again. Why wasn't she good enough for him to love her? What had she done that was so wrong? There was a knock on the front door.

"Daddy!" she shouted. She ran to open the door and her heart sank, Ricky.

"Girl you ready for this wood? Oh shit, what's wrong?" Ricky looked curiously at her.

"Not tonight, I can't," Lydia shook her head and closed the door in Ricky's face.

"Damn girl you could've called me or something. Lydia! SHIT!" Ricky walked away mad as hell.

Lydia lay in her bed crying like a newborn baby. All she wanted was her father's love and acceptance. To hear her father say I love you and you're beautiful would have meant the world to her. She decided not to tell her mother about what happened; she wouldn't care anyway.

That was so many years ago and yet it still felt like yesterday. She decided that reminiscing was a waste of time as she wiped the tears from her eyes. She hoped Anthony was quiet when he came home that night. She decided to concentrate on making love to Gregory and with that, she fell soundly to sleep.

CHAPTER FOURTEEN

Anthony walked down the sidewalk clutching the duffel bag tightly up against him. He was mad at himself for snapping on his baby sister but the thought of her with a man enraged him. In his eyes, she was pure and innocent; he didn't see her as a grown woman capable of making her own decisions. Anthony walked down 34th and Washington. He needed a pleasant distraction from all the bullshit that was going on in his life. He found the perfect place to drown his sorrows, Papa Mack's.

"Yeah, titties and ass and a few shots…damn right!"

Anthony walked into the dimly lit establishment and found refuge in a secluded booth near the back of the club but near an exit just in case he had to leave in a hurry. He surveyed the spot, getting familiar with his surroundings. The club was a dump and very outdated but it would serve its purpose for the night.

"What's good baby? What you sippin' on tonight?" the half-dressed waitress asked. Anthony looked her up and down admiring her physique.

"Let me get a Heineken and two shots of gin...Knotty Head...not that bottom shelf shit."

The girl winked at him and sashayed away. He sat the duffel bag on the floor between his feet with the strap resting on his knee. The waitress came back with his drinks but before she could turn to walk away, he told her to hold on. He downed the two shots of gin and took a long swig of his beer. He told her to bring another round and a bowl of peanuts.

She nodded and within minutes, she was back with his beverages. He could feel the effects of the liquor already. The gin had him feeling right...and horny. He looked around the room at the buffet of women; they all looked good to him. All of a sudden, the spotlight hit the stage, the beat dropped, and there she stood, the most beautiful woman he had ever laid eyes on. She came out in a white bra and G-string and white stilettos. She was so tall and sexy; it looked as if she could touch the ceiling. Anthony sat up in the booth and blinked several times to focus better on this beautiful creature.

She danced seductively to the music as if she was dancing only for him. She bent over and looked between her legs at the men gazing upon her. She slowly ran her manicured nails up her legs to her thighs and over her tight backside. She worked the stage as if she was in her own world and she worked the pole as if it was her lover. When she took off her top, dollars went flying from every direction onto the stage.

"Shit!" he said as he grabbed himself underneath the table. The beautiful vixen finished her routine, collected her money, and left the stage. Anthony was in awe. She was the finest female in the place. "Yo baby, the chick that was just danced, what's her name?" he asked one of the girls walking past.

"Hey sexy, you are fine as hell. You wanna lap dance?" the girl started swaying back and forth seductively.

"Maybe later mami...But right now I need to know the girl's name that was just on stage."

The woman looked disappointed. "Oh that was Alexis." She rolled her eyes and walked away.

Anthony sat staring at the dark stage. "Alexis. Anthony and Alexis. Yeah I gotta meet her. Definitely."

He ordered another round and watched for Alexis. He was determined to meet her. About twenty minutes later, she came from the back and made her way to the bar. She was wearing black boy shorts, a lime green bra, and green patent-leather shoes to match. She ordered a shot of Patron and downed it. She needed to stay buzzed to deal with this place. She leaned against the bar and looked around the club. The same tired lames that came every night were there.

"I swear it's always the same tired broke ass..." She stopped mid-sentence when she saw the sexy stranger staring her down. His eyes were instructing her to come over to his table. She liked his look; his dark caeser was on point, goatee shaped perfectly...damn his arms were huge!

She licked her lips and raised an eyebrow at him. She thought to herself that he looked like he might have a little money. He definitely looked like he could show her a good time in the bedroom. Alexis downed another shot and walked over to his table.

"What's good Alexis?"

She looked at him with curiosity, "Do I know you?"

"No, not yet sexy...but you should." He drank another shot of gin.

Alexis scooted into the booth next to him. "Why is that?"

"I think I can make you real happy. You need a man like me in your life." He picked up her hand and kissed it, "I'm Anthony."

She really loved his style. He might be a nice distraction from Gregory; Lord knew she needed something or someone to take her mind of the fact that he didn't want her. The two exchanged conversation, flirty glances, and slight touches. The chemistry was definitely there.

"Look sexy let's get out of here and go to your place," he said while staring at her breasts.

"Let's go to your place papi," she said rubbing in between his thighs. She could feel him getting erect.

"Nah baby. I stay with my sister right now. My uh...condo is under renovation at the moment."

Alexis gave him a suspicious look. She decided she didn't care if he was lying; she was drunk and horny and could use a different type of pole to ride.

"Alright let me get my stuff. You can follow me in your car."

Anthony let out a sigh, "My sister got my car baby. I'm gonna have to ride out with you."

Alexis started laughing. She got up and went to the back to get her belongings.

Anthony was so excited. He hadn't been with a chick as fine as her in a long time. He paid his tab, grabbed his bag, and followed Alexis out of the club.

■■■

Lydia had not seen her brother in two days. She called his cell but the recording said the phone service was temporarily disconnected. That was typical for Anthony, here one day...gone the next. Now it was early Friday morning and he still had not come home. Lydia decided she wasn't going into work that day. She was going to call out, something she never did.

"Oh ok Lydia, feel better. We will see you on Monday." Mr. Frasier said sympathetically.

"Thank you sir. See you on Monday."

Lydia hung up the phone and began to laugh hysterically. She had just lied to her boss and gotten away with it. She jumped out of the bed and went into the kitchen to start her coffee. She switched on the television to watch the news, and then changed her mind. The news was too depressing, she felt like laughing.

She flipped through the channels and found a rerun of Sex and the City. She loved that show! She always felt she had the heart of Charlotte, the savvy wisdom of Miranda, and the sex drive of Samantha. She longed for the fashion sense and talent of Carrie but she wasn't quite there yet.

Lydia poured a cup of coffee and continued to watch the love scene between Samantha and her lover. She imagined it was she and Gregory kissing and fondling each other. She imagined him devouring her breasts and fingering her shaved honey brown love spot hard and deep. She sipped her coffee slowly as she continued to watch the steamy scene and daydream about Gregory.

****

Gregory walked out of the hotel early Friday morning. He shielded his eyes from the bright morning sun that was peeking from behind the tranquil clouds. He got into his Corvette and yawned loud and long. The lady wore him out! To be almost sixty she had a lot of energy and was very flexible. He pulled the folded bills out of his pocket, fifteen hundred dollars. He couldn't believe she was willing to pay that much money for six hours with him. He had really put it on old girl too and she loved every minute of it, she had even paid for the expensive hotel room and room service.

Gregory decided to leave before she woke up just in case she wanted a morning session…besides her snoring woke him up so it was time to go. He drove home thinking about Lydia. He had to admit, she was very basic compared to the females he was used to messing with. He found her naivetés attractive. He looked at her like a blank canvas and he would create whatever masterpiece he wanted. Oh, the fun he planned to have with her.

He had already determined that she was the generous type after she graciously paid for dinner. She had several credit cards so he figured her credit had to be good. Then there was the icing on the cake, her occupation. If he could work his magic and make her fall for him, he could get his hands on credit card numbers. He laughed to himself. It could end up being his greatest hustle yet.

He decided to call Alexis to see what she was doing. The sixty year old he was just with didn't believe in giving head, which he found asinine, but for fifteen hundred dollars, he could live with it. But now he was craving it and he knew Lex would be down. He pulled out his cell and dialed her number. It rang several times then went to voicemail. Greg looked at the phone as if he had dialed the wrong number. When he called, she usually answered on the first ring.

He dialed the number again, the same thing. He tossed the phone down on the passenger seat and gripped the steering wheel tightly. He chewed his bottom lip as he felt himself getting hot. She always answered. ALWAYS. He knew she wasn't at work, so where the hell was she and why wasn't she answering? Was she with someone else? Someone from that bum ass club? He took a deep breath trying to calm down but it wasn't working. Alexis was not his woman at all, but he felt like she belonged to him, like he had laid claim on her.

"I'm going over there," he said out loud. He made a sharp U-turn and sped towards Alexis' house.

CHAPTER FIFTEEN

"DAMN BABY! Shit that was good!"

Alexis rolled off Anthony and collapsed on her stomach beside him. Anthony rubbed himself and looked over at her sweaty butt cheeks. He slapped her butt hard and she jumped. He stretched and looked around her room. Everything was decorated in black and red...black curtains, red lounge chair, black, red and white flowered comforter and shams, and an assortment of black and red stuffed animals. Her dresser and nightstand were black lacquer with gold trim. Anthony didn't really care for the décor but he was definitely comfortable in her bed.

"You thirsty?" She started rubbing on Anthony's hairy chest. She loved how his chest hair was straight and smooth. She thought it was unnatural for a man to shave his chest, as Gregory did.

"Yeah, I could use a drink after that workout. You got a beer?"

Alexis shook her head at him. *Who drinks beer at eight in the morning?* She thought to herself as she walked into the kitchen naked. Honestly, it was nice to have overnight company, he took her mind off her problems, but now it was time for him to go. She didn't want him to get comfortable; he looked like the clingy type. She went to the fridge but before she could open it, there was a knock at the front door. She instantly got an attitude. Who was at her door that early in the morning?

It better not be that damn Lawrence from the club. She already had a restraining order against him. She peeked out of the blinds to the curb, and there sat a shiny black Corvette.

"Oh my God! Gregory!" Alexis went back into her room and closed the door. She looked panicked.

"Where's my beer? Is someone knocking?" Anthony asked as he sat up in the bed.

"Yeah, just my neighbor. She always borrowing shit," she laughed nervously

The knocking grew louder and then Gregory yelled, "Lex! Lex! I know you here! Your piece of shit car is in the driveway!" Alexis let out a sigh and rolled her eyes.

"Hold up. Who is that?" By that time, Anthony was standing up and putting on his pants.

"It's nobody! Just be quiet and he will go away."

BANG BANG BANG

"ALEXIS OPEN THIS DAMN DOOR!"

Her cell phone rang, she looked at it, and it was Gregory. She didn't realize that she had already missed two calls from him. She was so busy sliding up and down Anthony's massive pole that she didn't hear her phone ring.

"Fuck that!" Anthony darted out of the bedroom door walking fast towards the front door. Alexis ran behind him, forgetting she was still naked. Anthony flung open the door and Gregory jumped. "What's up man?" Anthony said with his fist clenched and face tight.

Gregory looked Anthony up and down. Yes, Anthony was bigger than he was. Gregory looked at the tattoos on Anthony's arms. They were obviously prison tats; the quality was awful. Gregory started to laugh. He couldn't believe the dude actually opened Alexis' door. Alexis stood behind the door hiding because it finally dawned on her that she was completely naked. She couldn't get to her bedroom without Gregory seeing her so she stayed put.

"Look, I don't have no problem with you man...I just need to speak to Lex."

"And what do you want with my woman?" Anthony asked firmly. Alexis almost died, his woman? Yeah right.

"Your woman?" Gregory shook his head and chuckled, "My man, I think you got it twisted, that bitch belongs to me."

Alexis came from behind the door, enraged. "Bitch? Who the fuck you calling a bitch? And I don't belong to either one of you muthafuckas!" Alexis shouted rolling her neck; hand on hips and titties jiggling. At first, both men were fixated on her naked body but quickly snapped out of it.

"Either way, I'm in here and you out there so you need to step playa."

Gregory looked away then threw a punch at Anthony. Anthony moved away just in time then connected a right hand punch to Gregory's face then to his side. He doubled over but quickly got himself together and lunged towards Anthony. The two men wrestled each other knocking over lamps and her coffee table. Anthony slammed Gregory onto the floor and began kicking him. Alexis was screaming at the top of her lungs but the two men paid her no attention.

Gregory was balled up on the floor trying to protect himself the best he could as Anthony continued kicking and stomping him with his bare feet. Finally, she said she was calling the police and Anthony backed away from Gregory. The last thing he needed was the cops showing up and running his name. He had already missed two appointments with his parole officer so he knew he was wanted. Gregory got up as fast as he could but it was obvious he was hurting. Alexis stood behind Anthony; she was afraid Gregory might come after her next.

"You fucked with the wrong one," Greg shouted. As he headed for the front door, he spit a wad of blood onto Alexis' hardwood floor and gave her a sharp cold glare.

"Come see me then! Ain't nobody runnin'!" Anthony yelled with both arms up in the air.

Gregory left and Alexis slammed the door behind him. She looked around her living room, tears flowing down her cheeks. "Get the fuck out Anthony! Get out!"

Anthony stood with his mouth wide open. He couldn't believe it. He had taken up for her and now she was throwing him out? "Lex, I…"

"Don't call me that!"

"Oh his bitch ass can call you Lex but I can't? Who is he anyway?'

Alexis shook her head and exhaled deeply. "Someone I had a thing for but I guess not anymore."

Anthony was still mad but he could see the pain in her eyes. "Come here girl," he said quietly.

"I want you to go! I'm so serious right now," Alexis shouted between sniffles.

Anthony walked over to her and tried to pull her towards him but she resisted. He pulled her close again and bear hugged her. She wanted to pull away again but his embrace felt so good, so comforting. He hugged her and kissed her forehead. The tears continue to fall from her eyes down her cheeks. Anthony looked at her and gently wiped them away. What was it about her that had him feeling that way already? He just met her the previous night!

He kissed her as if he wanted to take all her pain away. He could tell she was a tough woman, and that she had been through a lot in life. He recognized the tough persona and the barriers she had because he was the exact same way. You had to be hard or people would take advantage of you, letting your guard down was not an option. She shivered in his arms. It felt different to her and honestly, she was a little apprehensive. She couldn't deny she still had feelings for Gregory…if she was completely honest; she loved him.

Anthony wanted her…all of her. He didn't want to share her and if that meant removing Gregory from the picture…then so be it. He picked her up and carried her to the bedroom. He kissed her body slowly, eagerly from head to toe. He kissed her as he had never kissed another woman. He put on a condom and slid deeply but slowly into her creamy wet spot, making sure she felt every inch of his rigid manhood. He stroked her steadily, keeping a deliberate rhythm while he kissed her.

Within minutes, the both of them climaxed together. Alexis was more confused than ever, she wasn't sure what was happening. She wanted Gregory and she knew she loved him but Anthony was making her feel desired and beautiful. It seemed like he really wanted to make her his woman. Should she give up on Gregory and concentrate on starting something meaningful with Anthony? Anthony decided he had marked his territory and she was his…and that punk ass Gregory had to go, no matter what.

Gregory drove away cursing at the top of his lungs. He drove recklessly, weaving in and out of morning traffic. How dare Alexis have that dude in her house and have sex with him! She didn't even take up for him. She should've told dude to leave as soon as she realized it was him at the door. He felt his eye and it was sore and tender to the touch. His bottom lip was busted. His whole body ached from being stomped. His ego was bruised more than anything else was. He was going to make that man, whoever he was, pay for what he did…and Alexis wasn't off the hook either.

He got home and threw his keys on the foyer table. It was nine thirty and he still needed to figure out what he was going to do that night as far as Lydia was concerned. He didn't want to take her to the sex party Renee was throwing. He didn't want to deal with Renee or having to sneak Lydia in. There was no way he was paying the thousand-dollar registration fee. He didn't want to come out of pocket for a hotel room but he definitely didn't want to bring her to his place.

He went into the bathroom to check his face. A red and purple bruise had formed underneath his eye and his bottom lip was slightly swollen. He blinked at the image looking back at him in disbelief. He felt himself getting mad again but decided to deal with all that later. He went into the living room and laid on the sofa. Where could they go that was cheap and couldn't be traced back to him?

He closed his eyes and was close to falling asleep when the idea hit him like a ton of bricks. He abruptly sat up and snapped his fingers, Brent! Brent said he was going to Renee's party so he could just use his apartment for a few hours. Perfect! He quickly dialed Brent's number.

"What's up Gregory?"

"Nothing much man. You working right now?"

"Yeah just made my rounds, now I'm chillin' at the security station. What's going on?"

Gregory paused for a minute then continued," I need a favor man."

"Talk to me," Brent said curiously.

"I need to use your apartment tonight."

"Hold on for a second."

Gregory sat on hold wondering what the problem was.

"Sorry Greg, I had to give someone directions to an office suite. Man why you wanna use my rinky-dink place? You got a condo on the beach."

Greg explained the situation to him hoping he would understand. Brent listened and didn't interrupt.

"So you wanna come up in my place, lounge in my living room, and screw this girl in my bed? I don't know dude. And I'm gonna have to take down my pictures and make sure all my stuff is put away. Man you're asking a lot!"

"Jesus Brent, is that a yes or a no?"

Brent sighed loudly, "Yeah ok but I don't get off till four thirty, and I'm not leaving the house until ten."

"That's cool, thanks man for real. I'm going to get her to meet me at your house around ten thirty, that will give me a thirty minute window to get right."

The two men talked for a few more minutes then hung up. Gregory hit star six seven and dialed Lydia's number. He wanted to make sure his home number was blocked before he called her. After the third ring, she answered.

"Hello beautiful, its Gregory," he rolled his eyes and smirked. "How's work going?"

Lydia smiled and giggled, "Hi Gregory. I've been looking forward to your call. I almost didn't answer; it came up as restricted. Where are you calling from?"

"Uh, from work. Yeah I had to stop by to drop off my office keys, you know since I'm not working tonight. I will be with you...sexy."

Lydia almost melted as she felt the hotness rise between her thighs. The way his words made her feel was indescribable. "So where are we meeting tonight baby?" She couldn't believe she had just called him that.

"My apartment."

"Really? Your place?"

"Yes 314 McDermott Street, apartment C. Can you be here by ten thirty?"

Lydia had the perfect idea. "Gregory, I called out of work today. I could come now and we could spend the day together!"

"SHIT." he mumbled.

"What? What's wrong?" she questioned.

"Oh I said shit, I can't. I have errands to run, I gotta go to the barber shop, and you know I gotta look good for you."

Lydia completely understood. She could use the time to pamper herself for their date tonight also. "I will be there at ten thirty. I can't wait to see you and your place."

"Cool. Talk to you later."

Lydia sat listening to her heart beating quickly. She laid on the sofa with her eyes closed, replaying their conversation in her mind. She was going to his apartment. That had to mean something right? He trusted her enough to bring her into his own personal space. She felt herself begin to drown in a sea of deep arousing thoughts. The doorknob began to jiggle; she sat up and looked at the front door.

"What you doing home? You sick?" Anthony asked while kicking off his shoes but still clutching the duffel bag.

Lydia's high quickly vanished. "No I'm not sick. I've been trying to call you but your phone is off."

Anthony reached into his pocket and pulled out his out of date phone and dialed his sister's number. "Your service has been temporarily disconnected, please call customer service to restore service."

Anthony shook his head, "My bad sis. I didn't know." He sat on the sofa and put the duffel bag beside him. He looked at his sister; she still looked the same way she did when she was twelve. The way she raised her eyebrows when she was curious about something, the way the corners of her lips curled up when she smiled and the way she twirled her hair when she was nervous.

"Hello? Ant! I'm talking to you!"

Anthony came to and laughed, "What?"

"I said where were you?"

He looked at his sister and laughed again. "How about you fix your big bro some grub and I'll tell you all about it."

Lydia rolled her eyes, "I know you were with some skank so spare me the details please!" Lydia walked into the kitchen to start fixing breakfast. As she was pulling the eggs out of the fridge, she decided it was as good of a time as any to drop the bomb on her brother. "Ant? I need to talk to you."

Anthony sat up and stared at his sister, "What's up?"

Lydia exhaled sharply, "Last night some crazy guy was banging on the door looking for you. He was knocking repeatedly and pretty much begging you to talk to him. It scared the shit out of me."

Anthony sat with his eyes as wide as saucers. His fists were clenched and tiny beads of sweat formed on his forehead. "Chica, what did he look like?"

"I don't know; I didn't go anywhere near the door until the banging stopped. When I looked out the peephole, he was gone."

Anthony got up and started pacing the floor. He was convinced it was someone sent by Big K. What the hell was he going to do?

"When do you plan on…leaving Anthony?" Lydia bit her bottom lip bracing herself for the impact of her big brothers temper.

Anthony stopped pacing and turned to face his sister. The look on his face made her cower. "Oh shit. You want me gone huh? Little sister wants her crib back so she can start whoring in private. That's what it is huh? That's cool, I'll leave tomorrow!"

"Ant please don't be mad, I just need my apartment back. Plus you said a few days; it's been a few weeks." Lydia didn't want to reference the tacky comment he made. She knew it would just cause even more problems.

Anthony sucked his teeth and nodded his head at her, laid back down on the sofa, and closed his eyes. He was done talking to her for right now. He had to figure out who was looking for him and what his next move was. His time and luck was running out.

"Ant? Anthony? I know you hear me!" He continued to ignore his sister's calls. She put the eggs back in the refrigerator, went to her room, and slammed the door.

"I don't need her, fuck her! I'll call my baby Alexis; she will let me crash with her." Anthony smiled then dosed off to sleep.

****

Gregory walked into Brent's apartment and looked around at the humble surroundings. He couldn't believe that Brent didn't live better than this. He was ashamed to "pretend" that this was his place. Brent didn't have nice furniture or the top of the line electronics. He had a thirty-six inch flat screen in the living room, which was the only television in the entire place. He had a red, green, and white plaid sofa with two wooden arms and a wooden backrest and an out of date wooden coffee table in the living room. A dusty fake tree occupied the corner of the room by the window. The light beige Berber carpeting under his feet had various stains throughout. Gregory frowned hard and shook his head. He now understood why every time he and Brent hung out, they hung out at his house. He was probably too embarrassed to invite him over.

He walked into the kitchen; it was very basic but spotless. The only appliances on the counter were a cheap black toaster and a white coffee maker. His bathroom was plain...definitely a bachelor's bathroom. He had a black shower curtain with the playboy logo on it and two black throw rugs on the floor. The bathroom was very tidy; at least that's what Gregory thought until he pulled back the shower curtain. Mildew lined the tile grout and the bottom of the tub was so dirty you could throw seeds inside it and start a garden.

Gregory quickly pulled the shower curtain closed and left the bathroom in disgust. His bedroom housed a king sized bed covered in a plain gray comforter and two pillows with black pillowcases. A matching painted black wood nightstand sat beside the bed and a matching set of dresser drawers decorated the wall on the side of the room by the door. In the corner sat an out of date treadmill. He had one window, which was covered in plain plastic white blinds.

"My man, you are killing me!" Gregory looked around in amazement.

"What? This is the Carlisle Estates! You better ask somebody!"

"Just because you have a fancy name like Brent Carlisle doesn't make this place fancy…at all."

Brent crossed his arms and frowned at his friend. "You don't have to use my place; you can find somewhere else to do your dirty work."

Gregory rolled his eyes and looked at his watch; it was ten fifteen.

Brent looked at Gregory's eye and frowned, "What's up with your eye?"

Gregory's anger began to grow again. "I got into it earlier with one of Alexis' punk ass boy toys. I got something for his ass though, her too."

"Why do you care Greg? She's just some trick you screw and do side jobs with. She is not worth fighting anyone over dude."

For some reason, the way Brent talked about Alexis made him upset. It offended him. "Just let it go ok?" Gregory said angrily.

"Cool," he said shrugging his shoulders.

Brent grabbed his stuff and jumped in his Jeep Cherokee and left. Gregory sat on the sofa feeling very out of place. The place was a dump compared to his beachfront condominium. Then it dawned on him, if Lydia saw how bad his place looked she would be more inclined to help him out financially.

"Yes this just may work out pretty well," Greg smirked and shook his head. He already had the wine chilling in the fridge; he had placed his bag of goodies in the room on the floor beside the bed. He turned on the television to find the music channels on cable, and then it occurred to him that Brent didn't have cable. Gregory tossed the remote on the coffee table and laughed. The guy was prehistoric. He went over to the radio that was sitting on the stand next to the TV and found a laid-back R&B radio station.

A soft knock on the door got his attention. He opened the door and there stood Lydia wearing a blue and white striped spaghetti strapped sundress and blue wedges. She wore her hair pulled back in a neat and tight ponytail. Her makeup was flawless and she smelled great, like fresh cut flowers on a hot summer day. Lydia felt very sexy in her ensemble. She had taken time to pick out just the right outfit for her date. She was really hoping he would like it. Despite the argument that she had with Anthony regarding where she was going, she felt wonderful.

"Come on in sexy. I'm glad you made it."

"Oh my God what happened to your eye?" Lydia gently touched his face. He was already tired of the question.

"Oh I just got into a little altercation at work this morning."

Lydia gave him a bewildered look, "But I thought you were just turning in the office keys this morning."

He thought quickly, "Yeah I did but my buddy Brent was escorting an employee out of the building that had just gotten fired and the guy snapped. I jumped in to help and caught a punch in the eye." Gregory smiled at his very believable lie.

"That's ridiculous Gregory, just crazy!"

He started to get a little nervous at her tone. "What?"

"It's ridiculous...that on your day off you got hurt, I'm so sorry!"

Gregory smiled at her, winked with his good eye, and told her to come in and get comfortable.

Lydia looked around, she was a little shocked and confused. Looking at the way Gregory carried himself, the clothes he wore, his presence...you would think he lived somewhere a little nicer, more upscale. Lydia didn't want to judge so she quickly dismissed the negative thoughts and concentrated on a wonderful evening with her baby. Lydia sat down on the sofa, Gregory looked delicious as usual. He smelled wonderful, she was spell bound by his fragrance.

"So how about some wine? I got a nice bottle of Pinot Grigio, almost like the kind we had at the restaurant."

Lydia nodded eagerly, "Yes please."

He went to the fridge and took out the chilled wine. He opened a drawer looking for a corkscrew. Nothing. He opened drawer after drawer, nothing. Unbelievable! The man did not own a corkscrew, which made sense; Brent was more of a twist off cap type of dude. Gregory closed his eyes and leaned against the counter, *Think man, think!*

"Gregory? Is everything ok?" Lydia could hear him rattling around in the kitchen.

"Yeah, I'm good. Be there in a second." There was no way he was going to let her know that he was having a problem opening a simple bottle of wine. Gregory grabbed a steak knife out of the drain board and carefully stabbed the cork. He put the bottle between his knees and carefully began to pull the cork forward. He got it half way out before the cork broke in half. "DAMN!"

Lydia jumped and looked towards the kitchen. She didn't say anything but continued to listen carefully. Gregory angrily pulled the broken piece of cork off the edge of the knife. By that time, he was sweaty and anxious. He stabbed the broken cork again trying to get a good grip on it. He almost had it, almost, but before he realized what was happening, the half piece of cork had slipped inside the bottle and was bobbing in the crisp white wine.

"FUCK!" Gregory yelled.

Lydia covered her mouth trying not to laugh out loud. She wanted to get up and see if he needed help but she didn't want to upset him more.

"Gregory, baby, are you…."

"I'm fine! Be out in a second!" He was beyond frustrated. He would just have to fish out any pieces of cork.

"Ok, wine glasses," he said softly to himself. He looked through the cabinets one by one.... nothing but plastic fast food cups and coffee mugs. What the hell? He finally found something similar to wine glasses; he found two plastic champagne flutes, which read "Congrats Cindy and Brian." Gregory felt like he was in the twilight zone but it would have to work, somehow. He poured the wine making sure there were no cork pieces floating. He came out of the kitchen, his forehead beaded with sweat. Lydia looked at him curiously, as she reached for the plastic flute. Gregory sat beside her and forced a smile on his face. He was mortified but there was no way he was going to show it.

"Who are Cindy and Brian?" she asked studying the engraving.

"Just friends of mine," Gregory took a long sip of his wine.

"Oh that's nice. How long have they been married?" she asked while staring into his deep brown eyes.

"Uh seven years, I think. I'm not sure."

Lydia nodded and finished her wine. She was feeling incredibly relaxed and she wanted another glass but she was too shy to ask. She looked around at the bare walls and windows. The apartment seemed so cold and impersonal. Maybe he needed a feminine touch to help him decorate, she would make a note to offer her help later.

"Let me refill your glass."

He went to the kitchen. He was ready to get her to the bedroom and fast. All this small talk and questions were getting on his nerves. He wished he had bought something stronger to drink for the evening. He knew Brent was a drinking man; he had to have liquor around here somewhere. He looked in the bottom cabinets and on top of the fridge, nothing. He opened the freezer, jackpot! An almost full bottle of ice cold Jack Daniels. He grabbed the bottle and two coffee mugs and went back out into the living room. He didn't say anything to her; he just poured a small amount of the potent beverage in each mug. He picked up his mug and downed the contents then poured another and downed that too. Lydia looked at him in amazement.

He looked at her and grinned, "Aren't you going to drink yours? Come on, relax with me." He reached over and rubbed her inner thigh. Sharp tingles shot up her spine, making her catch her breath. She grabbed the mug and swallowed the harsh brown liquid quickly. She coughed and gagged; Gregory patted her on the back. Lydia cleared her throat and shook her head. He poured her another shot and she willingly drank it down. Lydia was feeling overly relaxed now, her nervousness disappeared and she was extremely aroused. She looked at Gregory and licked her lips. She leaned over and kissed him lightly. He scooted closer to her and wrapped his arm around her waist while he kneaded her breast with the other.

Gregory didn't usually drink to get drunk but the Jack was going down so smooth that he had already consumed five shots. He was rock hard and ready to stroke.

They kissed hard and passionately, moaning, their hands exploring one another. Lydia could feel the heat between her thighs growing more and more intense, she longed for him to slide his hand up her dress and rub her swollen clit.... If he didn't do it soon, she would do it herself.

Gregory lowered the top of her sundress to bare her naked breasts. Her breasts were medium size, about a b cup and natural. He loved the darkness of her areola and her gumdrop-sized nipples. He planted his hot wet mouth on her nipple, swirling his tongue around her hard diamond. He took her hand and guided down to the bulge beneath his dress slacks. Lydia gasped! It felt so long, thick, and hard. She felt it jump and twitch every time she stroked her hand up towards the head. She had never felt a penis so big; she was a little intimidated but determined to have every inch inside of her.

She continued slowly stroking his manhood up and down, Gregory continued to suck and tease her nipples. Her breasts were her weak spot. She loved special attention on her nipples...it made her instantly wet. She began to unbutton his pants and undo his zipper. She was so anxious to see it, caress it, and taste it. It had been so long since she had a hard dick filling her mouth...she literally craved it. She loved having oral sex, more so giving than receiving. She loved making a man moan and squirm; she loved the control and power it gave her. Lydia felt her mouth getting wetter and wetter. Gregory sat up and looked at the expression on her face; oh, she was definitely ready; she was ready for "the monster."

"Let's go to the room." He picked up the bottle of Jack and walked down the short hallway towards the bedroom. Lydia followed behind him and admittedly, she was nervous. She knew sex with Gregory was going to be magical and explosive. It had been so long since she had something long and hard between her thighs. Gregory immediately began to undress. She stood watching; when he lowered his boxer briefs, she almost passed out. His manhood was long and hard with deep veins pulsating all over it. It bobbed and jumped as if it had a mind of its own. He had to be at least ten inches long, and not a stitch of hair…anywhere. Gregory loved the way she was admiring his body. He knew she wanted every inch of him inside of her and she was going to get it.

He walked over to her and slowly lowered her dress down to her ankles. She looked so delicious, so edible. Lydia tried not to keep staring at his large package but she couldn't help herself. Greg sat on the edge of Brent's bed, "Turn around and slowly slide your panties down to your ankles. Do it and bend over while you're doing it for me."

Lydia blushed. She felt so insecure and uncertain but she wanted to make him happy. She slowly turned her back to him. She started to slide her white lace panties down, bending over as she did like she was instructed. She got them down to her ankles and carefully worked them off, stepping out of them carefully as not to snag them on her wedges she was still wearing. Gregory's monster began to jump with happiness and anticipation. He adored the way her round honey brown ass looked. Lydia turned around to face him, unsure of what to do next.

"Come say hello to "monster" girl." A look of sexual longing covered his face as he slightly leaned back on the bed and spread his legs.

She looked at the throbbing organ between his legs. She walked over to him and he grabbed her arm and pulled her down to her knees. At that moment, she knew exactly what he wanted and she was more than willing to accommodate him. Lydia got on her knees and looked into Gregory's face, he was so handsome, and she couldn't comprehend why a man like him paid any attention to her.

Lydia slowly stroked Gregory's hardness, up and down, from the shaft to the tip, paying special attention to the swollen head. She watched as the clear pre cum oozed from the opening of his bulging brown tip. He watched her every move intensely while he moaned in approval. She put the tip in her mouth, swirled her tongue around it, and gently sucked it. He was enjoying her efforts but he wanted to feel his dick covered with her mouth. He put his hand on the back of her head and firmly pushed. She understood. She slid her mouth to the base and up again.

"AH SHIT!" he blurted out as he kept a firm grip on the back of her head. He guided her head up and down. Fast…slow…fast…slow. Lydia's jaws were on fire but she was determined to keep up with his demands. Gregory's breathing quickened and his body began to jerk. She tightened her jaw muscles tighter around his dick and braced herself for what was about to happen, but to her complete surprise, he pulled out of her mouth and let the hot juice spurt out of his manhood and down his hand as he continued to grunt and moan. The way it flowed down his still hard dick and onto his hand made Lydia want him more. She was so hot; she needed to feel him inside of her…NOW. He stood up and grabbed a towel that was hanging on Brent's treadmill.

Lydia got up and sat on the edge of the bed. She rubbed her clit; she was so horny now she could barely stand it. She looked at him wondering if he was satisfied. He didn't say anything to her at all, just got up and wiped his hands and crotch. He finally looked at her and smiled, "I see you got some skills huh?"

Lydia gave him a seductive smirk, "I know a little something."

He sat on the bed beside her and told her to lie back. She closed her eyes and leaned back on the bed; Gregory reached over to the side of the bed and pulled over the gray carrying case. He pulled out a small bottle of clear liquid and squeezed a small amount onto his fingertips. He began to massage Lydia's plump nub; she jumped from his touch. That was the first time she had felt his bare hands against her sweet spot. She let out a low moan as his finger teased and pleased her.

The smell of strawberries filled her nostrils and she wondered what he was using to produce the luscious aroma. He slowly inserted two fingers inside of her while still rubbing her clit with his thumb. She started grinding her hips to her own rhythm against his fingers. The sensation was so powerful, so overwhelming. He pulled his fingers out and brought them up to her lips, offering her a taste of her delicious dessert. She opened her lips and took his glazed fingers into her mouth.

She sucked her juices off his fingers, sweet...tart...and mmm strawberries. She lapped and licked his fingers hungrily, the taste of herself made her hot. He pulled his fingers from her mouth and put them inside her again…thrusting hard. She grabbed onto the sheet and moaned in delight. She felt the intensity building up; she bucked her hips harder against his fingers. By now, Lydia had her legs bent and both feet on the foot of the bed. Gregory fingered her harder; he kept envisioning her squirting like she did with Alexis.

"BABY,   I…I'M….UHHHH…YESSSS! COGERME! PAPI!" Lydia gripped the sheets tighter and rode the orgasmic wave until the end. Her thighs began to shake and knees began to buckle. She was seeing spots before her eyes and she struggled to catch her breath. She was literally worn out.

Gregory looked at his creamy fingers but he wasn't completely satisfied. Why didn't she squirt? He was working the shit out of her pussy! Lydia laid there breathing heavily and sweating. He rubbed her thigh, wiping his fingers off in the process. Gregory felt defeated. He wanted her body to submit to his touch. He stood up agitated, and flipped her over to her stomach. Lydia looked back at him smiling, but her smile quickly disappeared. He looked frustrated, almost mad.

"Baby, what's wrong?"

He fixed his face and smirked at her, "Nothing, I'm just ready to give you what you've been waiting for."

Lydia gave him a lusty look and laid her head down on the bed, arched her back and poked her butt up…giving him full access. Gregory squinted his eyes at her. He was going to make her body do exactly what he wanted.

He pulled a condom from his bag and slid it on. He pulled her to the edge of the bed and propped her ass up in the air. This was her favorite position but Jackson never wanted to do it. He was stuck on doing missionary and that was pretty much it. Gregory gripped both of her cheeks with each hand and slightly separated them then slowly slid into her wet hole. Lydia let out a loud groan; she could feel the pressure from his massive cock all the way into the bottom of her stomach. The intensity made her shudder. He stretched her hole wide with his thick ten-inch pole. He rammed her deep and steady, making sure he got every inch in each time, his balls slapping against her swollen clit. She buried her face into the bed and continued to moan and scream into the mattress.

Gregory put more lube on his fingers and inserted them between her butt cheeks. He then put the tip of his thumb into her wet "back door." Lydia clenched up and looked back at him with uncertainty. Gregory kept stroking and gently fingered her rear. Lydia had never done anal before, it was something that never fascinated her. When she was twenty, one of her lovers convinced her to try it but she was so scared and tense that he couldn't get it in. She used to watch adult movies and watch the women in the films cry out in pain and beg their lover to stop. She watched as the woman would reach back and try to prevent him from going deeper and harder inside her dark hole. She also remembered watching the women that enjoyed it and thought they were out of their mind. And now she was here...with Gregory, the man she desired and craved, and it was obvious that he wanted to go there with her. She was desperate to please him so if that's what he wanted, she would have to grin and bear it, so to speak.

Gregory continued to stroke her and finger her ass. He listened to her erotic moans mixed with whimpers of uncomfortableness and pain. He reached down into his bag and quietly pulled out "Monster Jr." Monster Jr. was seven inches long and jet back with veins running deep all over it. He kept pleasing Lydia with his hard dick while he rubbed the clear strawberry gel all over Monster Jr. He was like a kid in a candy store, anxious and excited.

"Does that feel good baby? Tell me it feels good. Say it!" he commanded as he sped up his pace.

"Tan bueno baby!" Lydia yelled out.

Gregory's eyes were as big as saucers. He loved the way she spoke Spanish. Damn that shit was sexy!

"Say something else in Spanish."

Lydia moaned. "Your polla es tan grande!" she cried out.

Gregory leaned forward close to her ear and whispered, "What did you say?"

"Your dick is huge!"

Gregory fought the urge to cum after he heard that. She sounded so good. He took Monster Jr., and massaged her asshole with the head. He put it in just a little then slid it out. Lydia tried to enjoy what was going on, but what exactly was going on? He was still stroking her tight hole but it felt like a penis and not his fingers. Lydia closed her eyes tight and griped the sheet tighter. He kept stroking, never breaking rhythm, as he slowly pushed the tip of the fake cock in further in her tight back door.

"Aye Papi! Please! No too much!"

Gregory was incredibly turned on by her pleading. "I'll be gentle, I promise. Make me happy Lydia."

Something took over Lydia's mind and body. He actually asked her to make him happy, that's all she ever wanted to do. She wanted his approval and desperately wanted him to love her. She already knew she would do anything for him…anything.

"Ok baby, I'll do it for you…anything for you." Those were the words that he had been waiting to hear.

Gregory smacked her ass and continued pounding away. He applied more gel to her backside. He slowly worked the large toy into her tight opening. Lydia cried out in pain, breathing heavily. It hurt and burned but she was determined to give him what he wanted. She buried her face deep into the mattress and clenched her teeth. He kept his pace as he slid the head of Monster Jr. in and out, teasing her. Lydia reached back hoping to slow his pace but Gregory pushed her hand away.

He wanted total control…he didn't need any help from her. She reached under and began to rub her swollen clit. Although she was in pain, the excitement of everything turned her on. Before she realized it, he had the fake penis halfway in her ass and still stroked her deep with his own member. Gregory listened as Lydia's moans of pain turned into cries of passion. She was actually beginning to enjoy the intense pleasure. Lydia reached back and rubbed his smooth thigh and tight stomach. He was so perfect. He looked at her and they locked eyes.

Gregory felt himself grow even harder inside of her. He kept working himself and the toy in rhythm, the black toy was covered in Lydia's thick white cream, and so was his long thick penis. She began pushing back on the two hard objects inside her. She kept rubbing her clit, her legs started to tingle. Her voice was almost gone from her screaming and moaning. Tears ran down her face and her mascara and eyeliner stained the sheets. Gregory massaged her golden brown ass with his free hand; he smacked it a few times until he could see the redness rise.

She continued to buck and grind, "I'm cumming! Baby oh my God, I'm cumming!"

Gregory tried to keep his rhythm going but her cries; her screams overwhelmed him. He began to jerk. He let go of Monster Jr., grabbed onto her round tight ass with both hands, and began to pound her hard and fast. Gregory began to shake as Lydia continued to shiver uncontrollably. His legs grew numb as he released the hot sticky nut into the condom. Gregory growled loudly over and over, as he made sure he released every single drop. Lydia lay panting on the bed with the black dick still hanging out of her ass. Greg slapped her butt and pulled out the greasy sex toy. Her back door was still gaping open. She immediately sat up and looked at her lover with her deep chocolate brown eyes.

"Did I make you happy baby?' she eagerly awaited his response.

Gregory stood there with the used condom on his still erect penis. "Yes very happy."

He walked away and went into the bathroom to clean up. She sat on the edge of the bed thinking about what had just happened. She had stepped outside of her comfort zone and it felt good, no great. She felt in control of her desires and wants...and she definitely didn't want to stop. She wanted more and she wanted it from Gregory.

She thought about all the wasted nights with Jackson, lying there miserable and unfulfilled. She thought of all the nights she sat in her tub covered in lavender scented bubbles masturbating but really wanting the touch of a man all over her wet slippery body. Now she had what she wanted, Gregory. He was her dream come true. She leaned over to pick up her panties off the floor and winched in pain. She was sore and on fire back there but she was still happy. She looked at the clock; it was almost one in the morning. Honestly, she hoped to get another round with her baby. She was addicted, hooked, and she didn't want a cure or a remedy. She wanted more...so much more.

"Man what time are you coming home?" Greg whispered into the phone with an attitude.

"Really? You calling me now dude?" Brent said with a bigger attitude.

Gregory peeked out of the bathroom door at Lydia who was now lying back on the bed almost looking as if she could fall asleep.

"Look, I'll be home probably around three or four. This chick I'm with tonight can't get enough of Big B! Besides I gotta work in the morning."

"Ok man, we will be gone before you get back. And...uh...yeah, you may want to change your sheets before you climb into bed dawg."

Gregory laughed and hung up before Brent could comment. He threw the filled condom in the toilet, flushed it down, and washed his hands. What had happened out there? He couldn't remember the last time he came so hard. Her voice and eye contact made him lose control. That was something new and he didn't like it. Gregory Summit never let a woman control him, physically or emotionally. He came out of the bathroom and walked to the bed. Lydia had dozed off, quietly snoring. He just stared at her. She looked so peaceful. Usually he would wake up his dates and tell them to carry their ass but for some reason, he didn't want to wake her up abruptly and tell her to get dressed; he actually wanted her to sleep. He looked at her smooth hairless lips and her pink clit peeking out at him.

He wondered how she tasted, if she was sweet or a little tart, or a combination of both. She wasn't a smoker so he knew she had to be tasty. He got on his knees at the foot of the bed in front of her. He gently slid her closer to the edge of the bed. He was face to face with her sweetness and he definitely wanted a sample. He separated her smooth lips and licked down the middle of her goodness. She stirred a little but fell soundly back to sleep. He laughed and lightly teased her clit with his tongue, flicking it back and forth, making it wet with his saliva.

He watched as her dark nipples began to stiffen. She quietly moaned in her sleep as she moved her hips in a circular motion. He put his finger into her deep moist hole while he continued to lick her now plump swollen bud. The smell of her excitement filled his nostrils, hypnotizing him. Lydia continued to moan; she reached down to touch Gregory's curly black hair. It was so soft and thick. She started grinding her hips up against the now two fingers he had inside her. He inserted his middle finger from his other hand inside her ass, Lydia let out a cry of pain and passion. He sucked and licked her clit while vigorously working her pink pussy and tight hole. She felt her eyes moisten as tears of ecstasy filled them; the feeling was overwhelming. She felt the wave of an intense orgasm begin to build. She tried to control it, she didn't want to explode yet, but the more she tried to fight the sensation the greater the wave felt. She couldn't hold it anymore and the feeling overpowered her. She let out screams of emotion and passion as her vaginal walls contracted.

Gregory pulled his fingers out of her various holes and held onto her thighs tightly as he continued to devour her, when he was finally done with her; his face was slick, sticky, and wet. Lydia lay huffing and puffing, trying to regain her composure. He stood up and hovered over her, smirking. He didn't make her squirt but that would happen in a matter of time, he would make sure of it. He went into the bathroom and wet a washcloth then came back to the bed and nudged Lydia. She barely opened her eyes and looked at her sexy lover.

"Here clean yourself up and get dressed," he said coldly and went back into the bathroom. Lydia sat up and sighed. One minute he was so passionate then the next withdrawn. Her feelings were a little hurt and she felt like crying but quickly blinked the tears away. She was pulling her dress up when he came out of the bathroom. He had his clothes and shoes on as if he were leaving too, not realizing he was blowing his cover.

"Are you going somewhere Gregory?" she asked sadly.

He looked at her with a confused look. "Yeah I'm going…" he stopped when he realized he was about to ruin everything. "I called a cab while I was in the bathroom. I've gotta walk you out when it gets here. I am a gentleman you know." He winked at her and she gave a slight smile then looked away. She wanted to stay with him, fall asleep in his arms while listening to his heartbeat. He looked at his watch; it was already three forty five. He hoped the cab showed up before Brent.

"When can I see you again Gregory?"

Gregory smiled and looked at her. "Soon, really soon. I'm still waiting on my phone so I can give you a number to reach me. I don't know why it's taking so long."

Sadness filled Lydia again, "I understand," she said softly. She sat thinking for a minute and came up with a great idea. "Gregory lets go to Zeta Wireless tomorrow and get you a phone! That way you don't have to wait for your replacement."

He thought about what she had just said. A new top of the line smartphone would be nice, especially if she was paying for it. "Wow sweetie that's a great idea, but...I don't have the money right now for a new phone. My hours at work have been decreased and I'm just making ends meet. I'm really embarrassed right now but I just can't swing that."

Gregory looked at her with a hurt look. He hoped his acting skills were up to par, at least enough to convince her. Lydia stood up and walked over to him. She kissed him deeply and passionately. She had never been so forward before… he brought out the untamed wild side of her.

"I'm going to take care of it love. I want to be able to hear your voice when I can't be near you." Lydia had just paid off her MasterCard and she was more than willing to splurge on him. She just wanted him to be happy.

"Are you sure? I mean I don't want you to spend a lot of dough on me Lydia. That wouldn't be right." His consideration was making her fall for him more.

"Yes Gregory, I'm positive. Call me tomorrow and let me know what time you want to go. I'll be free all day."

A horn sounded outside. Lydia gathered her things and walked towards the front door with Gregory following behind her. He turned her around and gave her a deep kiss while putting her hand on his still rock hard organ. She was so turned on; she didn't want to leave him. He could feel that she didn't want the night to end; that she was still longing to be with him by the way she was squeezing and stroking him. He backed away from her and touched her cheek.

"I will call you later alright?"

"Ok, I look forward to seeing you…and tasting you again Papi," she licked her lips and winked at him. Lydia walked to the cab and got in. Gregory watched as the cab went down the street, within two minutes Brent pulled up in his driveway.

"So, did you have fun? Brent asked his friend as he yawned.

"Definitely. She knows how to please your boy. She's definitely hooked now! How was your night?"

Brent plopped down on the sofa and let out a deep sigh. "It could've been better. This chick kept my face between her thighs man, but she did slip me five hundred so I guess it's all good." Both men laughed.

"Well, I'm outta here. I got three dates lined up for tomorrow so I can keep Renee off my damn back and Lydia's buying me a phone tomorrow."

"Ah and so it begins. The abundance of gifts. I tell you, you're a smooth muthafucka man. I'm telling you though, you still better be careful dude." Brent got up and headed to the kitchen. "She was looking for you too. I just told her I didn't know where you were." Brent opened the freezer looking for his bottle of Jack Daniels. "What the hell?"

Gregory took out his wallet and tossed a twenty on the coffee table. "My fault man, get a fresh bottle on me."

Brent shook his head and Gregory left. He walked three houses down and got into his Corvette that was parked on the side of the street. He drove home thinking about Lydia Morrell.

She would be the perfect woman for a man looking to settle down, he thought. Maybe in another time, in another place, she could possibly be the one, but in the here and now, he wasn't the man for her.

CHAPTER SIXTEEN

Alexis sat in the dressing room of the club staring at herself in the mirror. Her skin was dull and lifeless, pale and pasty looking; she had dark circles under her eyes. She was tired of being sick and tired. She loathed going to that shithole every night. It was taking its toll on her body not to mention her constant drinking every night. All her dreams and plans seemed like a distant memory. She wanted to become a nurse. She was taking classes during the day and working at the club at night to pay her tuition. Over time, she started to miss class because she would over sleep or was just too tired to get up. After a while, she stopped attending classes altogether.

The club, the fast cash became her life and now the fast life was consuming her body, mind and soul. She wiped away the tears and looked around the room making sure no one saw her crying. She looked at the shot of Patron sitting in front of her, it was always her go to...her tension easer, her pacifier, her friend.

She drank it down and felt the all too familiar burning sensation in her chest. The harshness made her feel calm and serene. She wiped her mouth and started daydreaming about owning her own club one day. It would be classy with gorgeous sexy women and men, and top shelf spirits for her patrons. A top of the line surround sound system with the best DJ money could buy. Plush crimson red carpet and shiny black "real" leather furniture would be the décor throughout the club. A smile spread across her face as she continued to imagine her dream establishment.

She would be the best owner and employer and Gregory... Gregory. Alexis' smile quickly disappeared. That muthafucka! She couldn't believe the way he acted. Who did he think he was?

She started tapping her long bright orange acrylic nails against the dressing room table in frustration. She was glad Anthony kicked his ass; he deserved it. He was probably with his Latina bitch now and not even giving her a second thought. Her thoughts faded from that fool Gregory to Anthony. He made her feel so good, so wanted. He made her feel like a true woman, not just some chick that strips at a club that he took home to screw.

She wanted to see him again but she was hesitant to call. She was scared to put herself out there. She had taken care to build her wall up around her and the thought of someone breaking through literally terrified her. No, he had her number; if he wanted to talk, he could call her. She checked her makeup and looked at the clock, three a.m. She prepared herself to do one last dance and call it night.

****

Anthony laid on the sofa in the dark staring up at the ceiling. The television was on but it was only background noise for his thoughts. He had so much going on he didn't know where to begin. Big K was after him, his sister wanted him out, and then there was Alexis. She was the best thing in his life right now. He wanted to take her away from that dumb club and make her happy. She was better than that dump. She deserved a man that would take care of her, pamper her, and love her. He thought about how great it felt to make love to her. Yes, in his mind, he had made love to her. The woman had his mind all twisted! He also realized she had baggage…that punk ass Gregory.

Who exactly was he? And why did he think he had claim over her? He couldn't believe he had the audacity to come to his lady's house and act a fool. Anthony clenched his teeth feeling himself getting hot with anger. Did she love him? Did he love her? He definitely needed answers because he refused to be number two in her life. He heard the front door open and he peeked over the back of the sofa. Lydia quietly closed the door and walked quickly to her room, hoping Anthony was asleep. She reached her bedroom door when Anthony's voice startled her.

"What's up baby sis?" Anthony said sarcastically. "Wow creeping in at three in the morning. That's not very ladylike now, is it?"

Lydia took a deep breath and turned around. "Ant, I'm tired. Please don't start!" She walked into her bedroom and closed the door. She barely made it to the bed before the door flew open.

"What's his name? He gotta name right?"

Lydia began to pull her pajamas out of her dresser as if she didn't hear him.

"What's the muthafucka's name Lydia?" Anthony said very loudly.

"Gregory," she yelled back to him.

Anthony laughed, "Gregory? That's a gay ass name. So he's your man or y'all just fuckin'?"

"None of your damn business! Get out of my room! Now!"

Anthony walked up on his sister and put his finger in her face, "You're turning out to be a whore, just like that bitch Sophia!"

Lydia pushed him away and began to cry. She was tired of his verbal abuse. She was tired of Anthony belittling their mother. No, she was not proud of what her mother had resorted to take care of them but she was still their mother. She could not and she would not take much more of it.

"That's why that bitch is suffering now and I'm glad she is! PUTA DE MIERDA!"

"GET OUT! GET OUT OF MY DAMN HOUSE ANTHONY!" Lydia screamed at the top of her lungs. Anthony gazed at her like she had lost her mind. Lydia was now sobbing uncontrollably.

"Ok I'm out! I better leave before I slap the shit out of your dumb ass!" He began throwing his belongings into his backpack. He grabbed the duffel bag and headed towards the front door. "When what happened to mom happens to you, don't come crying to me. I will have no sympathy for you because your ass deserved it!"

Anthony slammed the front door so hard that two pictures fell off the wall onto the floor. Lydia threw herself on the bed and continued to weep. She had always pushed the bad memory of what happened to her mother to the back of her mind but that night she couldn't fight it. All the awful memories came back, flooding her thoughts.

It had been six years since the senseless act of violence had happened to her mother, Sophia. Lydia still blamed herself and wished she could rewind time. It was her twenty-first birthday and Lydia was so excited! She officially considered herself an adult, a grown woman. She had planned to go to the Longhorn, a local bar that was very popular with the younger crowd.

Ricky was taking her and said he planned to buy her drinks all night. She had never really drunk before, a sip of wine or liquor here and there, but she decided to celebrate her birthday to the fullest. She was getting ready for her special night on the town when her mother came and stood in the doorway of her room. Sophia admired her daughter. She looked just like she did when she was twenty-one.

"Mi Amor, how about I cancel my date and you and I stay home and watch movies? I will cook all your favorite foods and make you a birthday cake! What do you think?"

Lydia frowned and looked at her mother. It had been years since her mother offered to spend time with her.

The two basically lived as roommates. Lydia didn't know her mother anymore and since Lydia began living her own life, she wasn't in any hurry to start reacquainting with her.

"Mom I have plans tonight. I can't change them now. Go on your date tonight and we can hang out tomorrow, ok?"

Sophia looked at her daughter and nodded her head yes and went back into the living room. She sat on the sofa and lit a cigarette. She felt the warm salty liquid sting her eyes. For the past few weeks, Sophia had an empty void in her soul, a longing for something that had been missing in her life, her daughter. She had missed spending time with her daughter and now she was a grown woman.

Lydia came out of her room wearing a beautiful knee length silver and black cocktail dress with strappy black high heels. She wore her hair in long shiny spiral curls that had taken her almost an hour to create. She didn't need a lot of makeup but she wore a little mascara and eyeliner and a soft pink lip-gloss.

"Te ves hermosa Lydia," her mother said softly. Sophia was now in her early forties but still looked young for her age. Lydia reminded her so much of herself.

"Thank you! I got this dress on sale at work, thirty five percent off!"

Lydia twirled around in the middle of the living room floor modeling for her mother. Sophia laughed and clapped for her baby girl. The two women laughed and smiled at each other. It was as if they were meeting again for the first time after so many years. There was a knock at the door and Lydia went to answer it.

"Damn girl! You look good as fuck. Oh I'm definitely getting in that a…."

"Ricky! Shut up boy. My mom is right there."

"Oh shit, hey Mrs. Morrell. How are you?" Ricky asked, fidgeting with his hands.

"I'm fine. You take care of my baby. Don't drink too much ok?"

"Oh yeah, yes ma'am. She's safe with me."

Lydia looked at her mother. The sadness was so evident on her face. She hadn't seen her mother look so sad in a long time but then again, she never took the time to stop and notice either.

"Mami, tomorrow we can watch movies and I will buy a bottle of that tequila you like and we can make margaritas. That will be fun, right?"

Sophia looked at her baby girl as if she was seeing her for the first time. "Oh baby, that makes me very happy! Now go, be careful, and have fun. Happy birthday." Lydia smiled and then left to celebrate.

Sophia put out her cigarette and began to get ready for her date. She wasn't exactly enthusiastic about spending the evening with Travis. She tolerated him because he never had a problem paying what she asked but she found him a little odd, almost creepy at times. She met Travis three months earlier at the hotel where she currently worked as a housekeeper. He was a maintenance man and had started around the same time as she did.

He was about 5'6", lanky, and Caucasian. He appeared to be in his late forties and always wore his long brown hair in a very neat ponytail with rubber bands going down the length of it. He was always clean-shaven and always smelled like the inside of a cedar chest. He wasn't what you would describe as handsome but his looks were very plain.

For the most part, he was very quiet and went about his day barely speaking to the other employees. He would occasionally smile at Sophia, revealing that he had several teeth missing at the bottom. She would always give him a little smile and continue working.

One evening, Sophia decided to stop at the bar downstairs located inside the hotel. She sat drinking and smoking her cigarette when Travis sat down beside her. He ordered a beer and looked at Sophia's glass.

"What are you drinking?" he said shyly.

"Vodka…on the rocks."

Before she knew it, Travis had ordered her a fresh beverage. She thanked him and soon they were talking and laughing. She told him that she was a single parent and how her husband deserted them. She told him that she had a hard time making ends meet and how sometimes she longed for male companionship. By that time, she had her hand on his thigh. Travis sat staring at her full lips and sweating. That night she took him home and had sex with him for hours. She could tell he was inexperienced but extremely appreciative of everything she was doing to him. He gave her four hundred dollars.

Sophia wanted to break her date with him but she was two hundred dollars short on rent and she knew she could get it and extra from him. She just hated the way he stared at her and how oddly quiet he was, even when they were having sex. The only way she knew he was cumming was from the one very low grunt he made when it happened. Afterwards, he always made it a point to leave quickly. He would get dressed, hand her the money and wave goodbye and leave. As strange as he was, she looked past it because he was always willing to pay.

Sophia sat at the vanity in her bedroom brushing her long black hair. A few strands of gray appeared and she reminded herself that she needed to buy hair dye the next day. Her hair used to be full and thick, now it was limp, thin, and dry. She noticed the crow's feet in the corner of her eyes and the thin lines forming around her mouth. Her youthfulness was surely fading.

She often wondered about George, her husband. In the beginning, she felt it was a blessing that he had left them, no more fights, no more abuse. Then she would think that if she had been a better wife, better woman, maybe he would have loved her more. They fell in love so young that maybe after all these years he had just grown tired of her and left. Her relationship with her son was nonexistent and she understood why. She did what she felt she had to take care of her babies and she didn't regret it, not one bit.

She did however regret losing her son. She loved him dearly and prayed for him every night. Once when she was getting off the bus after work and walking home, she saw him being handcuffed by the police. She wanted to go over to him and kiss him but she knew he would flip out. They made eye contact and he yelled out, "Keep walking whore." She lowered her head and quickened her pace. She realized that day that her only son would never forgive her for her transgressions.

Sophia stared at herself, consumed with her thoughts when she heard someone knocking. She got herself together and went to open the door for Travis. He came in and sat in his usual spot, the right hand side of the sofa.

"Hey Travis. How are you tonight?"

"I'm alright," he seemed agitated, "are we alone tonight?"

Sophia gave him a curious look. In the three and a half months, they had been seeing each other he never concerned himself with who was in the house.

"Yes we are alone. Today is Lydia's twenty-first birthday. I'm sure she will be out until very late. Do you want a drink? You seem upset."

Travis nodded his head yes. Sophia went to the kitchen, poured two shots of tequila, and grabbed two beers out of the fridge. She sat the drinks down on the coffee table and sat next to him. Admittedly, she was using Travis in a sense, but she did care about his well-being. He seemed so fragile and lost, like he just needed a friend. Travis slowly drank the tequila and gently placed the glass back on the table. He looked at the glass and then at her, as if he wanted to ask for more but didn't want to be rude. Sophia patted his knee and went to retrieve the bottle from the kitchen. She poured him another drink and he quickly swallowed it down. He let out a slight cough and rubbed his chest.

"Travis? What's wrong?"

"I'm getting put out of my apartment."

"Dios mio! When?"

"I have a week to come up with twenty one hundred or I'm done. I don't have that kind of money, not at one time."

Sophia drank her shot and gave Travis a sympathetic look. She genuinely felt bad for him, then she felt bad for herself, because she knew, she wasn't getting the two hundred dollars she needed.

"So I was thinking I could just move in here with you."

Sophia choked on her beer. She gave him a look of uneasiness. "Live here?" she asked.

"Well, yeah. I would live here, help with groceries and rent, we could ride to work together. You wouldn't have to ride that musty old bus anymore. You're always complaining about riding the bus."

Sophia didn't know if she should laugh or be upset. Why in the world did he think he could live with her? He wasn't her man and just barely a friend, more so a business arrangement. Travis looked at her with a slight smile. She frowned and looked at him annoyed. "You can't live here Travis, no."

His smile disappeared and confusion filled his eyes. He peered at her as if he couldn't comprehend what she said. She stared at the blank look on his face; she started to feel uneasy and didn't quite know what to do. Travis picked up his beer and took a long swig. He poured himself another shot of tequila and drank it down hard and fast.

"Like I was saying, when I move in, we could put my loveseat in our bedroom, yeah that would look really nice. I have a kitchen table that's bigger than yours, its cherry wood. I built it myself. You will love it."

Sophia's eyes widened and her breathing grew faster. Maybe he didn't understand what she had just said. Maybe the tequila had already taken effect on him. She scooted away a few inches from him and cleared her throat. "Travis, I said you can't, cannot move in with me and Lydia."

Travis began wringing his hands and slightly rocking back and forth. He sighed loudly and his forehead began to tighten. "It's your fault you know," he stated almost in a whisper.

"What did you say?"

Travis slammed his hands down on the coffee table making the shot glasses and beer bottles rattle. His face was a shade of crimson that Sophia had never seen before. "I said this is your fucking fault! I took care of you for three months and ended up screwing myself over!"

By now, he was standing up with his bony finger pointed in her face. Sophia cringed at the sound of his voice. She had never heard him yell, or even raise his voice. It boomed and vibrated like thunder during a bad storm on a hot summer day. She sat paralyzed with fright.

"I gave you whatever you wanted and now you're going to let me get put out on the street? You ungrateful bitch!"

Sophia jumped at the harshness of his words. She could not believe what was happening. The meek mild mannered man had turned into a raging monster right before her eyes!

"Leave Travis, Now!" Sophia stood up but Travis shoved her back onto the sofa. She tried to stand again and that time he pushed her back down with both hands. "Travis leave or I'm calling the cops!"

Sophia stood up again and Travis drew back his hand and slapped her as hard as he could. The burning pain took over the right side of her face, the taste of blood made her sick to her stomach.

"Stay down bitch," Travis commanded quietly yet firmly. He looked possessed. His green eyes turned almost black in color.

She held her face and began to sob softly. "Please, just leave. I won't say anything to anyone. I swear."

Travis bent over and looked her directly into her eyes. "Oh I know you won't tell; I'm going to make sure of that."

Sophia was certain she was going to die and as terrified as she was all she could think was she hoped he did it before Lydia got home.

Travis began pounding her with both his fists. She yelled and screamed as she tried to protect herself the best she could. She tried to fight back but her kicks and punches landed in vain. Travis grabbed a fistful of her black hair and dragged her from the sofa, kicking and screaming towards her bedroom. She tried to grab onto anything she could to prevent from being taken to the back of the house but the more she held on the harder he pulled.

At one point, it felt as if he was going to pull her hair clean out of her scalp. He yanked her inside the room, locked the door, and stood in front of it. She couldn't believe the nightmare that was unfolding. He was incredibly strong and full of rage. Sophia's mouth was full of her blood and her face felt like it was on fire. She tried not to cry out but the pain was excruciating.

"Get undressed," he said very calmly.

"Travis please, please don't do this!"

Travis smirked and shook his head at the poor beat up woman. "You owe me. Yep, you owe me a freebie and I'm not leaving till I get it."

Sophia slowly got undressed hoping that the crazy man would come to his senses and change his mind but he stood patiently waiting by the door. She sat on the floor naked and sobbing.

"Get up on the bed and lie on your back. Close your eyes."

Sophia did as she was told praying for her life and praying that the ordeal would be over soon. She could hear him moving around the room, opening drawers and her closet; she assumed he was looking for money...or a weapon. She heard him taking off his shoes, then the sound of his belt buckle, the sound of his zipper going down. She began to cry uncontrollably, shaking and trembling with fear. She felt him at the foot of the bed and she grabbed the sheet and tightened her face bracing herself in case he was going to hit her again. He leaned in before he raped her and whispered in her ear, "This is all your fault."

Travis raped Sophia repeatedly that night. He continued to beat her; he blacked both her eyes, broke three ribs, broke her jaw, and gave her multiple bruises. When he was finally too tired to gain another erection, he decided to shame her one last time, by peeing all over her. He had busted his knuckles during the attack so he went to the bathroom to wash up and then he left. Sophia lay lifeless on her bed.

Lydia came home that morning around two in the morning. She was incredibly drunk and just wanted to make a sandwich and go to bed. She opened the front door and noticed the empty beer bottles and shot glasses on the floor. The ashtray had been knocked over and ashes stained the already dirty brown carpet.

"What the hell? I'm not cleaning this up!" She went into the kitchen but decided just to grab a bottle of water and call it a night. She walked past her mother's door and heard low moaning. She assumed she still had her company so she didn't think twice to knock and check on her mother. Lydia went to the bathroom to shower and stopped dead in her tracks. Blood. Blood on the sink and the floor. Blood on the toilet seat and the lid was up. She backed out of the bathroom and ran towards her mother's room.

Fear grabbed ahold of her heart and she began to sweat as she knocked on the door. She didn't hear anything. She knocked again and slowly opened the door. The room was completely dark but she could make out the silhouette of someone lying on the bed from the moonlight gleaming through the blinds. She turned on the bedside light and let out a horrible, blood-curdling scream. There laid her mother naked, bloodied, and bruised. Her hair was wet and covered part of her face. The sheet was covered in so much blood it was hard to determine where it was coming from.

"MAMI...MAMI MAMI! Please wake up, please please wake up!"

She tried to get her mother up but she was heavy, like dead weight. Sophia let out a silent whimper. Lydia grabbed the phone off the nightstand and dialed 911. She covered her mother's naked body and continued to talk to her and ask her questions but her mother was in and out of consciousness and too weak and disoriented to talk. Who could have done that to her mother? If Lydia would have cancelled her date and stayed home like her mother asked, it would not have happened. It was all her fault and if her mother died then she would too because she would not be able to live with herself.

The police and the paramedics finally arrived and quickly checked her vitals, put her on the gurney, and put her in the ambulance. Lydia rode in the back with her mother. They asked her several questions, which Lydia had trouble answering because she was in a state of shock.

When they got to the hospital, they immediately took her mother to the critical care section of the hospital and instructed Lydia to wait in the waiting room. The police asked her several questions about the attack including where she was all night. Lydia felt like they were interrogating her. They told her that detectives would be contacting her because it was the third rape that month in the neighborhood and it could be linked together.

She sat crying for hours before the nurses let her go back to her room. Sophia looked awful. Her face was puffy and swollen; she had tubes coming out of her from every direction. She still was unconscious. Lydia grabbed her mother's limp hand and begged for forgiveness. She prayed that her mother would recover and that life would go back to normal. Lydia didn't leave her mother's side that night. The next day two detectives arrived at the hospital to speak with Lydia.

"Miss Morrell, I'm Detective Swinson, this is Detective Ormanson. We wanted to ask you some questions if that's ok."

Lydia nodded her head yes.

"Where were you when your mother was attacked?" Detective Ormanson asked as he pulled out his note pad.

"I was on a date, yesterday was my birthday," she said in between sniffles.

"Did your mother have any plans of her own last night?"

Lydia sat looking at her still unconscious mother, "Umm...she had a date too, OH MY GOD! HER DATE!"

Lydia looked at the men with fear in her eyes. She couldn't believe it didn't occur to her earlier. The man she had the date with last night had to have done it!

"Do you know who her date was with Miss Morrell?" Detective Swinson inquired.

Lydia was almost embarrassed to answer. Her mother dated several men and she had no clue who was coming to their house last night. She quietly shook her head no. Then she thought of something else.

"There was blood in the bathroom when I got home and the toilet seat was up!"

The two men advised her that they would be sending someone to her house to investigate. They told her they would do their best to catch the man that assaulted and raped her mother. If she remembered anything else to give them a call. Detective Ormanson handed her his card and the two men left. Lydia used the hospital room phone to call Anthony. She didn't know why she was wasting her time, she knew how he felt about their mother, but maybe it would open his eyes and make him think twice about forgiving her.

"Hello, who this?"

"Ant, its Lydia. I, I have some really bad news."

"What the fuck happened sis? Are you ok? Where are you?"

Lydia took a deep breath trying to fight the urge to start crying again. "Mami, she...she was raped and beaten up last night. She's in the hospital and she unconscious."

There was a long pause on the line. Lydia actually thought that maybe he hung up.

"Yeah? Ok, so are you ok? Do you need anything?" he asked nonchalantly.

"Yes! I need you to care Anthony! This is our mother lying in this hospital bed! She could have died!"

Anthony chuckled and Lydia grew angry. "Look little sis, this is the life she chose to lead. What did you think was going to happen? She tricking with this dude, that dude...it was bound to catch up with her...look if YOU need anything let me know. Love you, I gotta go." The phone line went dead and Lydia hung up the phone. After that day, she lost so much respect for her brother.

A few days later, Sophia regained consciousness and slowly began to heal and grow stronger. She told her daughter and the detective about the horrible ordeal regarding Travis. She explained that he was a friend from work but left out the part that she was taking money from him for sex. She later found out the Travis was already a wanted man and now he was nowhere to be found.

A year later Lydia got her own apartment and her mother moved in with her sister who lived two cities away. Lydia still blamed herself for not being there for her mother. As a result of the attack, Sophia was left permanently blind in her left eye and her jaw was slightly deformed from being broken in two places. Although Sophia never came right out and said it, she could tell that her mother had some type of resentment towards her. Although Lydia still kept in contact with her mother, their relationship was not the same and to be honest Lydia didn't know if it was because her mother blamed her for not staying home that night or if it was Lydia's own personal guilt eating her alive.

CHAPTER SEVENTEEN

Lydia woke up Saturday morning feeling tired but excited. She was looking forward to seeing Gregory again. She was excited that she was going to be able to call and text him after she bought him the phone. She laid in bed reminiscing about the love they had made. She couldn't believe how great he made her feel. He had taken her to a completely different world. She couldn't believe that she had anal sex but she didn't regret it one bit, she just hoped next time it would be his dick and not a fake one in her ass. Gregory was definitely a pleasant and needed change for her life.

She got up and went to the kitchen to make her coffee. She was so happy that Anthony was gone. As much as she loved him, she couldn't stand being around him. His negativity, his harshness, and his being in her business were more than she could deal with. He was just like their father. She checked her cell phone to see if Gregory had called. Of course not, it was only eight in the morning. As soon as she sat the phone down, it rang. She looked at the screen and although it wasn't Gregory, it was the second best thing.

"Francesca! Hey lady!"

"Hey woman, how have you been? I miss you so much!"

"I've been great and I miss you too. What's been going on?"

Francesca told Lydia that she had two weeks of vacation time and she wanted to spend at least a week with her. Lydia loved the idea of spending time with her best friend. She missed her so much. She missed their shopping sprees and Francesca's crazy sense of humor. Most of all, she missed having someone to talk to.

"Yes I would love that! When are you planning to come?"

"I'm thinking about next month. By then I should be done with this project at work and I will be totally free."

A smile spread across Lydia's face. "Sounds perfect! So what else is new with you?"

"Nothing spectacular girl. I've been dating here and there but men are all the same no matter what state you live in. I went out with this one guy from work two nights ago and he had the audacity to tell me only to order an appetizer because his cash was short. What the hell? Do I look like I go out just to eat appetizers? Why did you ask me out to dinner if you couldn't foot the bill? Dumb ass!"

Lydia started laughing and almost choked on her coffee. "What did you say?"

"Well you know me girl. I could've flipped out and caused a scene, which I normally would do, but I've been working on my self-control," Francesca started to laugh. "So I said ok that's fine. I ordered four appetizers, which came to the same price as an entrée! You should've seen his face! He was pissed!"

The two women fell out laughing. Francesca had always had crazy stories to share with Lydia. She was so animated.

"So what's up with you? You have a man yet?"

Lydia thought about her question carefully before answering, "Oh I'm seeing someone."

Francesca let out a squeal, "I know that's right! Who is he? Where did you meet?"

Lydia hated lying to her friend but she knew Francesca wouldn't understand if she told her the truth.

"I met him at the produce stand down the street. You know I still go every weekend. We started a conversation and have been talking ever since."

"Wow that sounds great. Where does he work? He does have a job right?"

Lydia smiled as she thought about Gregory and how sexy she bet he looked in his security guard uniform. "Yes, he works overnight as a security guard at the high rise building downtown."

"Oh a security guard huh? Has he been guarding your body Lydia?" Francesca let out a loud hard laugh.

Lydia laughed along with her. "Uh yes I suppose so."

"Ok you two have had sex right? Please tell me he's giving you the business girl!"

Lydia started to laugh. "Yes! Yes! Last night was fantastic! Dios Mio! He made me feel so good chica. I did something that I've never done before!"

"What? What did you do girl?" Francesca asked, almost panicked.

"I...I had anal sex." Lydia felt herself blush as she said the sentence aloud. There was a slight pause on the line.

"Oh my God! You didn't! Lydia I didn't know you had it in you woman! You little freak! This dude must be something special."

Lydia thought about how she felt about Gregory and yes, he was special to her. "Yes he's special Frannie. I want you to meet him when you come to visit. I think you will really like.... Oh hold on, I have another call coming in." She looked at the unavailable number and answered, "Hello?"

"Hey Lydia, its Gregory. Can we meet at the cell phone store in like an hour? I have a lot of things to take care of today."

"Sure, I can meet you there in an hour. See you soon...babe." Lydia still wasn't used to calling him that but it felt good.

"Ok see you there."

"Hello? Francesca? Are you still there?"

"Yeah I'm here. I was trying to make these pancakes like you do but mine never come out right, damn it! I need you to show me how you make yours again when I come to visit."

Lydia already knew what she was doing wrong. Francesca always flipped them too soon; she was so impatient. "I will be happy too but I have to go get ready, I'm meeting Gregory in an hour at the cell phone store."

"He's buying you a new cell phone? Go head girl! I am not mad at you!"

"No I'm buying him one." Lydia cringed as the last word exited her mouth.

Francesca tried to keep her cool, but that wasn't really in her nature. She didn't want to burst her best friend's bubble but she was not happy with what Lydia just revealed.

"What do you mean you're buying him a phone? What? Is this a loan? Why can't he buy his own damn phone?"

"Francesca calm down. He had a phone and it broke so he's still waiting for his replacement phone but I need to be able to talk to him whenever I want so I offered to buy him a cell phone."

"You know what; I'm going to let it go. I hope you know what you're doing girly. I still can't believe you're buying him a phone. That's just crazy."

"That doesn't sound like letting it go but ok." Lydia was upset that her friend flipped out. Just like her brother, her best friend treated her as if she were a child. She went to work and she made her own money, she was entitled to spend it any way she wanted. "I will call you later, ok. I'm looking forward to seeing you," Lydia said dryly.

"I'm sorry if I made you mad, you know I love you. I just don't want to see you get hurt that's all," her best friend said sincerely.

"I'm ok. I will call you later. I have to go get ready." Lydia hung up. She was mad at Francesca. She didn't know anything about Gregory and she was already being judgmental. She jumped in the shower hoping that she wouldn't be late. She put on a pair of jeans, a black t-shirt that said "Sweetheart" across the front, and her three-inch black sandals that she bought two days before. She left her hair down for a fun flirty effect. She checked herself over one last time in the mirror then went outside to hail a cab to meet Gregory.

Gregory jumped in his Corvette and rushed to the cell phone store. He was already late because he'd just gotten done with his date. She was one of his regulars from the escort service. Having sex with her was like watching paint dry. She just laid there moaning quietly. If he went deep in her, she would cry out in pain and ask him to stop. She was the worst but he had to go through with the date to keep Renee off his back and not to mention she paid four hundred dollars every time they were together.

Gregory rushed to park his car around the back of the building. He walked around the corner and saw Lydia getting out of the cab. He stared at her as if it was his first time seeing her. *Damn,* he thought to himself, *she looks sexier every time I see her.*

The way the tight fitting jeans hugged her ass and hips made him start to poke. He stood there looking around and trying to adjust himself. Lydia turned around and saw her baby standing there; he looked so good. She had never seen him in jeans before and he wore them well. He had on black and gray Jordans and a black muscle shirt. His hair looked a little unruly, like he had just gotten out of bed, but it looked so sexy to her. She felt the dampness forming between her legs as she walked up to him.

"Hey sexy, I hope you weren't waiting long."

"Not at all, I just got here," Gregory said, as he made sure his car keys were deep in his pocket.

The two went inside the cell phone store and looked among the hundreds of different phones. Gregory noticed the female employee checking him out and he winked at her. She blushed and looked at the computer screen in front of her.

"Gregory, you know I can put you on my phone plan that way the phone won't be that expensive and the bill may even be cheaper," she said with a big smile on her face.

Gregory stood thinking about what she said. If he allowed her to put him on her plan, she would get the bill each month and would be able to see who he was texting and calling. No that definitely would not work. Gregory glared at her and licked his lips. She smiled as she felt herself getting hot and bothered.

"Babe, I don't think that's a good idea. I don't want your bill to be higher because of me. Let's just do the prepaid deal and I will take care of the bill myself. My other phone was prepaid and it's just easier that way."

"Ok but that means I will have to pay full price for the phone," she said with concern. Lydia was not a big spender by any means. She remembered growing up without food, without nice clothes…just going without period. She never wanted to have to go through that again so she was very careful about how she spent her hard-earned money.

"Yeah I know but I promise whatever phone we get, I will pay you back. Yeah I will make sure I pay you back," Gregory reassured her even though he had no intention whatsoever of doing so. "I just want to be able to hear your sexy voice whenever I can."

Lydia loved the sound of that. They decided on getting the Max3, the newest smart phone on the market, four hundred and fifty dollars. Lydia pulled out her MasterCard and graciously paid for the phone. The ding of the glass door opening made Gregory looked in that direction.

"Oh fuck, Sasha!" he quickly turned around to face the counter. "Shit shit shit!" He didn't wanted that loud ass woman starting any trouble with him or Lydia and he definitely didn't want his cover to be blown. Lydia took the bag and handed it to Gregory who was now almost hiding his face in his chest.

"What's wrong with you?" she asked curiously.

"Huh? Oh nothing. Let's go." He tried to rush out of the store when he heard his name being called out. Lydia stopped and turned around to look at the very sexy woman.

She felt the jealousy build up inside of her. Who the hell was that woman? How did she know her Gregory?

"Hey what's up?" he said crossly.

"Nothing much, upgrading my phone. I tried calling you but I keep getting your voicemail. I guess you have a new number?" Sasha said looking at the bag in his hand.

"Nah, uh yeah I've been busy. Look we gotta run so it was nice seeing you." Gregory took Lydia's hand and literally pulled her towards the door.

He was almost in the clear when Sasha shouted out, "Call me so we can set something up." Gregory cringed at the remark as he hurried out of the door.

Lydia stood staring daggers at Gregory. She felt the jealousy rising in her chest and forming a lump in her throat. She knew he wasn't her man, that was just common sense, but her heart was telling her to find out immediately who that person was.

"Thanks for the phone Lydia. As soon as I get home I will activate it and you will be the first person I call," he said as he flashed his perfect smile at her.

Lydia's face didn't budge, not a smile or even the hint of a smirk, as she stood there trying to hold back the urge to breakdown. "Who was that?"

"She's just a friend. No one special."

"What kind of friend Gregory?"

Gregory didn't like being interrogated and if she weren't such a "cash cow," he would have told her to mind her damn business and left her standing on the sidewalk looking stupid. "She's just some chick I used to talk to. I ended it a while ago but obviously, she still got some feelings for me. This was way before I met you. This was before I saw you sitting in the park that day in December. Remember the really nice day in December when the weather was nice and it seemed like everyone just wanted to be outside?"

Lydia thought back to that day and she did remember. She had decided to eat lunch outside in the park instead of at her desk so she didn't have to deal with Katrina's fake ass or hear all the office gossip.

"Really? That's the first time you saw me?"

"Yes. And I knew I had to meet you," he said as he winked at her.

That wasn't a complete lie. Gregory had seen her in the park that day but it wasn't the first time he had seen her. He noticed her the day when she saw Jackson in the café with his new girlfriend. He saw how her face turned pale and how the tears rolled down her face. He saw how the sight of a man she once loved sitting with a woman that was more beautiful than she was broke her heart in pieces. That's when he decided he had to find out more about her because she was perfect…Perfect to manipulate.

Gregory had been with many women in his adult years and he could read them well. He knew Lydia was needy and lacking excitement in her life. He could tell by the way she walked and carried herself. He knew with the right amount of persuasion he could take over her mind and definitely her body. His plan was working perfectly so far, until that moment. That damn Sasha! He decided next time he got with her he was going to punish her ass and send her home that same night. That would definitely piss her off. Now he had to figure out how to calm Lydia down because he could see the anger and frustration all over her face.

Lydia stood thinking about what Gregory had just said. She couldn't believe that he had been watching her in the park that day. She offered him a little smile but she wasn't completely satisfied with his answer.

"Where do you know her from?"

Gregory sighed. "She used to work with me in the high rise building. She worked on the top floor with the lawyers." Gregory was over all the lying. He felt himself getting frustrated and was ready to leave her there and go home.

"But she doesn't work there anymore right?"

"Damn girl, I said she USED to work with me, meaning past tense ok? No she doesn't work there anymore," Gregory was almost yelling at that point.

Lydia's eyes widened and tears filled her eyes. She turned around and began walking away shaking her head.

"Fuck!" Gregory said to himself. "Lydia, come on girl, I'm sorry. I said I'm sorry!" She kept walking down the sidewalk and he caught up with her and grabbed her hand. Lydia stopped but refused to turn around and look at him. "I'm so sorry ok? I just got pissed because you were questioning me like…like you don't trust me. That crazy ass woman is my past."

Lydia slowly turned around and looked at her handsome lover. "I don't know if I should trust you. I don't know anything about you Gregory. And it's my fault because I haven't taken the time to really get to know you."

Gregory wasn't sure what to say. He couldn't tell her too much info but if he didn't give her enough he possibly risked losing her before he had a chance to work his magic and get his hands on her money and those credit card numbers. He pulled her close and kissed her, her cherry flavored lip-gloss made him want to kiss her more.

"Look whatever you need to know I will tell you but let's just take it slow ok. We have plenty of time."

She looked at him trying to study his face. She saw some sincerity but also some doubt. Her mind was telling her to be careful, as Francesca suggested but her heart said to give him a chance because so far he was the best thing that had happened to her in a long time. Lydia wanted him to be part of her life more than anything.

"Gregory, why don't you come back to my place and let me make you some lunch. I'm a great cook. We could hang out and talk."

Gregory smiled but in his mind, he wanted to scream. He didn't want to go to her house. He wanted to get in his car with his new Max3 and go home and chill until his next date at six pm. He looked at the way the sun make her brown eyes glimmer. He looked at how her breasts looked in her form fitting t-shirt. He felt monster twitch in his pants. He looked at his watch, eleven am. He decided he had time to chill with her but he didn't plan to do a lot of talking. He agreed to go with Lydia to her house for a couple of hours. He just hoped his baby would be ok parked around the side of the cell store building.

****

Anthony sat on Alexis' sofa watching rap videos and eating cereal. He had called her last night once she got off work and asked if he could crash at her place for a little while. Alexis was skeptical but didn't want to see him out on the street so she agreed he could stay but just for a couple of weeks. She couldn't understand why his sister, his own flesh and blood would put him out. What kind of bitch was she?

Alexis had just gotten out the shower and walked in the living room wearing a towel. She didn't like the way Anthony was spread out on her sofa. She was so used to being alone in her apartment that the sight of him almost irritated her. She looked at his book bag and shoes in the middle of the floor, her living room smelled like feet. She noticed the duffel bag on the floor within arm's reach of him. She noticed the bag the first night they met at the club and her curiosity was getting the best of her. She really wanted to know what was in that damn bag.

"Anthony! You got my whole living room smelling like corn chips," she said as she grabbed her Hawaiian Breeze air freshener and started spraying.

"Girl stop trippin'! My feet don't smell...and stop spraying that shit, it stinks."

Alexis rolled her eyes and went into the kitchen for a bottle of water. She came back in the living room, pushed his feet out of the way, and sat down.

"What's in that bag right there?" she asked almost with an attitude. Anthony glanced over at the bag but instead of answering her, he grabbed the remote and started flipping the channels. "Oh? You didn't hear me? I said, what…is in…that bag right there?" she said pointing at the duffel bag.

"Just my stuff. Nothing important. Damn stop being so nosey. Why don't you worry about what's behind this zipper!" He slowly unzipped his jeans.

Alexis gave him an icy stare. She knew there had to be something really important in that bag because he was acting too suspicious. She was determined to find out what it was, but in the meantime, she would play his little game. She got on her knees and pulled out his stiff manhood. She licked her hand then began to stroke him hard and fast, sliding her hand from the bottom to the top making sure to bring the foreskin from his uncircumcised penis up over his swollen head. Anthony leaned his head back and closed his eyes. Alexis's head game was absolutely the best.

She knew exactly how to make a man feel like a king. She licked her lips and went in on his hard dick, swirling her tongue along the head, licking his erection from one side to the other. She deep throated him several times, making him moan and grab her head. She slid his penis fully into her mouth and bobbed her head quickly making the tip bounce off the back of her throat.

Anthony bucked, fucking her mouth as if he were inside her tight wet spot. Alexis felt his manhood jerk and throb and she knew he was getting close. As soon as he was about to release, she lifted her head, got up, and walked away.

"Hey what the fuck!" Anthony grabbed himself and started jerking as if his life depended on it until the hot thick creamy liquid spilled out and flowed down his hand. He sat breathing hard and sweating. "Alexis, what the hell? What's up with that?" he said angrily.

She stood in the doorway of her bedroom as she let her towel fall to the floor revealing her freshly shaved spot. "When you decide to tell me what's in the bag, that's when I will decide to swallow." She started laughing as she went in her room and closed the door behind her.

CHAPTER EIGHTEEN

Renee parked her black Range Rover in Gregory's driveway. She needed to talk to him about his performance at work and since he wasn't returning her calls, she decided to go to him. She got a call from his date on Saturday morning saying that Gregory was rude and didn't really give her the "special attention" that she needed. The woman also stated that Gregory almost made her feel like she was bothering him.

Renee guaranteed the woman that he would be reprimanded but that didn't satisfy her, she wanted a complete refund of her three hundred dollars. Renee agreed to refund her money and quickly hung up, now she was at Gregory's, and she was determined to get answers. She got out of her truck and walked towards his door, the sound of her stilettos beating against his cobblestone driveway. She rang the doorbell as she peeked through the glass of his designer front door. She tapped her foot impatiently as she waited for him to come to the door.

She rang the bell several more times and peeked through the door again. The inside of his house was immaculate. Black shiny granite countertops graced the kitchen from one end to the other. A top of the line blender, juicer, and toaster sat on top, all stainless steel. She turned her head and pressed it against the door to see the black microfiber living room set and glass tables. His hardwood floors were shiny like mirrors.

"What the hell? Look at the size of that damn flat screen!" Renee said aloud.

She walked over to the garage, the sounds of the ocean waves crashing and the cool breeze blowing through her now black and blonde hair made her smile. She always loved the beach. It reminded her of the many summers she stayed with her grandmother. They would visit the beach almost every day, digging holes and making sand castles. Renee would collect as many different shells as she possibly could.

One summer her Grandmother built her a display box to place her beach treasures in for safekeeping. She absolutely loved that box. Her Grandmother had made it out of oak and painted it baby blue and sea foam green and she glued different color gemstones all over the lid of the box. One summer she decided to leave the box home instead of taking it with her to her Grandmother's house. It was already so full that she couldn't possibly squeeze another shell inside. When she went back home after summer vacation, the precious box was left behind with most of her other possessions when they were evicted from her family apartment. Her mother hadn't paid the rent all summer so on September 1st they were put out. Renee stood watching the waves as her face tightened with anger. She was only eleven but she hated her mother for letting the eviction happen more so because she had to leave her treasure box behind.

"Girl get the fuck over it!" she said shaking herself out of her trance. She looked through the side garage door; Gregory's Corvette was not inside. She called his cell phone and it went straight to voicemail. She opened her purse and pulled out a piece of paper and a pen, and jotted a quick note, "Call me ASAP! I need to talk to you! Renee." She folded the note and slid it between the front door and the pane.

She stood thinking to herself about Gregory's lavish abode. How could he afford all of it? He was barely going on dates during the week and she was certain he didn't have a second job. Yes, she would definitely get down to the bottom of it. She got back into her Range Rover and sped off.

****

Lydia opened her apartment door and welcomed Gregory in. He looked around at the quaint one bedroom apartment. He didn't see anything special about her place, of course, it wasn't nice like his condo, but it really did suit her.

"Have a seat, get comfortable," she said. "Are you thirsty?'

"Yeah I could use some water. Bottled please."

"Of course." She went to the kitchen and got two bottled waters. She sat down beside him on the sofa and flipped on the music channels. "What kind of music do you like babe?"

"Whatever you pick is cool," he said as he picked up the Sports Illustrated off the coffee table.

She sighed and patted him on his knee. "I'm trying to find out your music preference. When you're home what type of music do you relax too? I saw a Miranda Lambert and Blake Shelton cd in your cd rack at your house. I didn't think you were a country music fan."

Gregory looked at her puzzled. "Country? I don't listen to no damn country."

Now Lydia was confused, "Then whose cds were those?'

It finally dawned on him that she was referring to Brent's house. "Oh, those were probably my buddy Brent's cds. He's one of those good old boys from the country. That's his thing not mine. I like R&B, some hip hop, Jazz."

Lydia turned to the smooth jazz channel. The song that was playing was so beautiful. The laid-back sound of the saxophone made her feel sexy. She looked at Gregory as he thumbed through the magazine and bobbed his head to the sensual beat coming from the television.

She scooted closer to him so she could smell his cologne, God it was so intoxicating. She soaked in his essence; she let it wash over her like a cool summer breeze. She wanted this man. She needed this man. She longed for this man. She couldn't remember the last time she ever wanted something so badly. She shook her head; she knew she was getting carried away. She didn't know much of anything about this beautiful person but she was dying to find out.

"Gregory, what's your last name?" She felt so stupid asking that for the first time. They had known each other for five months now and she didn't once think to ask him.

Gregory glanced up from the article he was reading, "Turner," he said with a smile. Yet another lie, his last name was Summit.

"When's your birthday?"

Gregory almost rolled his eyes but caught himself. "May 15th."

Lydia got excited, that was three weeks away. "Oh we have to plan something special for your..." she realized she didn't know exactly how old he would be. That was embarrassing. "How old will you be?"

He tossed the magazine down because obviously she wasn't going to let him read in peace. "I will be thirty three."

"Well we will have to plan something special for your thirty third birthday."

Gregory looked at his watch; he was ready to go. He didn't like all the questions Lydia was asking. The less she knew the better. He didn't like lying to her either, that was just more information he would have to remember.

"Umm, you don't have to worry about lunch. I'm kind of pressed for time and I should probably get going."

Lydia's smile quickly vanished. She always hated when they had to part ways but at least he had a cell phone now. She really didn't want him to go. She leaned over and kissed him on the cheek. Gregory looked at her and recognized that look. He knew exactly what she wanted.

He leaned over and kissed her lips while rubbing her arm slowly moving towards her breasts. He gently circled her hard nipple with his finger through her shirt. Lydia felt the goose bumps rise all over her body. She reached over to feel his hard erection. Gregory let out a low moan, her hands on him felt so good. He began to unfasten her jeans, fiddling with the zipper. She offered assistance by standing up and pulling off the skintight jeans revealing orange lacy panties. Gregory unzipped his jeans and pulled out his massive wood. She loved it; she loved everything about it.

"Come ride me," he said while stroking monster.

"Let me get a condom."

Lydia went into her bedroom and opened the nightstand drawer. She was happy she decided not to throw out the condoms that Jackson left behind after they broke up. She took off her t-shirt and bra, baring her perfect breasts. She slid off her panties, took a deep breath, and slowly walked back into the living room with the condom. Gregory loved what he was seeing. Damn she was sexy as hell; he couldn't deny it. Lydia walked over, opened the condom, and slid it onto her new best friend. She went to straddle him but he stopped her.

"What's wrong?"

"Turn around and slide down on me."

Lydia did as she was told, the entire time grinning. She slid down on his thick penis; the feeling was intense.

She let out a gasp as she began riding and grinding on him. She watched their reflection in the television screen...She loved the way they looked together. Gregory held her by her waist controlling her movements.

The sight of her tight ass jiggling made him almost explode instantly. She was so tight, squeezing his manhood just right. He pulled her legs up on the sofa and pulled her back up against him. She continued riding him while he squeezed and pinched her hard nipples. Her sounds of passion turned him on so much. She sounded beautiful.

"Aye, aye papi I'm cumming!" Lydia grinded harder and deeper, faster.

"Ah shit, I'm cumming too!"

Gregory couldn't hold it anymore. They both released at the same time, holding and griping on to each other as the wave of ecstasy took them over. Lydia got up and collapsed on the sofa beside him. She was hot, sweaty, and extremely satisfied. Gregory took off the used condom, stuffed it inside the wrapper, and tossed it on the coffee table. He'd definitely needed that.

Lydia went into the half bath and got him a wet washcloth. She went into her bedroom, quickly cleaned up, and put on an oversized t-shirt that came down to her knees.

"Baby that was so good. I can't believe we came together. You know what they say about that right?'

Gregory tossed the wet washcloth on the table beside the condom wrapper and looked at her with raised eyebrows, "No. What?"

"A couple that cums together stays together for life," she started to giggle.

Gregory looked at her with a blank stare. He didn't see the humor in what she just said. *Couple,* he thought to himself. *Stay together for life?* Yeah he knew she was sprung but damn that chick had fallen hard and fast!

Gregory gave her a dismissive laugh as he zipped his jeans. He wasn't even going to entertain that comment.

"Babe what about your parents? Do they live around here?"

"My mom died two years ago and I never really knew my father. He left my mother and me when I was almost one. All I know is his name and that's more than I want to know."

Lydia saw the pain in his eyes so she decided to let that subject go. She knew exactly how he felt and maybe one day they could have a heart to heart about how their fathers abandoned them.

BANG BANG BANG

The knocking at the front door made them both jump.

"Yo Ant! Ant! You here man? Come on dawg! I need to holla at you!"

Lydia couldn't believe it! Was that the same guy that was there the other night? Even though Anthony was gone, she still had to deal with his bull.

"Who is that?" Gregory said curiously.

"Someone looking for my brother. He stayed with me for a few weeks. I guess whoever it is doesn't know he's not here anymore."

BANG BANG BANG

Gregory laughed. "Are you going to answer it or what?" It wasn't his house and he wasn't planning on getting involved in any mess her family had going on.

"No, I'm scared. You don't know the kind of people my brother hangs out with. There's no telling who's on the other side of that door and what they want."

He could literally see the fear in her face. That was too much. He didn't want to get in the middle of it but he didn't want her sitting there scared either. He got up and went to the door. A very dirty not to mention smelly looking man stood there cowering.

"Hey my man. What's good? Is Ant here?"

"Nah dude, he's not. He doesn't stay here so I suggest you don't knock on this door anymore...ever." Gregory stepped towards the obviously homeless man.

He quickly backed away, "Ok, ok I don't want no trouble. If you see him tell him Paco looking for him." Gregory slammed the door and looked at Lydia. She looked relieved.

"Thank you. I hope he doesn't come back."

"He won't. If he does let me know."

She smiled. He actually did care about her, so she thought.

"So how long have you been doing collections?" Gregory asked.

"About three years. I'm somewhat tired of it though. I get tired of fighting people to get them to pay their debt. It's crazy. They create all these charges then they don't want to pay. And everyday someone is always disputing the charges. People will say anything to get out of paying their bills."

Gregory sat listening closely. "So if they have a dispute with a charge, what happens then?"

"We send it over to the fraud department. They have to investigate the charges and sometimes it takes a while. Sometimes it takes too long and the customer gets mad and threatens to close their account. That's when they usually take it as a loss and credit the funds back to the customer's account."

Gregory sat intrigued. It might be easier than he thought. The hardest part would probably be getting Lydia to be down with the plan. He picked up his bottled water and took a long drink, almost drinking most of its contents.

"Well babe, I really got to get going. Thanks for...everything," he said as he winked at her. "I will activate the phone and call you as soon as it's charged."

She walked him to the door and they passionately kissed goodbye. Lydia closed and locked the door. She was absolutely in heaven. He made her feel so wonderful inside and out. The actual thought of him gave her goose bumps. She sat on the sofa in a daze. The way he chased the stranger away from her door made her feel so special. He cared for her; she just knew it. They had actually climaxed together.

Of course, she didn't believe the saying about couples that climax together stay together for life; but it was nice to think that it could be true. She laid on the sofa engrossed in her thoughts until she dosed off with her wonderful man on her mind.

****

Gregory rode in the cab back to the cell phone store to get his car; his mind was racing. It was the greatest hustle ever. He could get at least one to two different credit card numbers and make online purchases. He would have to figure out where to have the packages delivered though. Brent may be down and if he could get back in Alexis' good graces, she would definitely be willing to help. He wished he didn't have that date at six so he could stay home and brainstorm. He had to figure out the right time to bring it up to Lydia and where he would send his purchases. He would make sure he would switch which credit card numbers he used often so that it wouldn't look too suspicious.

When the customer finally got their statement, they would just call and dispute the charges. His name wouldn't be attached to it. If anything, they would probably connect Lydia to it, if and when they were caught. Yes, that was just the hustle he needed. Gregory was still smiling when the cab pulled up to the cell phone store. He jumped out and headed towards the side of the building. He hit the keyless entry button and heard the familiar chirp of the doors being unlocked. As he rounded the corner, he stopped dead in his tracks. His front two tires were slashed and a long scratch went from the back of his Corvette up the passenger side to the front of the car.

"WHAT THE FUCK! OH MY GOD!" he was screaming at the top of his lungs as people stopped and watch the temper tantrum. Who would do that to his baby, his precious car? He blinked back the angry tears as he looked at the damage. He noticed a white piece of paper stuck under the windshield.

He snatched it and opened it, "Watch your back punk ass!" He balled up the piece of paper and threw it on the ground then leaned up against the car. Who could have done this and why? It could have been that guy that Alexis was fucking with or damn it could have been Alexis. She would definitely pull some crap like that. He stood there staring into space. Sasha! It definitely could have been Sasha's ass! Whoever it was he was definitely going to get to the bottom of it and when he did there was going to be hell to pay!

CHAPTER NINETEEN

The weekend had gone by quickly and Monday was already there. Lydia dreaded going into her place of employment. She wished she could quit but she needed the job until she found something better. She did her usual routine. She logged into the computer, put her purse in the bottom drawer of the file cabinet, and put on her headset. She stared at the screen waiting for the dialer to begin calling the thousands of American Express customers that owed money.

She couldn't take her mind off Gregory. She loved that she was able to call and text him now. She was disappointed because she couldn't talk to him like she wanted last night. He said he wasn't feeling well and he was going to bed early. She offered to come over but he said that he didn't want her to get sick too. He was so considerate.

The first three calls that came through on the dialer were wrong numbers. She knew it was going to be a long day. Customer after customer gave the same excuses and many of the businesses that were called weren't open yet so they would be put back in queue to be called again. As the phone rang, she looked around the office. She noticed Katrina wasn't there. She had a habit of not being in on Monday mornings so she wasn't surprised. She was surprised to see Michael shuffling in late. He looked a mess! Lydia covered her mouthpiece with her hand, "Michael come here."

Michael sat his briefcase down and slowly walked over to Lydia. His eyes were red as if he had been crying. His skin was pale and pasty looking and he actually smelled like liquor.

"What's wrong Michael?" she said as she grabbed his hand.

"He left me…That selfish son of a bitch left me," he fought hard to fight the tears that were welling up in his eyes.

"I'm so sorry sweetie. Were you guys having problems?"

Michael grabbed Katrina's chair from her desk, wheeled it over to Lydia's desk, and sat down.

"Honey no. I thought we were happy. He wasn't acting strange or anything. Sunday morning we made hot passionate love, by Sunday evening he was packing his shit, and telling me it was over."

Michael reached in his pocket fishing out a used tissue to blow his nose. Lydia felt so bad for him. He was the sweetest most genuine person she knew and to see him like that just broke her heart.

"Did he at least tell you why?" she inquired.

He closed his eyes tightly as if the pain was excruciating. "He left me for another man. He has been having an affair for the past two months."

Lydia covered her mouth and shook her head. She couldn't believe what she was hearing. Michael and Robert were the perfect couple. It didn't matter that they were gay; they were the prime example of how love was supposed to be. Lydia used to find herself envious over their relationship, now just like that, it was over, and Michael was a complete mess.

"I stayed up all night drinking and crying. I begged him not to leave me Lydia. I told him I would do anything to make it right, ANYTHING! He just looked at me like I was nothing and said he didn't love me anymore."

Michael broke down and began sobbing loudly. The other employees were looking around trying to find out where the noise was coming from. Lydia grabbed her friend and hugged him tightly. She began to cry herself as she tried to console him. The memory of her begging her father to stay flooded her mind.

She literally felt Michael's pain. She knew the agony, the humiliation of begging for the love of someone just to have them turn around and leave you broken and crushed. She cried with her friend and also for herself.

Mr. Frasier came around the corner with a stern look on his very round face. "What in the world is going on here? Michael why aren't you at your desk working?"

Lydia looked at her boss with an aggravated look as Michael continued to cry quietly. "Mr. Frasier, Michael needs to take a personal day today. He needs to go home."

Mr. Frasier threw his hand up in frustration, "Fine. Go home Michael. Next time you're having personal issues either call out or leave them at home and come to work!"

He turned around and walked fast and hard back towards his office. Lydia let go of Michael and took several napkins out of her desk drawer. She cleaned herself up and gave him some to do the same.

"Go home Michael. Go home, take a shower, and get some rest. I will call to check on you later ok sweetie?"

Michael looked at his friend and nodded his head ok. He slowly walked back to his desk, grabbed his belongings, and left the building. Lydia sat thinking about her friend. How could Robert do that to him and how did Michael not see any signs? Two months was a long time to cheat on someone and not show any signs of it.

She knew he would be ok but it would take time. He was madly in love with Robert. He was his first relationship with a man. She took her cell phone out of the desk drawer. She sent a text to Gregory, "Miss you babe." She sat eagerly awaiting a response. She looked at her monitor, thirty-six dropped calls. "Damn it!" she whispered to herself. She began working again all the while glancing at her phone waiting on Gregory's response.

Gregory was finally getting his car back. He laid in bed replaying things repeatedly in his head. Who the hell messed his car up like that and who left that note on the windshield? Why did Renee come to his house Saturday? He reached over to look at the note she had left in his door. He didn't feel like dealing with her at all but he knew there was no way around it. She couldn't be mad about him not going on dates and bringing money in because lately he'd been going on three to four dates a week.

He hoped she didn't want another round with him because he was not sleeping with her again, no way. Then there was Alexis. He wasn't sure what to do about that situation. He didn't know why he was tripping over her having old boy there, she wasn't his woman. Why should he care? He knew he had to find out who dude was because there was no way he was going to disrespect him and get away with it.

He heard his new phone buzz and looked at the screen. He typed, "Miss you too," and hit send. She wanted to talk the night before but he was busy getting head from one of his clients. He had to cut Lydia short when the woman made his dick touch the back of her throat. His phone buzzed again, the incoming text read, "Are you feeling better?"

Gregory texted back, "Yes much better thanks." He tossed the phone on the bed and thought about Lydia. Maybe he would use one of the credit card numbers and purchase a one-way ticket out of the States. He needed a change, a big one. Truth be told, he was tired. He didn't want to keep screwing random women for money; it was getting old and he was over it. He needed to find another way to make his money. He knew he wasn't ready to settle down, he didn't think he ever would. He just wasn't that type of man.

He made up his mind that after he did this one last hustle he was done, done with Renee and Premier Escorts, and done with sleeping with women for money. He looked at his phone, "Will I see you tonight?"

Gregory texted back, "No I have to work." He actually had two dates he had to take care of that night. One for the escort service and one of his own personal clients.

Lydia looked at her phone in disappointment. She was looking forward to spending time with him but she understood he had to work. Maybe she would swing by Michael's and check on him. She was sure he needed someone to talk to. She texted Gregory back, "Ok love, I understand. I will talk to you later. Muah!"

She put her phone back in the drawer. She felt so good about Gregory and how their relationship was progressing then the vision of Michael sobbing took over her thoughts. Could she really trust Gregory? Had he ever lied to her? She sat back in her chair staring off into space.

She tried not to overthink or over analyze but the feeling was nagging at her. Technically, he wasn't officially her man, they had never had that conversation, but it definitely felt like it was heading in that direction. Was he seeing other women...like Alexis? She felt anger building up inside of her... if she was committed to him then he should be to her!

She logged off the dialer and grabbed her phone out of the drawer. She went to the bathroom and dialed Gregory's number. The line rang and rang. She hung up and dialed the number again. The line rang forever and then she got the message saying that this person hasn't set up their voice mail account yet. She was pissed. What was the point of her getting him the damn phone if he wasn't going to answer when she called?

She sent him a text, "wyd? I'm calling you and you're not answering. Call me back."

She sent the text and paced the bathroom floor waiting for a response. She couldn't stay in the bathroom forever; she was already dropping calls left and right. She knew her numbers would be awful today and she may even be written up. She looked at her phone, nothing. What was he doing? Where was he? Her imagination was getting the best of her and she didn't like it. She left the bathroom and sat back at her desk.

She decided that after work she would go see Michael and then go home. Maybe she would surprise Gregory by stopping by his place. She could make him a nice dinner before he went to work. All of her panic-stricken thoughts disappeared and she became excited at just the thought of seeing him. She put her headset back on and got back to work.

Gregory inspected his car; it looked like new. He decided to go see Renee and get it over with. He drove down Windsor Avenue towards the agency. He was already pissed that she came to his house, that shit was unnecessary! If she called him and he didn't answer then she should have just waited until he got back to her. He pulled up to the agency but he didn't see her Range Rover. He decided to go in anyway just to be nosey and see what was going on. He walked into the waiting area; the smell of lavender assaulted his nose. He hated that smell! Renee was always spraying lavender oil everywhere in the office.

"What's good baby?" he said to the receptionist.

She blushed and looked down. "Hey Gregory. How have you been?" Kristie asked.

"I'm good now that I've seen that sexy smile of yours. When are you going to go out with me?"

"You know I can't date the employees," she giggled and looked away.

"Then I quit. Ok so now when are you going to go out with me?"

Kristie laughed at his advances. "Renee is looking for you. She's in a mood today."

Gregory rolled his eyes, "Damn she's here? I didn't see her car."

Kristie looked at him and nodded her head, giving him a sympathetic look. He looked at her office door and let out a long loud sigh as if he were a student going to the principal's office. He took out his cell phone and looked at the time, three o'clock. Then he took out the cell phone that Lydia bought him, three missed calls, and one unread text message. He looked at the text message and frowned. He didn't like being kept tabs on. Just like he was going to tell Renee, if you call and I don't answer, wait until I get back to you, plain and simple.

He knocked on her office door. "Yeah come in!" she shouted. She was sitting at her desk painting her toenails. *How ghetto,* he thought to himself.

"Well well look who chose to grace us with his presence. You're a hard man to get ahold of G."

Gregory cringed. He hated being called that. He felt himself getting pissed already. "Why did you come to my house Renee? You don't have any business on my property. If you need me call or text. I will get back with you...when I get the time. Understand?"

Renee gave him an icy glare. Who the hell did he think he was talking to like that? She took a deep breath and stood up from behind her desk taking care not to mess up her fresh pedicure.

"I can go wherever I damn well please. You know that you are primarily on call so it's part of your job to answer when I call you. I went to your house because you chose not to call me back! Speaking of houses, yours is pretty laid out for someone with a job like this. What's up with that?"

Gregory stood up and walked over to the mini bar she had set up in the corner of the office. The bitch was asking for it. He decided to have a drink before he snapped and lost his job. He poured himself a small drink of scotch and swallowed it down. Renee stood there with her hips on her hands waiting for him to respond.

"Don't come back to my house Renee. Don't come looking for me. I will call and check in just like everybody else. DON'T COME BACK TO MY HOUSE!" Gregory slammed the glass down and walked out of her office slamming the door. The receptionist stopped what she was doing a stared at him as he walked out. He took his new phone out of his pocket and called Lydia.

"Hey sweetie," she whispered, "I'm not supposed to be on the phone. I still have an hour left at work. What's up?"

"Listen, if you text or call and I don't answer just wait for me to call you back ok? Don't fuckin blow my phone up like that; that shit is unnecessary and it pisses me off. Got it?" The line went silent.

"Gregory I was just trying to get ahold of you. Where were you?" she whispered.

"See that's what the fuck I'm talking about. You do not need to know my whereabouts every minute of the day. I'm a grown ass man and I don't have to answer to anyone, that includes you. I'm handling my business. I'll talk to you whenever." Gregory hung up.

Lydia looked at her phone like there was a snake in her hand. She was appalled. He had actually snapped on her and then hung up before she could fully explain herself. In her mind she didn't do anything wrong and he had blown everything out of proportion. She was so mad she wanted to cry but she refused to do so. She was going to give him time to calm down and then call him later to straighten everything out.

CHAPTER TWENTY

Lydia stopped by Michael's house to check on him. It was obvious he had been crying and drinking. Slow sad music played on the stereo. She sat on the couch and looked at him lovingly. "Are you ok sweetie?"

"I will be eventually. He stopped by to get the rest of his things. He just walked in here like we were roommates and he had gave his thirty day notice." He blew his nose loud and hard. She felt so bad for him.

"Lydia have a drink with me babes. I'm so tired of drinking alone."

Michael poured her a glass of chardonnay. She took it but told herself she wasn't drinking too much because her plan was to stop by Gregory's house before he left for work.

"I will have a couple of drinks but I can't stay long. I have to be somewhere by seven."

"Where do you have to be besides home in front the television?" he asked with an attitude.

Lydia gave him a sharp look, "I'm going to see my man before he leaves for work thank you!" she drank her glass of wine in one long gulp and held her glass out for more.

"Oh do tell! Your man huh?" Michael said as he looked at her with an, "I don't believe you" look.

"Yes Gregory Turner. The guy that sent me the bear and roses at work that day. Remember?"

Michael poured her another glass of wine as he raised his perfectly waxed eyebrows. "So this Gregory is your man you say? Have you slept with him?"

Lydia sipped the second glass of wine and looked at him sarcastically, "Oh course I have."

"What part of town does he live in?"

"He lives over in State Square on McDermott Street."

"Oh that's nice. That's a nice quiet area. Middle class. Where does he work?"

Lydia was getting a little annoyed by all of his questions. She understood that he was hurting and having issues but that was no reason to interrogate her and her relationship with Gregory. She drank down her second glass of wine and smiled at Michael, "I have to go."

"I'm so sorry girlfriend. I apologize for making you uncomfortable. I am having some major trust issues right now and I just don't want to see you hurt like me. These muthafuckin men will tell you anything to keep you quiet and happy while the whole time they are out screwing somebody else!" he started to cry again and Lydia felt herself getting upset. She didn't believe that all men cheated, some men were faithful and trustworthy, and she wanted to believe that her Gregory was one of them. She hugged Michael and kissed him on his cheek.

"I will call you tomorrow sweetie, I promise." He wiped his face with his robe sleeve and looked up at her.

"Lydia take my car. You can use it for a couple of days. I'm not going anywhere."

Lydia looked at him with a puzzled look, "But what about work or if you need to go to the store?"

"I've got everything I need and I already talked to Frasier. I told him I would be back on Wednesday. Just swing by and pick me up on Wednesday morning ok?"

Lydia smiled at her friend and shook her head ok. She leaned over, kissed him on the forehead, and thanked him. He walked her to the garage and opened the door. She looked at his emerald green Ford Taurus. It was a newer model, 2012. She was happy that she wouldn't have to catch a cab for the next couple of days. She got in and back out of the garage and waved to Michael as she drove off. The leather seats felt so good caressing her body.

She played with the radio until she found a contemporary jazz station. She rolled the windows down and let the cool evening breeze blow through her long brown locks. She couldn't wait to get to Gregory's. She suspected that maybe he just had a bad day because of the way he spoke to her earlier. She was going to go to her man's place and calm him down, and give him some nice relaxing head. That's all he need was her undivided attention. She pulled up in front of his apartment. There was a gray Jeep Cherokee in the driveway. She stared at the jeep for a few minutes; her thoughts were going into overload. She didn't want to think the worse but after having that conversation with Michael; she couldn't help but feel a certain kind of way. She bit her lip and sat in Michael's car listening to the sultry tune and wondering what to do next. She took her phone out of her purse and dialed his number but it went straight to voice mail. She decided to go knock on the door.

As she walked up to the front door, she heard country music playing loudly from inside. She smiled and instantly thought of their conversation about his friend Brent. *He and Brent must be hanging out before he goes to work,* she thought. She knocked on the door and the music ended abruptly. She almost passed out when the door opened. The man standing before her was magnificent. His blues eyes sparkled sharply in the sunlight. His short red hair was so shiny and bright. His arms were humongous! He had to be a body builder because no average man could have arms like that. She looked him up and down studying his every feature. She was in complete awe.

"Can I help you?"

Brent's deep country accent threw her off guard. He looked at the amazing looking woman. She was beautiful; there was no other word to describe her. Her shiny hair moved gracefully in the breeze. Her golden brown eyes shimmered as she stared at him in silence. Her body was amazing. Brent examined her from head to toe. He was upset that she came to the wrong door because he definitely could do some things to her.

"I'm sorry. Is Gregory here?"

"Gregory? Gregory Summit?" he asked in confusion. Lydia shook her head.

"No Gregory Turner." She turned and looked at the street and around the neighborhood. She was certain she had the right house.

"I'm his girlfriend Lydia. I wanted to see him before he went to work tonight."

Brent looked at her and didn't know what to do. He didn't want to blow Greg's cover. "Oh um come in, he should be home soon. I'm his friend Brent. Did you try calling him?"

"Yeah but I keep getting his voicemail. He seemed upset earlier so I just wanted to talk to him."

Lydia walked in and sat down on the couch. Brent sighed in frustration. He didn't care what Gregory did but when it started involving him, he had a problem with it. Lydia tried to call him again but it went straight to voicemail.

"I will be right back I need to go in the back real quick," Brent said nervously. He walked quickly down the hall and into his room. He took his cell phone out of his pocket and called Gregory, on his other number.

"What's good B?" Greg answered on the first ring.

"What's up? Your girl is here! That's what's up man!" Brent explained while peeking out the cracked door at her. He watched her as she looked around the living room. She was so beautiful he couldn't take his eyes off her.

"My girl? Man what the fuck you talking about?"

"Lydia!"

"Oh shit! Stop lying, she's there for real?" Gregory pulled out of his date and sat on the side of the bed. He couldn't believe that she actually showed up unannounced!

"She said she's been calling you but it's going straight to voicemail. Funny I call you and you answer right away."

Gregory looked at the phone that she had bought him and it was dead. "She was calling me on the phone she bought me but I didn't know it was dead."

Brent couldn't believe he was getting caught up in this mess. "Well what do you want me to tell her? I'm not trying to be in the middle of this mess man! I knew I should've never let you use my damn place! Shit!"

"Hold up man! Who are you raising your voice at?" Gregory shouted angrily.

"I'm talking to you! This is what the hell I'm talking about, you, and all your bullshit games. You had better call her and let her know something! This is fucked up!"

Brent hung up the phone and peeked back out of the door. Lydia sat looking down at her phone. The look on her face looked so hopeless. She looked confused and hurt. Brent genuinely felt bad for her. Although Brent did work at the escort agency, he never disrespected a woman. He never led them to believe it was anything but a business situation. He heard Lydia's phone ring and he leaned against the door to listen.

"Hey sweetie! What time are you coming home? I have a surprise for you." Lydia's happiness quickly vanished.

"Are you fuckin crazy coming to my house unannounced? I just got done telling you about blowing up my phone and you took that as a sign to pop up at my house? What the hell is wrong with you?"

Lydia sat quietly listening to Gregory yell at her. "I know baby, I'm sorry. I thought you were having a bad day and I wanted to come see you."

Gregory was pissed. Not only was he mad at Lydia but also he was mad at Brent for coming at him the way he did. He was starting to think that the hustle might be more trouble than it was worth

. "Listen, just go home. I don't know what time I'm coming back and honestly I don't feel like seeing you or dealing with you tonight." The line went dead. Lydia looked at the phone. She couldn't believe what just happened. She tried to hide her emotions but the unbearable feeling took over. She began to cry...she tried to stop but her feelings were so hurt. She couldn't bear having Gregory reject her. Brent heard her crying and felt his heart sink. Brent was always a softie when it came to women crying. He hated to see a woman sad or upset. Brent's father died in a chemical fire at the plant where he worked when he was fifteen. He quickly became the man of the house, watching over his mother and three sisters. He became an expert at comforting women and being a protector. Now he stood in his room listening to this beautiful stranger sob uncontrollably. That fucking Gregory. He walked down the hallway back towards the living room. He grabbed some toilet paper out of the bathroom. He didn't know what he was going to do. Even when she was crying, she was beautiful. He had an overwhelming urge to hold her and ease her pain. He walked over to her and handed her the tissue.

"I'm so sorry I didn't mean to break down like this." She quietly blew her nose. Brent sat down beside her. He could smell her vanilla scented perfume. He watched her as she wiped her eyes and tried to get herself together. Brent wasn't quite sure what to say.

"It's ok. What did he say?" Brent was curious.

"He's mad at me because I showed up without telling him. Honestly, I didn't think I was doing anything wrong. I just wanted to see him before he went to work tonight."

Brent raised his eyebrows. *Work tonight?* he thought to himself. Surely, she didn't know where he really worked.

"He will get over it soon. Just give him time. Please stop crying." He reached over and rubbed her back.

"She is so beautiful," he kept thinking to himself. She looked at him and smile, and it melted his heart.

"Do you want a drink? I think there's wine, water and some Jack Daniels in the kitchen."

Lydia thought back to that night with Gregory and how they almost drank a whole bottle of jack.

"Yes if you don't mind can I have a glass of wine?" she smiled at her gracious host. Brent went into the kitchen and poured her wine into a coffee mug. He poured himself a shot of jack and went back into the living room. The two sat and talked for almost an hour. She told Brent about the craziness at her job, about Michael and Katrina and he told her about his family and when he was in the military. They laughed at each other's stories. Brent couldn't remember the last time he had a genuine good time with a female and no money exchanged hands. She was a breath of fresh air and the type of woman he could see himself settling down with.

Before he could rationalize what he was doing, he leaned in and kissed her lightly on the lips. Lydia pulled back and looked at him. Why would he do that? Wasn't he Gregory's friend? Brent touched her hand and smile at her. Lydia felt her heart skip a beat. He was so amazingly handsome. He had a genuine kindness in his face that she was drawn to. His clear blue eyes made her feel at peace and safe. Brent picked up her hand and kissed it. He kissed her wrist and up her arm, the whole time looking into her eyes. Lydia knew she should have pulled away or said stop but her body craved more. She looked into his piercing blue eyes and felt hypnotized. He pulled her in and kissed her, at first gently and then very passionately. She let out a small moan, his mouth felt so great on hers. She hated to admit it but he was a much better kisser than Gregory was. He touched her face as they kissed and she felt the goose bumps form on her arms. She touched his chest. She could feel the hardness of his muscles through his shirt. He pulled her in closer by her waist. She put her arms around his neck and ran her fingers up his neck then through the back of his red hair. She felt her panties moisten. What the hell was she doing? Brent stood up and scooped her off the sofa in one quick motion. He carried her to the bedroom while he was still kissing her. He didn't know if he was wrong for what he was doing but at the moment, he didn't care, he would deal with that later. He sat her on the bed.

"Are you ok? I mean; I don't want you to do anything you don't want to do," he said quietly.

Lydia stood up and began undressing. She wanted him. She wanted every inch of his hard muscular body. Brent began to pull off his shirt as Lydia sat on the bed in just her panties and bra. She saw the bulge grow bigger underneath his flimsy basketball shorts. He pulled his shorts and underwear down and Lydia grinned from ear to ear. He was huge and the carpet definitely matched the drapes! The fiery red hair around his massive hard dick turned her on. She didn't like pubic hair but his red hair intrigued her. He walked over to her and slowly pulled her crimson red lace panties off. He stood admiring her smooth shaved sweet spot. He rubbed her and his fingers were drenched. He knew she wanted him and he definitely wanted her. He went into the nightstand drawer and pulled out a condom, opened it and slid in on his erect member then he leaned her back hovered over top of her kissing her lips, her neck. She moaned and rubbed his strong back moving her hands down to his waist to his ass. She wanted to feel bad about what she was doing but at the moment, she didn't have it in her. This man was making her feel so superb; the way his body melted against hers felt so natural. He reached down and guided himself into her, she gasped for air. The sensation took her breath away, literally. He filled her damp whole, stretching her wide. She let out a low yell.

Brent stopped and looked down at her. "Am I hurting you? I can stop."

Lydia grabbed onto his ass tighter and pulled him towards her more, "No. Don't stop, please."

She pulled him and again and he continued to slide into her. Brent worked his stiffness slowly inside of her, making sure he stroked her carefully. Lydia wrapped her legs around his waist allowing him to go deeper inside her. She rocked her hips trying to keep up with his rhythm. Brent leaned forward and licked up and down her neck while giving her little kisses. He tongued the inside of her ear and he could feel her getting wetter and wetter. She moaned and wrapped her legs tighter around his waist as she used her leg muscles to pull her butt slightly off the mattress.

"Hold on around my neck," he whispered to her. She did as he said and Brent wrapped his arms around her waist and picked her up off the bed. Lydia held on tight around his neck with her legs still wrapped around him. He reached down, grabbed onto both her ass cheeks, and worked his rock hard dick deep inside her. Lydia let out passionate screams and moans, even calling his name. He glided her up and down while pumping in and out of her. Lydia had never felt such ecstasy before. She loved the way Gregory made her feel but Brent was bringing something totally different to the table.

She felt like she would pass out but she hadn't even came yet. He sat down on the bed with his manhood still inside of her. Now she was on top. Lydia began grinding against her new friend, the sound of her wet pussy gushing against his dick made her even hotter. She put her feet up on his thighs so she could slide down on him deeper. Brent grabbed onto her breasts and teased her rock hard diamonds with his thumb and index fingers. He was enjoying seeing them get hard. Her breasts were her weak spot and that was a sure way of making her cum. She quickens her pace, grinding hard, and fast. Her swollen clit was rubbing up against his red hair causing unbelievable friction. He let go of her breasts and grabbed her hips, holding on tight; he moved his hips in rhythm with hers. He felt it building up…he didn't want to cum yet but he didn't know how much longer he could hold on.

"VOY A CORRERME! ADIOS MIOS!" Lydia yelled out grabbing tightly onto Brent's arms. He had no idea what she said but whatever it was, it was sexy as hell and just enough to take him over the edge.

Brent growled like a Lion in the wild," AWW SHIT! FUCK!" He started bucking his cock in and out of her hard and fast until he drained all his semen out. Lydia collapsed forward onto his sweaty heaving chest. They laid there for a while holding each other in complete silence, listening to each other breathe heavily. Brent rubbed his big hands up and down her small smooth back. She was so tiny compared to his 6'5" 300 lb. frame. He had an intriguing desire to protect and comfort her.

"We can never tell Gregory," she whispered meekly.

Brent rolled his eyes at her comment. He lifted her face and looked into her eyes.

"Are you and him together? I mean are you really a couple?" Brent knew Gregory's intention but he wanted to know how far gone she was when it came to him.

Lydia stared back into his crystal blue eyes. For a moment, all she wanted to do was kiss him and forget about everything else but she knew that wouldn't erase the fact that she slept with another man. Not just another man, but Gregory's friend... in Gregory's house, in the Gregory's bed. She softly smiled at Brent and shrugged her shoulders.

"We've never officially talked about it. We are in the beginning stages you know. Getting to know each other better."

"Then why are you buying him things and giving him money? That's something that a girlfriend does for her man, not two people getting to know each other." Lydia frowned at him and he could tell that maybe he said the wrong thing.

"How do you know about all that?" she asked firmly.

"He told me...more like bragged about it. I am his friend; of course he's going to tell me." Brent knew he was overstepping his boundaries but at the moment, he didn't give a damn. Lydia tried to get off Brent but he pulled her back down on his chest. His limp member was still inside her and he felt himself getting aroused again.

"I'm not trying to hurt you Lydia. But if you are so committed to Greg and everything is good, then why are you laying here with me?"

Lydia felt angry and she wasn't quite sure why. She didn't like Brent questioning her about her "situationship" with Gregory, even if he was right. She pushed herself off him and started to get dressed.

"I really hope you don't plan on mentioning this to Greg when he gets home. And don't slip up at work and mention it either." Brent propped himself up on his elbows.

"Work?" he questioned.

She looked back at him and gave him an agitated look. "Yes work, the high rise building! I know you work days and he works nights but I'm sure you see each other sometimes right?"

Brent shook his head. Not only did the asshole use his place as a front but also he told her he worked at the high-rise building with him? That was too much. Lydia finished dressing then sighed loudly. She was more confused than ever now. Gregory was mad at her and she had just slept with Brent. Why would Gregory brag to him about the favors she had been doing for him? Yes, she admitted she had bought him the phone and had given him at least fifteen hundred dollars over the past few weeks, but she didn't want her man to want for anything. Her man. The undeniable truth was that Gregory wasn't her man and after what she learned today, she wasn't sure if she wanted him to be.

"I've got to go in case Gregory shows up."

Brent pulled the used rubber off and quickly put on his shorts, "Let me walk you out."

Brent walked her to the front door and grabbed her hand before she could open the door.

"When can I see you again?" he kissed her hand never taking his eyes off her.

"See me again? I don't know if that's a good idea," she looked down at the floor," what about Gregory? I feel awful we had sex in his house and in his bed. Don't you?" she asked searching for some type of remorse in his face.

Brent pulled her close and kissed her hard, "No I don't feel bad at all and if you are completely honest with yourself you wouldn't feel bad either." Lydia felt the familiar feeling of sadness and uncertainty forming inside of her. She had felt this feeling so much in her life.

"Brent, will you be here when Gregory gets home or are you leaving before he gets back?" Brent searched her face. She was so gentle, so delicate. Why did Greg have to pick her to screw over?

"Yes I will be here...all night. But Greg won't he here. He will be home." Brent knew there was no going back now. Lydia shook her head at him. She was completely confused.

"What are you talking about Brent? This is his home." Brent smiled at her. He went into the kitchen and pulled a small envelope out of one of the drawers he folded it tightly and placed it in the palm of her hand.

"I want you to look at this once you get in the car. It should answer your question."

She wanted to look at the paper now but she would wait. He walked her to Michael's car and opened the car door for her. He kissed her cheek and closed the door. She watched him walk back into the house then she headed down the street. She got to the stoplight and quickly opened her hand and unfolded the envelope. It was a utility bill.

"Why did he give this to me?" she wondered aloud. She turned on the light inside the car and read the address, "Brent Carlisle 314 McDermott Street Apt C." She reread the address again in disbelief. Gregory had lied to her; that was Brent's house! Lydia drove home, furious and devastated. Now she understood why he was so mad at her for showing up unannounced…he was scared that she would find out he was lying. She wasn't sure if she should be mad at Brent, he did tell her the truth and what he said made a lot of sense. If she was so head over heels for Gregory then why was it so easy for her to have sex with Brent? Maybe her feelings for Gregory weren't as strong and genuine as she thought. And now that she knew the truth about Gregory lying to her and bragging about the money that she had given him, she was even more confused about her feelings. She was going to find Gregory tomorrow and he was going to tell her the truth about everything!

CHAPTER TWENTY-ONE

Alexis left the club around two Tuesday morning. She was extremely tired and didn't feel like dealing with Anthony when she got home. They had developed a love hate relationship. It always started out with an intense screaming match over his stinky feet or him leaving beer bottles all over the living room and would end in rough passionate lovemaking. She just wasn't in the mood for the same song and dance tonight. She walked to her car when she saw headlights flashing at her. She reached in her oversized red bag for her mace as she walked quickly to her car. She tried to get her keys in the car door but dropped them. Then she heard a car door open and close. "Oh shit oh shit!" she said as she grabbed her keys off the ground.

"Alexis!" the voice called out to her.

"Get the fuck away from me!" she yelled as she held her mace up ready to spray."

"Put that shit away, it's me Gregory," he yelled with his hand up in front of her face. Alexis lowered her hand and leaned against the door.

"What the fuck! You scared the shit out of me!" she looked around him at the shiny black escalade that he had gotten out of.

"New ride?" she said with an attitude.

"Nah, one of my ladies let me use it while she's out of town. What's up girl, I miss you." He looked at her and licked his lips seductively. She glared back at him with dismissive look. Truth be told she missed him too but she was not going to tell him that.

"Well I don't miss you. I've been extremely busy," she said while rubbing on her left breast. Gregory caught the hint but he wasn't buying it.

"Busy doing what? Teaching old boy how to fuck as well as me?" Gregory started laughing but Alexis didn't find his remark funny.

"No he doesn't need any instruction. He has it down packed. He knows exactly how to lick this cat." Alexis started rubbing herself on the outside of her skirt. Gregory felt monster rise in his khaki shorts. He loved when Alexis played games; it just fueled the fire within him.

"Come sit in the truck with me," he winked at her. Alexis knew what he was up to. She decided to play his little game.

"Ok, let me put my stuff in the car first." Alexis unlocked the door and tossed her things inside. She followed Gregory over to the truck, he opened the door for her, and she got in.

"Oh this mutha trying to be a gentleman all of a sudden," she laughed aloud.

"What's funny," he said curiously

"Nothing. So what do you want? Last time I saw you I was a bitch. Remember? Are you still playing with your little Latina bitch?" she rolled her eyes at him.

Gregory smirked, "You know I didn't mean that shit. I was just mad as fuck that dude came at me the way he did. And yeah I'm still working my magic on her. You still dealing with that loser?"

Alexis checked her makeup in the rearview mirror, "Yes, we live together."

Gregory looked at her like she was crazy. "You moved his ass into your crib? Are you fuckin' kiddin' me?

She loved it that he was getting jealous. "Yes, I moved him into MY PLACE, where I pay rent and utilities. What the hell is wrong with you?"

Gregory was mad as hell but he wasn't going to let it show. He leaned back in the seat and looked out of the window.

"What's his name anyway?"

"Anthony," she said making her tongue seductively touch her top teeth as his name rolled out of her mouth.

"Well Anthony better watch himself 'cause I haven't forgot how he disrespected me."

"Get over it Gregory!" she gave him a dismissive wave. "He sure in the hell ain't thinking about your ass. Believe me."

"You're thinking about my ass though aren't you?" He reached over and rubbed in between her thighs. Goosebumps covered her bare arms as she began to tingle. She slapped his hand away and he laughed. He touched her thigh again but this time he slid his hand all the way up to her hot center. He found his way easily to her bud, especially since she didn't have any panties on. She jumped at his touch.

"You need to get your hands off me," she said as she opened her thighs wider. She wanted him but her hard to get game wasn't working very well. Gregory began fingering her hard and deep, she moved her pussy up against his two fingers, she felt herself getting wetter and wetter. He pulled his fingers out and put them in her mouth. That was it; Alexis couldn't fight the temptation anymore. Gregory moved his seat all the way back and unfastened his belt and unzipped his shorts. His erection popped out like a jack in the box waiting to be played with. Alexis looked over at her friend; she did miss him.

"I know dude ain't got what I got," Gregory said as he stroked himself. She looked at him and rolled her eyes. Truth be told, Gregory was bigger than Anthony down below. He reached in his pocket and pulled out a condom. He tossed it over to her and continued to stroke monster. Alexis was speechless. She couldn't believe that he actually wanted to have sex with her, she was sure he just wanted a blowjob. She didn't want to give him the satisfaction of him knowing she wanted him but the temptation was too strong, she just couldn't resist him. She unwrapped the condom and reached over to slide it on him. She climbed over the middle console straddled him. She slowly eased her wet slit down onto his hard erection. Alexis grabbed onto the back of the seat as Greg scooted down a little. She began grinding up and down, rotating her hips in a clockwise motion. A few times her ass hit the steering wheel, causing her to honk the horn. They both laughed but never slowed their rhythm. Gregory played with her breasts, taking time to suck and tease each nipple.

The windows began to fog as she rode his dick harder and harder. He could tell by the way she was giving it to him that she was frustrated with him but he didn't care, the way she was riding him felt great. Gregory's body began to jerk, he couldn't hold back anymore and he came hard. Alexis didn't get a chance to get hers but of course, that wasn't his concern. She got off him and climbed back over to the passenger's seat.

"Well it was real but I gotta go, "Alexis got out of the truck and walked back to her car. She was mad and disgusted with herself. She had once again let Gregory Summit manipulate her into getting his way. She got in her car and drove off, never looking in his direction.

****

Lydia had made arrangements with Gregory to meet after work. She had purposely distance herself from him because she wasn't sure what she was feeling. At one point and time, she craved the man. He was all she ever thought about. But now Brent was invading her thoughts. She had opened the utility bill that he gave her and found his phone number. Ever since the night they slept together, she's been dying to call him. She wondered was he thinking about her too. She decided to call him because she couldn't take the suspense.

"Hello?" Brent asked puzzled.

"Hi, is this Brent?" she asked embarrassed.

"Yeah, who's this?" Brent looked at the number on his phone.

"It's Lydia," she said quietly. What if she read all the signs wrong? What if he didn't want to talk to her or see her again?

"Hey girl? How are you?" He knew he said he sounded excited but he didn't care.

"I'm good," she was at a loss of words," uh I just wanted to call to say hello." She rolled her eyes at herself.

"I want to see you...now," Brent could feel himself getting worked up. Ever since that night, she was all he thought about but he didn't have a way to contact her. Lydia blushed. She had plans to meet Gregory but now all she wanted was to spend time with Brent. She was completely torn now.

"I want to see you but Gregory's supposed to meet me at my house."

Brent frowned, "So tell him you have to change your plans. I can meet you at your house or you can drive to my place." He had made up his mind that she was going to be with him tonight. Lydia thought about what he was saying. It wasn't like her to lie to get out of something but she decided she needed to be with Brent.

"OK I will call him. I guess you can come to my place but it's going to take me awhile to get there. I don't know where all the cabs are right now."

"You work at the collection place on Rockford right?"

"Yes. But how did…"

"Stay put, I'm on my way to get you." Brent hung up grabbed his keys and left work an hour early.

Lydia called Gregory's number and he answered right away. She told him that something had come up and she couldn't see him tonight. He tried his best to interrogate her because he found it odd, very odd that she would cancel an opportunity to see him. She reassured him that it was nothing major and she would call him later. As she hung up Brent pulled up in his Cherokee. He got out and smiled at her, opened the car door for her. He looked even more handsome today than he did the other night. Maybe it was his dark blue security uniform that he wore. She got in and glanced around, his truck was very clean and organized. He got in and grabbed her hand and kissed it, she loved when he did that. He was so tender and gentle.

"So your place or mine?"

"Mine is good, if that's okay?" she blushed.

"You're place it is baby girl."

He winked at her and she smiled and looked out the window. It felt so right to her. He held her hand the entire trip. They drove to her place in silence with only the faint sound of the twang of country music playing on the radio. She tapped her finger to the song thinking to herself that the music wasn't as bad as she thought. Twenty minutes later, they were at her apartment. Before he could put the truck fully in drive, he was out of the vehicle rushing around the front of the car so he could open her door for her. She was greatly impressed. It was nice to have a man pick her up instead of having to catch a cab. She knew it wasn't Gregory's fault he didn't have a car but it was a nice change of pace.

Brent liked the look of her place, very gentle and feminine like her. He sat on the sofa and for some reason he was nervous. Lydia grabbed two bottles of water from the fridge and sat down beside him. She would rather have a glass of wine but she wanted to keep a clear head tonight. She wanted to make sure what she felt the other night was true and genuine. "Thank you for picking me up. I appreciate it," she said as she brushed her hand across his.

"No problem. What happened to your car, the one you were driving the other night?"

"That was my friend's car. He let me use it for a couple of days since he wasn't feeling well but he came back to work early." She was glad Michael got himself together and came back to work. Maybe it would take his mind off Robert.

Brent opened his water and took a long gulp, "Oh ok. I know my car is not as nice as Gregory's but she's mine and I take good care of her." Lydia looked at Brent in complete confusion. Did he just say what she thought he said? *Gregory's car?*

"Gregory doesn't have a car Brent," she smiled as she shook her head. Brent sat back on the sofa took off his clip on tie and loosened his top button. He knew exactly what he was doing. He knew that Gregory never told her about his shiny black corvette for fear she would be able to track him down. He wasn't trying to hurt Lydia but he felt she deserved the truth.

"Greg has a car. A shiny black corvette. And his last night isn't Turner, its Summit."

He stared at her to see what her reaction would be. Lydia looked back at him, staring at his mouth as if she could see the words exiting. She was in complete shock. Gregory had told her two lies, two lies that she fell for hook, line, and sinker. Brent rubbed her back trying to bring her out of her trance.

"Where does he really live Brent? Please tell me."

Brent was digging himself deeper and deeper into a hole. He knew once Gregory found out about what he did he would be furious. He may even come after him. Was telling all his secrets worth risking his friendship with Gregory? He looked at Lydia. He touched her soft wavy hair, then her smooth flawless face. He traced his finger down the side of her cheek to her chin. He was in awe of her. He decided yes it was worth it. He didn't care about Gregory because Gregory was a dog and a manipulator.

"He lives in a beach front condo on the Southside. He drives a black corvette. That's the truth Lydia."

"But how can he afford that on a security guard's salary?" She was completely floored by the information she just heard. Brent looked at her and it took everything in him not to laugh. He had to give it to Gregory; he had really played his role well. He had the poor girl completely fooled. He wanted to tell her everything, he felt compelled to be completely honest with her. If he decided to tell her everything, that meant coming clean about himself too. He wasn't sure if he was ready for that.

He turned to face her. He took a deep breath trying to prepare for what he was about to say.

"Lydia, Gregory doesn't work with me at the high rise building." Brent felt the lump of anxiety forming in his throat threatening to choke him.

"He works at Premier Escorts."

The words stung her like a thousand bees. Premier Escorts? She was trying to make sense of everything. She didn't call the escort service so why was he approaching her? Why did he lie? She stood up, walked over to the kitchen window, and stared out into the darkness. Emotions flooded her fragile soul. She gripped the sink as she swayed back and forth. She felt dizzy and nauseous. Brent saw her swaying, jumped up, and ran over to her. He turned her around to see the salty hot tears flowing down her face. Her bottom lip was quivering. She let out a low moan as her hurt and pain came pouring out of her.

She couldn't stand on her own. Brent held her up and held her close in his bulging muscular arms. He felt like the biggest jerk in the world. Was he wrong for telling her the truth? Was he selfish for snitching on Greg because he wanted her to himself? He walked her over to the sofa and sat her down. Seeing her cry was breaking his heart.

"There's something else," Brent said.

She looked up at him in disbelief, "What else could you possibly have to tell me? Is he married? Does he have something?" She felt the panic overwhelming her.

"No that's not it." He looked away from her. He wished he hadn't said anything now.

"Tell me Brent. Please!"

"He approached you because, because he wanted to make you fall in love with him. He wanted to make you fall in love so you would.... give him credit card numbers from your job."

Lydia felt all the breath she had escape her. That was it. The last straw. The rage filled her quick and fast.

"So what Brent? You knew all this shit; and you were part of the scam? That's what's going on here? Oh what you had a change of heart now?"

Brent shook his head no fast and hard and tried to reach for her hand but she quickly pulled it back. She was outraged.

"Yes I knew but that was before I met you Lydia! After I met you, after I made love to you, I wanted to tell you everything! I'm so sorry baby! I just wanted you to know the truth about that lying bastard!"

Lydia jumped up and walked over to the door, "I want you to leave Brent."

Brent sat on the sofa. He felt the tears sliding down his face; he didn't even realize he was crying. He looked down at the floor in shame, "I work there too."

Lydia's mouth opened wide. That was too much for her. Gregory's horrendous lies and now Brent telling her he was an escort also.

"Were you planning on taking advantage of me too, weren't you?"

Brent looked up quickly, tears streaming down his pale cheeks. "Fuck no! Oh, my God baby girl. I only work there for extra money to make ends meet. Gregory's the one that does this shit full time and he loves it. You know he does side jobs too right? Him and that skank Alexis!"

Lydia almost fell over. She hadn't heard that name in a long time. At first, she wondered if Gregory and Alexis were an item but now she had her answer. Brent got up and walked over to her. He put his arms around her hoping she wouldn't reject him. He hugged her tight as she cried.

"I will give it up; I will walk away from that place, for you. All I want is you. I want to give us a chance." Lydia broke down and the two cried together.

Greg decided to drive past Lydia's house. He had an uneasy feeling. He knew Lydia was sprung over him…and monster. Now all of a sudden she was cancelling their get together? She seemed cold and distant when they talked on the phone too. Something was not right. He turned down her street and slowly crept past her house. He saw a familiar vehicle parked on the street in front of her place. He blinked hard to focus, a gray Jeep Cherokee. His heart began to beat fast and sweat beads formed on his head even though his air conditioning was blasting. What the fuck was Brent doing at Lydia's house? He drove past staring at her apartment. He could see the silhouette of two people embracing by the light of the lamp in front of the window in the living room. Gregory gripped his steering wheel tightly. So, that is why Lydia had been so distance the past couple of days? Brent was supposed to be his boy and that is what he was up to? Gregory squealed his tires and sped down the street. Brent and Lydia stopped embracing long enough to glance out the window to see where the noise was coming from.

"What was that?" Lydia asked through the sniffles.

"I don't know. I don't care. All I care about is you, right here and right now."

Brent kissed her as he had never kissed another woman before. She took his hand, led him to her bedroom, and closed the door.

CHAPTER TWENTY-TWO

Anthony watched Alexis as she walked around the apartment getting ready for work. She seemed different to him. She was withdrawn, distant, and sometimes downright cold towards him. At one time, he actually thought he was in love with her but now she was turning out to be a stuck up bitch just like the rest of them. He tried to get some love from her that morning but she turned him down flat saying she didn't feel good. He wasn't buying that. She was a freak and always wanted it. He wondered had she been back in contact with that punk ass dude from before. Anthony had seen him one day leaving the mall with a beautiful older blonde woman. He had at least six bags in each hand. He had to give it to him he was a true playa; he knew how to get what he wanted, even if that meant getting Alexis.

"What time did you get off last night," he asked looking at her suspiciously. He pretended he was asleep when she came in two hours late that morning.

"Why?" she said with her hands on her hips.

Anthony crossed his arms and smiled, "I'm just asking babe. Why you getting so upset chica?"

Alexis rolled her eyes and continued to get her belongings together for work. She was in such a bad mood because once again she fell for Gregory's crap. She was at the point where she just wanted to be by herself. She needed time to get herself together.

"Anthony when do you plan on getting your own spot? This just ain't working out anymore."

"Where the hell is this coming from?" Anthony knew there had been some tension between them but he didn't expect her to ask him to leave.

"I just need my space. I don't want a roommate and that's what you've become. An overbearing pain in the ass roommate. All you do is lie around funking up my place. I'm tired of you!"

That was it. Anthony couldn't control his anger and before he knew it, he had Alexis by the throat squeezing tightly. Alexis grabbed at his hands trying to loosen his grip. She tried to grab for his face but she was getting weaker and weaker as she tried to fight for air. Anthony shoved her up against the wall still holding onto her. She managed to let out a small whimpered plea for help. Anthony let her go as her semi-conscious body slid down the wall to the floor. She held her throat coughing and trying to breathe again. He stepped back and glared at her with rage in his eyes. He was tired, tired of the rejection from his family, and so called friends. He was tired of dealing with whores like his mother. He thought Alexis was different but she was a filthy whore just like the rest of them.

Lydia was turning into a slut too, creeping in at all times of night after being with that dude Gregory. He was determined to find out who the guy was that was banging his sister. He didn't care if she was grown. Anthony grabbed his things, including the black duffel bag and headed for the front door. Alexis sat on the floor crying, she was scared to look at him. She couldn't believe that he had put his hands on her. She thought he was going to kill her.

Anthony looked at her and chuckled, "You're pathetic, a pathetic slut. I should've left you at the trifling ass strip club where I found you." He turned and left. Alexis balled up on the floor in the fetal position and sobbed uncontrollably.

Anthony didn't know where else to go but to back to his sister's house. He had to get rid of the duffel bag and soon. Once he did that, he would get out of town, for good. He hoped on the bus and rode fifteen minutes to his sister's house. It was only nine thirty so he assumed she would be home. He knocked on her door, no answer. He forgot he still had his key so he let himself in. He went straight to the fridge and grabbed a beer. He plopped down on the sofa and noticed her bedroom door was closed. He wondered was she in the shower, maybe that's why she didn't hear him knocking. He tapped on her bedroom door before slightly opening it. The room was dark, but he heard breathing.

Maybe she turned in early, he thought. He was going to close the door until he realized the breathing wasn't just breathing, but moaning also.

He listened closely as he heard his sister utter, "Oh Papi, no se detienen." Anthony opened the door wide and flicked on the light. There was Brent in all his glory pounding his massive dick in and out of Lydia and her legs wrapped tightly around his waist. Anthony saw nothing but red.

"Oh my God, Anthony! What are you doing here?" Lydia yelled out pushing Brent off her and trying to cover her nude body. Brent sat on the bed confused.

"Who the fuck is this?" Anthony said so vehemently that spit flew from his mouth.

"Is this that muthafuckin Gregory? This the dude you been creeping around with?"

Lydia was trying to cover herself but she was shaking so badly with the fear she thought she would vomit. Brent looked at Lydia for some type of explanation but he could tell that she was paralyzed with fear.

"You better speak up slut! This dude Gregory?"

Brent stood up completely naked, but he didn't care.

"Yo man, you need to calm the fuck down for real. First of all, no I'm not Gregory and second who the fuck are you and why are you in her apartment?" Brent could feel his adrenaline flowing. He didn't know who this person was but he was ready to knock him out cold.

"Damn sis, you got a whole line up going now huh? You are truly your mother's daughter!" Anthony let out a loud sarcastic laugh and clapping his hands. Lydia looked at Brent with embarrassment. She didn't want him to think that she was sleeping around with a bunch of men. That was her past and she wasn't like that anymore.

"Dude why don't you leave ok? We all need to calm down right now."

Brent sat back down and rubbed Lydia's back trying to calm her nerves. She felt uncomfortable with him touching her with Anthony standing right there. Anthony laughed at Brent's good old boy southern accent. He wasn't going anywhere and if Brent didn't shut up he wasn't going anywhere either.

"I ain't going nowhere! You need to get dressed and leave, before someone gets hurt."

"Are you threatening me man?" Brent stood back up breathing heavily. His fists were balled up tight.

Anthony watched Brent getting worked up and he loved it. He wanted him to jump so he could beat his ass. Brent was much bigger and a lot taller than Anthony was but that didn't faze him at all.

"I hope Gregory ain't a bitch like this dude Lydia. You sure know how to pick them!"

"Stop comparing me to Gregory! I ain't nothing like his punk ass! If I can help it he will never see your sister again!" Lydia looked at Brent and revealed a slight smile. She couldn't believe how he was taking up for her.

"Gregory is nothing but a liar and a manipulator, screwing as many women as he can. He's probably somewhere right now getting head or fucking that bitch Alexis."

Anthony couldn't believe what he just heard. Did he say Alexis? No he couldn't be talking about his Alexis?

"Hold up, Alexis? Alexis who?" Anthony's face was screwed up with confusion and denial.

Brent bent down to pick up his underwear and pants never taking his eyes off Anthony. He started to get dress, "Alexis from that strip club on 39th and Washington."

Lydia slid out of bed and began to put her clothes back on. She didn't know what was going on. Why was Anthony so eager to know about Alexis? She thought back to the night that she and Alexis were together. She vowed that she would never tell Brent about that but then again he probably already knew. She was sure that Gregory bragged about that too.

Anthony leaned against the door. He was trying to put two and two together. Alexis and Gregory? Was Gregory the dude that came to her house? He felt his head tightening. That meant that Lydia's boyfriend was the same dude that came to Alexis' house that morning. The same guy that claimed Alexis as his. What the hell was going on?

"Ant, what is wrong with you?" He was sweating and mouthing something to himself.

"Do you know Alexis Lydia? Don't fuckin' lie to me!" he pointed straight at her face. Lydia didn't want to answer. She wasn't sure how he knew her and the wrong answer could make things go from bad to worse.

"No I don't know her Anthony. How do you know her?"

"She was my girl. That's who I've been staying with."

"Oh shit! You're the dude that fought Gregory that day at Alexis' house? Oh man!"

Brent let out a loud laugh. It took a minute but it was becoming clear to Lydia. The night she went to Gregory's "house," he had a black eye. He said he got it at work but now she realized he had gotten into a fight with her brother over Alexis. Anthony walked over and sat on the foot of the bed with his head in his hands. Brent continued to stand watching him just in case he decided to go off again. Lydia felt bad for her brother but she wasn't sure what to do. She sat down beside him and rubbed his back. She glanced at Brent and he shrugged his shoulders in confusion. It was evident that Gregory Summit was the common denominator in this completely crazy mess.

Brent finished getting fully dressed and stepped out in the living room to give them some privacy. He sat on the sofa and stared out into space. The entire situation was getting out of control and now he was a part of it. He was glad that Lydia had lied to Anthony about knowing Alexis. He knew that they knew each other; he knew that they slept together; of course, he had seen the DVD. He told himself he would never tell Lydia that he saw it. He wasn't even sure if she was aware that she had been videotaped that night. If she didn't, she wasn't going to hear it from him. He didn't want to hurt her any more than she had already been hurt. It was only a matter of time before Gregory found out everything and when he did, it was going to be war. Anthony came flying out of the bedroom door towards the front door, Lydia was chasing behind him.

"Anthony calm down, don't go over there right now! You're too upset! Just calm down!"

"No fuck that! She owes me some answers! Don't you want to know why your man is sleeping with that bitch?" Anthony yelled as he glanced over at Brent.

"My man, don't you want to confront this dude for hurting my sister?" Brent thought about what he had just said. He was mad at Gregory. He was mad that he had mistreated and used Lydia.

"Let's go to Gregory's house first then we will deal with Alexis," Brent said as he grabbed his keys.

"That's what the fuck I'm talking about," Anthony stood pounding his fist together.

"I'm going too!" Lydia grabbed her black flats out of the living room closet. Both men looked at each other quietly laughed and shook their heads.

"No baby girl, you stay put. We don't need you getting hurt." Brent walked over and kissed her on the forehead. She pulled away from him and frowned. She was not going to stay home because this involved her also. She was the one that was lied to and she was the one that had given Gregory money. She was the one that Gregory had planned to scam. There was no way she was going to stay put.

"I said I am going!" Lydia slipped on her shoes and stood by the front door with her arms crossed like a hot-tempered five year old. Brent looked at Anthony for back up.

"Yo don't look at me. She said she's going so let's go." They got in Brent's Jeep and headed for Gregory's beachfront condo.

* * * * * * * * * * * * * * * * * *

Gregory was so mad he couldn't see straight. Brent, his good friend, was seeing his girl. In his heart, he knew he had no claim on Lydia but he couldn't believe that Brent would move in on her. Was he trying to steal his hustle? That had to be it! Brent was driving that raggedy ass truck and look where he lived! That rundown apartment could use a lot of upgrading. He didn't have the latest electronics or nice furniture. Gregory grew more upset by the second. His no good country ass was trying to steal Lydia from him so he could get the credit card numbers from her! He was tempted to turn around and go back to her house but then he thought what he might do to Brent...and her so he quickly changed his mind. He needed to relax and take his mind off what he just saw so he decided to go grab a drink and maybe a lap dance at Papa Mack's.

He was hoping he would run into Alexis too. Alexis had always been there for him. She was almost like his best friend...with benefits of course. He did feel bad for calling her a bitch but he was mad and jealous. The thought of her with another man made his blood boil. He did care for her a lot, maybe even loved her. He parked his corvette and walked into the shabby establishment. He went straight to the bar and ordered Hennessey on the rocks. He looked around and thought about the first time he met Alexis. He came in that night looking for another candidate for his selfish endeavors. He loved the way she carried herself, like she owned the club. She was classy. She was definitely ride or die material. He really hoped she was there so he could talk to her. He had two more drinks and felt great. He looked at his watch; it was just about midnight. If she were there, he would have seen her by now.

"My man, Alexis working tonight?" he questioned the bartender.

"Nah, she called out."

Gregory raised an eyebrow. Alexis was all about her money, even though she hated working at the club she would never call out. He pulled out his cell phone and dialed her number but there was no answer. He thought maybe she was sick or maybe she called out to lay up with her new man. He had to find out. He felt like he was losing his mind. Between Lydia, Brent, Alexis, and that dude Anthony he felt like he was seriously going to hurt somebody. He paid his tab and was about to leave when he saw Renee and Big Kendrick walk in. Big Kendrick aka Big K was the biggest drug dealer on the Southside. Gregory wasn't surprised to see the two of them together because that was the type of company Renee kept. They came in walked straight to the VIP section. Gregory called the bartender over again.

"Changed your mind man? You want another hen?"

Gregory shook his head, "No but how often does Big K and that chick come in here?"

The bartender stretched his neck to look over at the VIP section. Gregory rolled his eyes because the bartender was being so obvious and he wasn't trying to draw attention to himself.

"Oh they come here a lot. They will be the new owners next month."

Gregory was intrigued. The biggest drug dealer in town and the queen of the escort service were going to be co-owners of a strip joint.

"Have you heard anything about any renovations or changes to the place?" he asked the guy.

"Oh man! They planning to lay this place OUT!" The bartender was loud as hell. Gregory told him to calm the hell down and stop being so loud. He gave Greg a "whatever" look and kept talking.

"Man they talking about putting all new furniture in here and new carpet. I heard Big K say they putting a top of the line sound system in and building a new DJ stand. And the bar! SHIT! The bar is going to be bangin'! I hope they get some better looking bitches in here though. These hoes are tired as fuck. You feel me? My man, you gonna leave me hanging?"

The bartender had his fist out ready to dap Gregory but he was too busy staring at the two new owners in the corner. All he saw was dollar signs. He wanted in on the action. A top of the line strip club would bring in thousands maybe even millions. Big K's money was long and strong and Renee wasn't hurting for anything either. He definitely was going to have to step to Renee about the new business venture. He got up and slipped out the door trying to avoid Renee seeing him. He got to his car and sat there for a few minutes. His mind was on overload. He decided he was going to go check on Alexis and see if she knew anything about the new plans for the club.

Brent, Anthony, and Lydia arrived to Gregory's condo. Lydia got out and looked around in amazement. This is where Gregory actually lived? The smell of the sea salt from the ocean filled her nostrils. She could feel the cool breeze from the beach blow through her hair. The sound of the waves crashing seemed to soothe the pain that had buried itself deep in her soul. She closed her eyes and for a brief second she was in paradise.

"Man look at this shit!" Anthony looked around the grounds.

"This dude living like this and trying to hustle my sister? Yeah I gotta bust his ass…again!"

Brent walked over to the garage and peeked through the door. He wasn't home. Anthony kept talking to himself and getting worked up as he looked through the windows and door of the condo. Brent saw that Lydia was enjoying the breeze from the ocean and that she was shivering. He walked over to her and embraced her with his huge arms. The warmth of his body made her feel so good, so safe. She thought about all the guys she had slept with in her younger days and how she felt she needed their acceptance and approval. She thought about the rejection from her father and how it made her feel less than worthy. If her own father couldn't love her then how could any man? She thought about Jackson, how she longed to be in a relationship that she didn't even care if she had to settle for a boring predictable man. At least she wouldn't be alone. Then when she and Jackson ended, she found herself alone anyway.

She was longing for excitement and passion. That's when she met Gregory and she thought her prayers had been answered but it was just the beginning of a nightmare. What if she had given him credit card numbers from work? What if she'd gotten caught? She would have gone to jail for years and lost everything. She began to cry as Brent continued to hold her. He looked down at her and kissed her forehead, her nose, and then her lips. He could tell that she was thinking about the crazy situation. He wished he could take her pain away.

"Anthony, let's go man." Brent yelled as he walked Lydia back to his truck.

"We got to find this muthafucka man, tonight!" Anthony wouldn't be satisfied until he was face to face with the man that had planned to hurt his sister.

CHAPTER TWENTY-THREE

Gregory arrived at Alexis' apartment. He walked up the stairs and knocked on the door several times.

"Who is it?" Alexis called out.

"It's Gregory girl, open the door."

"I'm not in the mood for company Gregory, please just go away."

Gregory looked at the door. First Lydia now Alexis? He couldn't believe that Alexis was turning him away. What in the world was going on? He knocked on the door again. He wasn't leaving until she let him in. Alexis cracked the door. It was very dark and still inside her place.

"What the fuck? I said I don't want to be bothered right now!" she snapped at him. He could see that she was upset. He needed to know what was going on so he pushed past her and let himself in. The only light that was on was a small lamp in the corner of the living room. He turned around and looked at Alexis but he could barely see her. He walked over to the light switch and turned on the overhead light. His mouth dropped open. Alexis looked a terrible mess. Her mascara and tears were running down her face, her lipstick was smeared to the side of her face. He looked closer and he could see red marks around her neck. She stood looking down at the floor as if she were ashamed. He had never seen her like that.

"What the fuck happened to you?" Gregory's bedside manner needed improvement.

"Please just go. I'm not in the mood to deal with you or anybody else right now."

She walked over to the sofa and lied down. Gregory followed her, moved her feet, and sat down. He stared at her waiting for her to say something but she just laid there with her eyes closed.

"Lex, talk to me," he said smacking her thigh.

"Anthony attacked me."

Anger took over Gregory's body like a parasite. He felt his heart beating out of his chest.

"He put his hands on you? He put his hands on you and you didn't call me? What the hell is wrong with you Lex? Sit up and answer me!"

Alexis sat up and tried to blink away the tears but she couldn't. They started to fall and roll down her cheeks onto her chest. "I don't know what happened Gregory. I asked him when he was planning to move out and he just snapped. He grabbed me around my throat and he wouldn't ease up. I tried to fight him but, but I couldn't breathe. I though he was going to kill me!"

She put her face in her hands and continued to cry. Gregory grabbed her and held her close. He had never seen her so broken and he didn't like it. He was livid and ready to find Anthony and kill him but he had to take care of her first.

"Where is he now?"

"I don't know, after he finally let me go he just grabbed his shit and left. I hope he doesn't come back."

"If he does he will have to deal with me."

She smiled at him letting him know that his words made her feel better. Alexis got up and went into the bathroom to clean herself up. She glanced in the mirror and the image scared her. She was a wreck and she couldn't believe Anthony left marks around her neck! He was definitely going to pay for that!

"I went to the club looking for you," Greg yelled from the living room.

Alexis wiped the makeup off her face with a wet washcloth, "I couldn't go in after what happened. Why were you looking for me anyway? I thought you would be boo'd up with Miss Lydia." She continued to wash the layers of makeup off her face.

"Some shit went down tonight and I needed to talk to you. Hey did you know about Renee and Big K buying Papa Mack's?"

Alexis came out of the bathroom. Gregory stared at her as if it was the first time he had ever seen her. She was beautiful! He loved the way she looked without all the heavy makeup on her face. That was the first time he had seen her without makeup and he was very impressed. She looked at him then became uncomfortable.

"What the hell are you staring at boy?" she laughed.

"I've never seen you without makeup before. You look nice."

Gregory wasn't accustomed to giving sincere compliments. Usually his compliments were just a ruse to get what he wanted but that time was different. Lex smiled at him and grabbed two beers out of the fridge. She handed him one and sat down.

"Yeah I heard about the club and I don't care. I don't plan on being there much longer."

Gregory frowned, "And where are you going?"

Alexis's shook her head stared into space, "Anywhere but here. I can't take it anymore. The club, this life. I was supposed to be a nurse Greg. I'm just a washed up stripper with no future." Gregory was taken aback by her harsh words. She always walked around as if she was the shit; he would have never thought that she felt that way about herself.

"From what I heard they are going to build the club into something spectacular. Don't you want to be a part of that?"

"A part of what? Just because the club will look and feel brand new, bottom line I will still just be a stripper. Period."

He looked at her with curiosity. "What if you could be part of the action? Like a partner?"

Alexis rolled her eyes at him; "You know damn well I don't have money like that and what makes you think that those two are trying to bring me in as a partner? Get real." Lex drank down her beer and let out a loud burp.

"Well I'm trying to get some of the action. That will be a million dollar business with Big K running it. Do you know how much they will probably make just on the reopening? Hell no, I'm not letting this opportunity pass me by."

"You do what you want Gregory, you always do. So what bullshit were you talking about that happened earlier?"

For a split second, he had totally forgotten about everything that had gone down. "I think Brent is trying to make a play for Lydia."

"Brent? From the escort service? How does he even know her?"

"I used his place once to bring Lydia over. I didn't want her to know where I really lived. So, the girl goes to his house Monday night trying to surprise me, but guess what? I'm not there! So, Brent being the good old boy that he is, lets her in and calls me. I was already preoccupied so I called her and fussed her out. I'm thinking that's that and she went home."

Alexis was now sitting on the edge of her seat listening to every word coming out of his mouth.

"So Tuesday afternoon me and her were supposed to hook up and she calls and cancels. That's not like her. She would never cancel on me. So, I got suspicious and drove past her house. Guess who was there?"

"Brent right?" Alexis eagerly answered as if she was a contestant on a game show.

"Yep. And I saw them hugging. I'm telling you, Brent trying to move in and take over my hustle I had planned."

Alexis sat shaking her head. In a way, she was happy the whole thing was falling apart. Maybe now, he would take his focus off Lydia and back on her where it belonged. Alexis looked at the clock on the wall; it was three am.

"I'm going to bed. Are you coming?" she said as she winked at him.

He chuckled, "Yeah I'm coming."

****

Brent, Lydia, and Anthony decided to call it a night and look for Gregory in the morning. Everyone was tired and full of emotions. They decided to go back to Lydia's house to crash. There was no point going to look for Gregory or going to Alexis' house that time of the morning. The three walked to the front door. As Lydia opened the door, she let out a scream. Brent and Anthony pushed past her and looked around. Her apartment was turned upside down. The cushions on the sofa had been slashed and feathers were everywhere. The coffee table was turned over and the lamps were broken on the floor. Everything was pulled out of the closets and thrown around the living room.

Brent stepped over the items on the floor and looked into her bedroom. Her room was ransacked too. The bathroom was a mess. Things pulled out of the medicine cabinet and utility closet. Anthony started rummaging through the things all over the floor; Lydia stood crying by the front door. Brent rushed over to her and held her tight.

"Who would do this?" Lydia was looking around at the mess.

"Anthony man what the hell are you looking for?" Brent was getting more frustrated by the minute.

Anthony ignored him and kept flinging things around and cursing. He was panicking and sweating. How could he have been so careless? He couldn't believe he didn't take the duffel bag with him.

"Lydia," he said as he pulled her out of Brent's arms.

"Did you see where I put that duffel bag before we left?" she looked at him and blinked a few times.

"Yeah, when I got my shoes out of the closet I tossed it in there on the floor." She pointed towards the closet by her bedroom door. He ran back over to the closet but it had been emptied out. Lydia watched her brother's face as fear overpowered it. He actually looked as if he were going to cry. Lydia had never seen her brother cry.

"Man what's going on? What was in the bag?"

"We gotta get out of here. Now!" Anthony grabbed his backpack that had been emptied out and tried to find his belongings to repack. He looked at his sister as if she was crazy.

"Go pack something! Hurry up!" Lydia jumped and ran into her room to grab some clothes. Brent shook his head in disbelief. What had Anthony gotten himself into? Anthony was making so much noise that Brent didn't want Lydia's neighbors to come out of their apartments being nosey. He went to close the door and froze in place. Lydia came out of the room with her bag in her hand and let out another cry. She dropped her bag and covered her mouth. Anthony looked at her then looked in the direction of the door.

"Fuck me," he said quietly. There on the back of the door was a note attached by one of Lydia's kitchen knives, "IT'S NOT OVER. YOU AND YOUR SISTER ARE DEAD!"

CHAPTER TWENTY-FOUR

Brent looked at the note like it was bomb. What the fuck was going on and what was in that damn duffel bag?

"Anthony. What the hell was in that bag man? For real, what's going on?" Brent was scared but he had to stay calm. His military training taught him to never panic but stay calm and access the situation.

"We don't have time for that right now. Let's get the fuck out of here and I will explain on the way!"

Anthony grabbed his backpack and headed towards the front door. Lydia picked up her overnight bag and followed behind her brother. She couldn't believe this was going on. Who would come into her home and tear it to pieces? They hurried out of the door looking up and down the street. Anthony looked down the street to his left. He could barely make out the black Excursion sitting with no headlights on. Everything in him told him to yell, scream, and run but he was paralyzed. Brent guided Lydia to the car not paying attention to Anthony or the truck on the street. Wheels started squealing and the Excursion was barreling towards them. Brent and Lydia looked in the direction of the noise but Anthony stood frozen in place. Brent pushed

Lydia to the ground then ran towards Anthony yelling his name.

"Ant get down, get the fuck down!"

Gunfire filled the air, the loud noise of the popping was deafening. Brent dove and tackled Anthony, knocking him hard to the ground. Lydia lay on the hard concrete by Brent's truck screaming with her hands over her ears. The Excursion sped off down the one way street.

"Shit! Fuck!" Brent rolled off Anthony but Anthony laid still.

Brent shook him, "Come on Anthony, they're gone. Ant? Ant, come on man!"

Lydia jumped up and ran over to her brother. Neighbors were coming out of their homes and gathering around the two men. Brent turned him over on his back; a bright red stain covered the middle of his yellow t-shirt. Anthony had been hit right in the middle of his chest.

"Anthony nooooo!" Lydia fell on top of her brother crying and begging God to save her brother.

Brent looked at the blood on his hands. The last time he had that much blood on his hands was when he was in the military. Anthony seemed lifeless, but Lydia could see he was still hanging on. He kept repeating, "I'm sorry" over and over. Brent picked him up, put him over his shoulder, and put him in the back of his truck. Lydia sat on the ground crying.

"Lydia lets go, NOW!" Brent yelled at her. Lydia got up, ran to the truck, and jumped in.

Brent comes to a screeching halt in front of the emergency room doors at Prodigy Central Hospital. He lifts Anthony's stiff body out of the truck and rushes into the hospital. Lydia slowly follows behind him in complete disbelief. How could this happen? Who shot her brother? Was it Gregory or one of Anthony's crazy friends? What was in that black duffel bag? The nurses see Brent walking in with Anthony and immediately jump into action. They put him on a gurney and rush him to the hallway. The nurses behind the desk are asking Brent questions but he can't answer. All he can do is concentrate on the blood on his hands. Lydia sits in the waiting area staring out into space.

"Ma'am? Ma'am? Please I need to ask you a few questions. The man that you brought in tonight, who is he? What's his name?"

Lydia slowly looked up at the nurse; she noticed how kind her eyes looked. She opened her mouth but nothing came out at first. Then she cleared her throat and spoke, "Anthony Morrell...he's my brother." Lydia looked down at the white linoleum floor. Brent came over and sat beside her.

"Is he allergic to anything?" the nurse inquired.

"No. I don't think so."

The nurse decided to give them space and she went back behind the counter.

"Lydia, do you need to call your parents?"

She looked at him with glassed over eyes, "My mom maybe. I don't know if she will care or not. I don't know where my dad is." Brent handed her his cell phone. Lydia carefully dialed her mother's number.

"Hello?" Sophia answered. It was about four thirty in the morning and she was still groggy from being awakened by the ring of her bedside phone.

"Mami, its Lydia." She glanced at Brent and he gave her a reassuring nod.

"Mami, we are at Prodigy Central, Anthony...he's been hurt. Shot."

"I am on my way," and with that Sophia hangs up.

"My mom is on her way. I can't believe this! My brother was shot tonight Brent! They actually tried to kill us!" Lydia got up and looked out of the window of the emergency room.

"I'm sure he will be ok, he seems like a fighter," Brent tried to make her feel better.

Lydia walked to the nurse's station. "What is going on with my brother? Why hasn't anyone told us anything?" she was getting hysterical.

"Ma'am he is in the back with the doctor. As soon as we know anything, we will surely notify you. I promise." Before Lydia could sit back down the doctor called her name.

"I'm Lydia, how is my brother?" she braced herself for bad news. When they brought Anthony in he didn't look good at all and he was in and out of consciousness.

"We did remove two bullets from his chest. One was dangerously close to his heart. He's lost quite a bit of blood and we are going to need to give him a blood transfusion. We ask that family members donate blood also." Lydia leaned against Brent for support; she grew weaker and weaker by the minute.

"He is in critical condition right now and we are taking him to the ICU. We will prep the lab to receive you and your family to give blood. Is there anyone else who can donate besides you and your husband?"

Before she could correct the doctor, Brent spoke up, "Yes her mother is on the way as we speak."

"Very good, the more donations the better. Please let the nurse know when your family is ready."

The doctor offered a weak smile and turned to go back through the heavy double doors. Lydia held onto Brent tightly. She nuzzled her head into his broad chest and closed her eyes tightly. She loved her brother with all her heart. If anything happened to him, it would kill her. She didn't know why they shot at them and at the moment she didn't care, she just wanted her big brother to live.

"Lydia, Mi Amor," Sophia stood looking at her daughter. Lydia let go off Brent and quickly hugged her mother. She was in her fifties now but she was very frail and looked almost like she was in her seventies. Deep wrinkles invaded her face and her eyes looked dark and dull. Her once long black hair was now fully gray. Lydia looked at her mother with pity. Her jaw was still disfigured from when Travis attacked her and although she was blind in one eye, she still had to wear glasses for her one good eye.

"What happen to Anthony?" she said wringing her frail hands.

"Mami, someone shot at us and he was hit, twice. Brent tried to knock him to the ground but it was too late." Sophia looked around her daughter at the tall handsome stranger standing behind her. He gave her a smile and Sophia nodded hello to him.

"Mami we have to give blood right away. Anthony needs it. The doctor said the more the better. Who else can we call?"

Sophia thought for a moment. She hadn't kept in touch with any of her family. Her sister that she moved in with after the attack had passed away from lung cancer several months ago.

"Lydia, there is no one…just me and…" Sophia stopped and stared into space. Lydia and Brent looked at each other then back at Sophia.

"Mami what's the matter?"

Sophia slowly walked to the nearest chair and sat down. She felt the weight of anxiety bearing down heavily on his chest. Lydia sat down beside her and grabbed her hand. Sophia looked at her and tried to speak. Her bottom lip began to quiver as tears filled her eyes.

"What's wrong? Please say something!" she was growing impatient with her mother. Brent stood by the vending machines trying to give them privacy but listening at the same time.

"There is one more person that may be able to help." Sophia spoke almost in a whisper.

"Really? Who? Who is it?"

"You're half-brother."

Lydia let go of her mother's hand gave her a bewildered look. She felt all her blood race to her head and she felt dizzy and nauseous. She must be mistaken. She didn't ever remember her mother being pregnant with another child. There was no way the information could be correct.

"Mami, I-I don't understand. You're saying Anthony and I have a half-brother?"

"Yes my love," Sophia continued looking down.

Lydia looked at Brent with confusion. He walked over and sat beside Lydia, putting his hand on her shoulder. He knew whatever was about to transpire was going to be huge.

"Mami, when did you get pregnant again? How did you hide it and what happened to him?"

Sophia smiled at her baby girl. She was still so beautiful and caring. She touched Lydia's cheek then touched her long hair.

"No sweetie, different mother, same father."

Lydia felt her heart about to beat out of her chest; she actually thought she was having a heart attack. Sweat began to bead on her head and nose. She felt her hands turn clammy. She couldn't understand what her mother had just told her. Her father had a child, a son, by another woman? Lydia stood up and paced the floor, occasionally looking at her mother.

"When? When did this happen?"

Sophia took a deep breath. She swore she would never tell her children about the son their father had a year before Anthony was born but now it was time to tell everything.

CHAPTER TWENTY-FIVE

"Your father was desired by all the women in the neighborhood. He was handsome, a great dresser and he had charm and charisma. He always had money and he didn't mind letting everyone know. When your father expressed interest in me, I was flattered…and hesitant at the same time. I wasn't anything special. I wasn't as beautiful as the other girls that were after him, but I did love the attention. Oh the other girls would give me awful terrible looks but your father would tell me to enjoy it and that they were just jealous"

Lydia gently smiled at her mother while Brent put his arm around her and rubbed her arm. He looked at Sophia and he could see where Lydia got her looks. If you looked past the wrinkles and pain in her face, you could see the spitting imagine of Lydia Morrell.

"When your father proposed to me of course I said yes. It was a dream come true. I knew your father wasn't perfect…and I knew he still had other women, but I didn't care. I loved him and the way he treated me. When we got married and moved into our little home, I was so happy Lydia. I swore I would be a great wife and one day a wonderful mother. One night your father came home drunk and told me he had a ten-month-old son but he had ended it with the child's mother before he proposed to me. I was devastated because we had been trying to have a child of our own and then I find out he already had a son. I wanted to leave him, but I couldn't. I loved him."

Lydia was holding her mouth as tears streamed down her face. Brent was shaking his head; he didn't know what to say.

"Your father later told me his son's mother was Yvonne, the black lady that worked at the convenience store on Tillman Street."

Lydia blew her nose with the tissue Brent had handed her earlier, "Didn't she die not too long ago?"

"Yes I believe so."

Before Lydia could ask another question, the nurse came into the waiting room to let them know they needed to donate blood immediately. Anthony's blood pressure was rising and falling and they needed to begin the transfusion to help stabilize him. The three walked back to the lab.

****

Alexis laid in Gregory's arms listening to him breath. She was enjoying his presence. That was the very first time in the two years they had known each other that she actually got to lay in his arms. No threesomes, no money exchanging hands…just the two of them in their own little private world. They had had sex the night before but this time it was different. It wasn't rushed or tainted. It was slow and deliberate. She glanced up at his sleeping face. He was beautiful. She knew she was in love with Gregory and she hated to admit it. He was not the kind of man you fall in love with and expect him to feel the same. Not Gregory Summit. He would use and abuse you then throw your heart away like yesterday's trash. She rubbed his smooth chest and he stirred a little. Alexis started thinking about herself. Was she wifey material? Was she the kind of chick that a man would introduce to his mother? She was a stripper at a nasty ass club. She drank too much and had nothing to offer any man, but a lap dance. She chuckled to herself. Who was she fooling? Maybe she would stay at the club after Big K and Renee took it over. Gregory did make some sense, with their influence and money there would be a lot of high rollers and big spenders coming in, which meant more money for her. She wasn't convinced about him becoming a partner with them. Big K was a dangerous man. He had killed so many people and over half of the bodies were never found. He wasn't the kind of man you wanted to cross. She could handle working with him but Renee was a different story. She couldn't stand that bitch. She walked around like her shit didn't stink. She always walked around with those ridiculous looking weaves. She could see herself slapping the hell out of her one night. Maybe she should reconsider her decision. Gregory stretched and yawned loudly. Alexis closed her eyes and pretended she was still asleep. He peeked at her, then kissed her forehead, got up and went into the bathroom. She waited for the door to close and then smiled ear to ear. It was the attention from him that she longed for and she was finally getting it. She rubbed her neck; it was very sore. She frowned as she thought about the night before. Anthony had put his hands on her, no, he tried to kill her, and she was going to make sure he paid dearly.

"Yo Lex, get your ass up and fix me some breakfast," Gregory yelled from the bathroom.

"Muthafucka after the work I put in last night your ass should be taking me out to breakfast!"

Gregory cracked the door and looked at her, "Shit alright. Get ready."

Alexis gave him the finger and sat up on the edge of the bed. She heard vibrating and looked around for her phone but realized it wasn't hers; it was Gregory's. She picked it up and looked at the screen, Brent C. Alexis started laughing, "Oh this shit is gonna be good! Gregory, your phone's ringing. It's your boy Brent.

****

Lydia, Sophia, and Brent walked back into the waiting area. The doctor explained that they would start the transfusion process to stabilize him and keep him under observation. Brent stepped away to call his job to let them know he would not be in that morning. He wasn't concerned about calling Renee about his dates for later because as far as he was concerned he didn't work there anymore. He wasn't a stupid man. Brent knew that his place was run down and basic but he had a roof over his head, electricity, and food to eat so he was content. His security job paid his household bills and he banked the escort money. Brent had plenty of money to fall back on until he found a more respectable second job. He wanted to make Lydia happy; she was a good woman. He came back inside after calling out and sat next to Lydia. Lydia stared at her mother. She was dying to talk about this so-called half-brother. She didn't know whether to be happy or sad. She didn't know if the half-brother even knew about her and Anthony. Anxiety was building up inside of her and she couldn't take it anymore.

"Mami, my half-brother, do you know where he is?"

Sophia patted her daughter's knee. "No I do not know dear. The last time I saw him, I was seven months pregnant with your brother, and Yvonne came to the house with him looking for your father. She cussed at me and called me a whore and a home wrecker. She said that your father was a lying bastard and she was going to make sure he paid for getting her pregnant and not taking care of their child." Lydia shook her head in disbelief.

"So he is a year older than Anthony? They probably went to the same high school and everything then right?" Everything was getting so deep. Their half-brother could have been a friend of theirs, the local neighborhood paperboy, and the guy working at the fast food restaurant. The room started to feel hot and Lydia felt light headed.

"Do you know his name? Maybe we can locate him. He may still be living in the city."

Sophia rubbed the spot on her arm where they had inserted the needle. Her skin was very thin now and the area was very sore. She was tired. Tired of talking about the past, tired of her estranged relationship with her only son who was now lying in a hospital bed from being shot twice. Now her daughter was showering her with all these questions, she was sorry she decided to tell her the truth.

"Greg Summit, I believe. Yes, that's it."

Lydia let out a loud gasp and Brent jumped to his feet. He couldn't believe the name that just came out of her mouth. Brent jumped up so fast that it startled Sophia.

"Lo que esta mal?" Sophia asked grabbing her chest. Lydia sat completely still; her eyes were wide open. She looked as if she were in a trance.

"What...did...you...just...say?" Lydia asked very slowly in a low monotone voice.

Brent was now standing with both hands on top of his head. He heard the name Sophia said very clearly. "Fuck me!" he kept saying while shaking his head.

Sophia turned to face her daughter. She didn't understand what was happening. She gave her daughter a confused look and repeated herself, "Greg Summit." Lydia slowly looked up at Brent. He was now holding his head as if he were in excruciating pain. She felt the bitter taste of bile forming in her throat; her mouth became watery. She tried to control her gag reflexes but it was no use, Lydia vomited all over the shiny white-waxed hospital floor. Sophia started crying and speaking Spanish, Brent tried to pull her hair back and rub her back, but she kept pushing him away. The nurse ran over and asked did she need medical assistance but Brent told her no, that everyone was okay. The nurse called for a janitor. Lydia tried to stand but she was too weak. It felt as if her legs were paralyzed. Sophia sat rocking back and forth crying; she just didn't understand what was happening.

"I-I need..." she pointed towards the restroom.

"Ok baby, I got you. Come on." Brent scooped Lydia up in his arms and carried her to the ladies restroom.

"Ms. Morrell, please give us a few minutes ok? I promise we will explain everything." Sophia nodded ok and gently sat back down. She put her head in her hands and continued to sob. Brent proceeded to take Lydia into the restroom, the nurse was about to say something regarding him going into the ladies room but he gave her a sharp look and she looked away. Brent sat Lydia down on the toilet seat. He wet a few paper towels in cold water and began to wipe her forehead and her mouth. She was acting like an invalid; it was obvious she was in shock.

"Baby? Baby girl? Please say something. Speak to me." Brent stroked her hair and rubbed her face. She sat completely still like a statue. Brent opened the bathroom door and asked the nurse for a plastic cup. She reached under the desk and handed him a Styrofoam cup. He went back in the bathroom and filled the cup with cold water and handed it to Lydia; she didn't take it. Brent didn't know what to do. He sat down on the floor and rubbed her leg. Gregory was her half- brother! WOW. Random thoughts filled his head as he continued to rub her leg. Looking at Gregory, he looked completely African American. Brent knew his mother was black; he met her before she passed but Gregory never really talked about his father, and why would he. He didn't know the man. He only knew what his mother had told him while he was growing up, that his father left them for another woman. Poor Lydia. He looked at her and tears started to form in his eyes. He couldn't imagine the pain, hurt, grief, disgust, and embarrassment she was going thru. She had fallen in love and slept with her half- brother. The thought made Brent nauseous and pissed off all at the same time. A knock at the door made him jump.

"Yeah someone's in here!" he yelled out while wiping the tears from his face.

"Lo siento, it's Sophia. Is everything ok?" Brent got up off the floor and opened the door. Sophia stepped in. She was uncomfortable being in the ladies room with the tall muscular white man. She looked at her daughter; she looked pale and despondent.

"Sir what is wrong with my Lydia? Why did she get ill?"

"Ms. Morrell, please call me Brent." He reached out to touch her shoulder but she flinched so he quickly pulled her hand back to his side. Brent didn't know if it was his place to tell her mother the news. How could he even begin? Before he could muster the strength to begin to tell Sophia the horrible news, Lydia grabbed his hand. He bent down to kiss her on her forehead, "Baby are you ok? Here, drink this water."

Lydia cautiously took the cup and took a sip. She exhaled deeply and looked at her mother.

"Brent, can I be alone with my mother please?"

Brent fumbled with the doorknob trying to get out of the ladies bathroom in a hurry. He walked out of the glass double doors into the warm spring air. He looked at his watch; it was a little after eight a.m. He pulled out his cell phone. He was going to call Gregory so they could meet somewhere and talk. He wanted to be the one to tell him that he was in love with Lydia and that she and

Gregory were half brother and sister. He didn't want Lydia to tell him, there was no telling the reaction he would have.

Brent knew if Gregory got violent with him, he could handle it. He also wanted to be around when she told Anthony. He had witness how violent Anthony could get and he wanted to make sure he didn't put his hands on her. Brother or not, Brent wasn't going to let that happen. Gregory was already fuming over the fact that Anthony was seeing Alexis and that he beat his ass but when he finds out that Anthony is Lydia's brother, he was going to flip out. It was now becoming obvious that Gregory and Anthony shared the same father. Something occurred to Brent as he stood watching an ambulance pulling up to the emergency room entrance. If Gregory doesn't know that Anthony and Lydia are related, that means that Alexis doesn't know either! When Anthony finds out that his sister slept with his girlfriend, he is going to try to kill someone! "Oh shit!" he said aloud. An elderly lady walking past gave him a harsh look and kept walking. The shit was about to hit the fan definitely. He would go back inside, check on Anthony, Lydia and Sophia, and then call Gregory to set up a meeting.

Anthony was now in stable condition and there wasn't much else to do but to wait for him to wake up. Brent took Lydia and her mother to his house. There was no use of going to her apartment. It was still a mess. He urged Lydia to call the police but she said there was no use. Whoever ransacked her house got what they came for, the black duffel bag. She couldn't wait for Anthony to get well so she could find out more about the bag and more importantly, who wanted them dead. She thought about how Gregory was going to take the news. She felt queasy just thinking about it. She knew she had to tell him, the sooner the better.

"I want to tell Gregory today Brent. Can you call him and ask him to come over?" Brent looked at as if she had lost her mind.

"Babe, it's too soon. Come on now. Let's give it a few days." Brent didn't want her to tell him, he wanted to bear that burden for her. She has been through enough.

"Don't you want to wait until Anthony is better? We can tell everyone at the same time."

"No I want to tell him today!" Her words resounded with anger.

"I want to see his face when I tell him that I know all about the plans he had for me!"

Lydia peeked down the hallway towards his bedroom. Sophia was lying down and she didn't want to wake her. Brent sat down on the sofa beside her. He stared into hers; he could see the hurt and pain. He didn't think she was thinking rationally.

"Let's call him tomo----"

"NO! TODAY. RIGHT NOW!" Brent shook his head and pulled his phone out of his pocket.

"Yeah," Gregory said coldly. He couldn't believe Brent had the audacity to call him.

"Hey man. Uh, are you busy?" Brent was nervous.

"Nah, what's up?"

"Can you come to my place in an hour? I need to talk to you about something important." Brent didn't want to disclose the fact that Lydia and her mother were at his apartment also.

Gregory was getting pissed. He already knew about him and Lydia and now Brent wants him to come to his house to chitchat about it? He had some fuckin nerve! Gregory decided he was going to humor him.

"Yeah man, I can do that. Everything good?"

Brent glanced at Lydia who was glaring at him, hanging onto his every word.

"Yeah I just need to talk to you. See you in an hour." Brent hung up. He felt exhausted, completely drained.

"So? Is he on his way?" Lydia was very impatient.

"Yes babe. I'm telling you, this is a mistake. It's too soon. You are a ball of emotions."

"I'm fuckin pissed. That's what I am!" Brent raised his eyebrows. He was shocked at her language.

"Lydia, you have to calm down. We need to focus on finding out who wants you and your brother dead and what was in that damn bag. Gregory can wait!"

He grabbed her and hugged her hard, "I could have lost you last night, do you realize that? I haven't even begun to make you happy yet. The first time I laid eyes on you, I knew I wanted you—not just sex, but you. All of you. I want to be here for you. I want to help you get through this."

Lydia heard every word that Brent said but right now, her anger was overpowering every other emotion she had. She was livid! She was mad at Sophia for not telling her years ago about Gregory. How could she have known that the man she was falling for was related to her? She was furious with Anthony. He was always getting himself involved with the wrong people, always involved with something illegal. And now some kind of way he had gotten her involved in his madness. Someone had actually shot at her the night before. She thought about Brent. How could she trust him? He was Gregory's close friend. She found it hard to believe that he had no clue who she was. Did he have an ulterior motive also? Like Gregory? Last but least she was mad at herself. All of her life she let men use her, abused her. She was so dumb and naïve. She always thought she needed the approval of a man to be considered acceptable. She gave her body repeatedly to several different men in her lifetime and in the end, they all ended up doing the same thing, leaving her. Brent wasn't any different. It would just be a matter of time before he would use her body and toss her aside like yesterday's newspaper. She decided today was going to be the last day that she let a man take control of her. No more dumb, naïve, Lydia Morrell. She was going to take control of her life and anyone who got in her way would be sorry.

****

Gregory tossed the phone on the bed and started laughing. This dude had some nerve. His best friend, there was definitely no loyalty.

"So what's up Gregory? What did he say?" Alexis sat on the edge of the bed, anticipating his answer. She loved the drama. She didn't know Brent too well but if his plan was to take Lydia away from Gregory, she was thankful to him. She was determined to make Gregory her man. He actually showed her his sensitive side the night before; he actually cared about her. She just needed to get that distraction out of his life so he would concentrate on her and hopefully getting a piece of the action at the club after the new owners take over.

"He asked me to come over so we can talk. Can you believe that shit? This muthafucka want me to come over so he can telling me he fuckin my bitch!"

Alexis smiled quickly disappeared. He was still stuck on that bitch. After the way they sexed the night before, she should be the last damn person on his fuckin mind. She felt her anger and jealousy rising, she felt hot and shaky.

"Why the fuck do you care so much about that damn girl Gregory? Obviously she don't care about your ass as much if you think if she fucking Brent right?" She gave him a sideways look. Gregory gave her a sharp look. Alexis didn't know what she was talking about. There was no way that Lydia wasn't feeling him anymore, not after the way he dicked her down. She was still hooked on him; he knew it. Brent was just a temporary distraction but that was about to end in less than an hour.

"You don't know what the hell you're talking about. I'm about to get dressed and go see what his punk ass is talking about."

"Damn, I wanna go!" Alexis jumped up and ran to her closet to grab clothes.

"Wait, wait, wait, hold up. You're not going!" Gregory finished buttoning his shirt and laughed at her. She was like a little kid.

"Please Gregory! I won't get in the way, I swear!" she was sliding on a pair of skintight jeans.

"You always gotta be in the middle of everything don't you? Hurry up, bring yo' ass!" Gregory headed towards the front door. Alexis threw on a tank top and her sweater and a pair of flip-flops and hurried out the door behind Gregory.

CHAPTER TWENTY-SIX

Gregory and Alexis pulled up to Brent's apartment. He tapped the steering wheel while staring at the door. Alexis was looking at him with a disgusted look.

"Well let's go! What's wrong with you?"

Gregory rolled his eyes, "Shut the hell up! I knew I should've left your ass at home. Give me a second." Gregory knew it was going to be trouble. He knew he would lose his temper and set it off in that apartment. Most of the time, he could control himself but he had a feeling the situation was going to get the best of him. He took a deep breath and got out of the car, Alexis followed close behind him on his heels. He knocked hard on the door.

The loud knock made Lydia jump. Brent got up and put his hand on the doorknob.

"Baby are you sure you want to do this?" he looked at her with pleading eyes, hoping she would change her mind.

"Open the damn door Brent." he didn't like the dull look in her eyes. It was almost frightening.

"Hey Greg...Alexis? Why are you here?" Brent said almost in a whisper. It was going to be really bad. Gregory had bought the drama queen with him.

"I asked her to come. So? Is there a problem?" Gregory pushed past Brent and his eyes locked onto Lydia's. She looked different to him.

"Well I see the gang's all here huh?" Greg said sarcastically.

Alexis looked at Lydia with hatred. Why wouldn't see just disappear? She was ruining everything for her.

"Have a seat y'all." Brent went and sat down beside Lydia. He went to put his arm around her but she shrugged her shoulders letting him know that she didn't want him to touch her. The gesture hurt his feelings but under the circumstances, he understood.

"Nah, I'm good standing. What the hell is all this about?"

Greg stood stiff with his arms folded while Alexis sat down on the recliner shooting icy glares at Lydia. She couldn't believe that just a couple of months ago she was fingering her and licking her pussy. Lydia shot back the same icy looks at her. She knew she had something to do with Gregory's plan. She was on her shit list now too.

"I know all about you. I know everything, Gregory Summit." Lydia said the words so calm, so serene. It was scary. The room was eerily quiet. Gregory's eyes got large and he looked at her with uncertainty. He let out a nervous chuckle.

"What do you think you know? Besides my real last name?" He looked at Alexis and shook his head. She looked at him with a smirk on her face.

"I know you're a lying asshole." She looked at him square in the eye. She didn't blink not once. Gregory was getting uncomfortable but he never let it show.

"I know all about the plans you had for me Gregory Summit. I know you're nothing more than a man whore working at Premier Escorts. Let me ask you something? How did you get to Brent's apartment? By cab or your shiny black corvette?" Alexis fell out laughing. It was so obvious that Gregory had been busted! She loved every minute of it. Gregory shifted his weight from one foot to the other.

"I got here in my shiny black corvette that I never let your tired ass ride in. You just weren't good enough."

Brent was getting pissed but he decided to play it cool.

"And it's funny that you drove your shiny black corvette to Brent's apartment. Or is this your apartment?" she squinted her eyes at him. She held her mouth tight. She had never in her life been this furious.

Gregory laughed, "Hell nah this dump ain't my place. You weren't good enough to go there either!"

Alexis sat up straighter in the recliner and smiled at Lydia. She thought she was the Latina princess when in actuality she was just another one of Gregory's hustles.

"Yes I've seen where you live. Nice place, right on the beach." Lydia winked at him. Gregory frowned.

"You've been to my house? What the fuck were you doing at my house?" He started walking towards Lydia and Brent stood up to block him. Greg looked at his former friend. The sight of him made his blood boil.

"And you. You just couldn't wait to get her all to yourself. Your ass wishes you were me, don't you?"

"You need to back off man." Brent stood stiffly; ready to throw a punch if he had to.

"So what else does she know Brent? I know your snitching ass told her everything she knows. Yeah tell her everything and soften her up so you can go in for the kill. I never thought my so called best friend would stab me in the fuckin back!"

Alexis sat giggling at the entire situation. She thought it was hilarious that these two were arguing over Lydia. She looked at her. She wasn't anything special. Yeah she was pretty but so was she. Alexis knew her body looked better than hers did and she knew her bedroom game was much better than hers was. She just couldn't see what was so special about her. The door to Brent's bedroom opened and Sophia slowly walked into the living room. She had been awake for a little while and heard the loud talking in the front room but was afraid to come out.

"Lydia, is everything ok?" Sophia looked around at the two unfamiliar faces in the room.

"Yes Mami, go back in the room. I will come talk to you in a few minutes, ok? Do you want anything to drink?"

"No I'm fine. We need to get back to the hospital to check on Anthony."

"Yes we will Mami. I promise. Go back into the room."

Alexis had a strange look on her face. Did that old lady just say Anthony? And why was he in the hospital? Gregory had moved away from Brent when the older lady came into the living room but he kept his eyes on him.

"Who was that?" Gregory inquired.

"Lydia's mother." Brent replied.

"Fuck all that," Alexis stood up.

"Who is in the hospital? Did she say Anthony?"

Brent scratched his head hard. This was it. He knew the ugly truth was about to come out into the open and he wasn't sure if he or anyone in the room was ready for it.

"Yes Anthony is in the hospital. He was shot twice last night." Lydia looked at Alexis as if she was garbage. She couldn't believe that she had let her put her mouth on her. She and Gregory deserved each other.

"Wait. Tall, around 6'2", low cut, goatee? That Anthony?" Alexis felt panicked. She could sense Gregory staring a hole in the side of head but she didn't care.

"Yes, Anthony. Anthony Morrell, my brother!" Lydia was now on her feet with both hands on her hips.

"Damn! Get the fuck out of here!" Gregory couldn't believe it. He looked at Alexis with his mouth wide open. Alexis didn't know what to say. Anthony, the same man that nearly choked her to death was Lydia's brother. Gregory started laughing.

"I don't know what the fuck you laughing at; he whipped your punk ass not too long ago. Remember?" Gregory quickly shut up and looked at Brent. He was smiling as he looked at him.

"Your brother put his hands on me. He damn near killed me. I'm not letting that shit go."

"Bitch are you threatening my brother?"

Alexis jumped up out of the recliner, "Who the fuck you calling bitch? I will drag your ass through this apartment. I wasn't a bitch when I was eating the hell out of your pussy now was I?"

Lydia stopped breathing. She felt the heaviness on her chest. She couldn't believe she had just said that in front of Brent. And did her mother hear her? She looked at Brent and he looked down not because he was mad but because he was embarrassed for her.

"Yessss honey, I was working that ass wasn't I Lydia? Had that tight pussy squirting all over my face and you loved it."

"Shut the fuck up! SHUT UP!"

"Oh nah, I'm not shutting up," Alexis was doing a little dance as she spoke, "tell everyone how much you loved my wet tongue on your clit. As a matter of fact, you don't have to tell us. We can watch it anytime we want." Alexis sat down and crossed her long legs and smirked at her while she let the info she disclosed sink in.

"You taped me? Us?" she felt a lump forming in her throat.

"Yep. Gregory's idea." Alexis pointed up at him with her long manicured acrylic nail. He stood behind the recliner with a blank look on his face. Honestly, he was getting bored with the entire conversation. He didn't care if her brother was in the hospital. Whatever happened he deserved it. Next time maybe he would think twice before he pissed someone off. He was annoyed with Alexis. Why the hell did she tell Lydia about the DVD? It didn't matter; there was nothing Lydia could do about it. Brent could have her; he was done. She was more trouble than she was worth.

"Look folks it's been fun but I'm out. Let's go Alexis."

"I'm sorry to hear about Yvonne. She passed from cancer right?" Gregory turned around fast and hard.

"How the hell do you know about my mother?"

"I remember Yvonne. She used to ring up my candy at the convenience store. She was always so nice to me and my brother." Gregory's breathing began to quicken. What the hell was going on? Why was she bringing up his mother? Alexis stood by the door looking equally confused.

"I'm going to ask you one more time then I'm going to snap the fuck off. Why are you bringing up my mother?"

"What's your father's name Gregory?"

"Why are you asking about him? Look I'm done. Let's go Alexis."

He turned to open the door and he heard Lydia say, "George. His name was George. I know because---he is my father too."

Brent sat waiting and prepared for Gregory's reaction. Alexis couldn't believe her ears; Gregory and Lydia were related? He turned around looking as if he was going to pass out. There was no way he and Lydia could be related. She was making this shit up trying to get back at him and he wasn't falling for it.

"How did you know my father's name?"

Lydia began to tear up. "George Morrell is mine and Anthony's father Gregory. I swear I'm not lying. Your mother got pregnant with you by my father. He left her and married my mother. My mother was the reason he left your mother. A few months later she was pregnant with Anthony."

Gregory shook his head violently like he was trying to shake the toxic information out of his head.

"Lydia, listen to what you're saying." By now, Alexis had sat back down but Gregory was still standing by the front door. Lydia was still standing and Brent was right behind her.

"Do you think I would make some shit like this up? The very thought of this makes me sick to my stomach Gregory! Do you realize, do you understand? I fell in love and had SEX with my half-brother!"

"Oh shit! That's nasty as hell!" Alexis didn't think before speaking, which wasn't uncommon for her.

"Wait how you know this for sure?" He was convinced that there was some misunderstanding.

"My mother told me last night at the hospital. Someone is trying to kill Anthony and me; I have no idea why. He was hit twice in the chest and he lost a lot of blood so we all donated. I asked my mother was there any other family member that could come and give blood, that's when she told me about my father's son that he had before either one of us were born. She knew your name Gregory."

Gregory felt himself swaying. He grabbed onto the back of the recliner stared at the floor. Incest? No...no way, not him. He started to grow angry. Why the hell didn't her mother tell her and Anthony years ago about this? Why didn't his mother tell him that his deadbeat father had other children? Or did Lydia already know and that was her sick twisted way of making him look like a fool? He was furious and ashamed. He bet that Brent knew about it too. It wasn't going down like that.

"I don't believe a fuckin' thing you're saying! You're a liar! I swear to God I will kill you and your weak ass brother if I ever see you again. Mark my words."

"Yo man, don't be threatening her like that!" Brent stepped in front of Lydia. He understood that Gregory was mad and embarrassed but he wasn't going to let him threaten her.

"You shut the fuck up!" Gregory pointed his finger directly at Brent.

"You think I don't know what this is all about? I'm not stupid man! You moved in on her so you could work her over and get those credit card numbers. I saw you two the other night hugging each other, you're the reason she cancelled on me. I knew something had to be up but I would have never thought that my best friend could be so low." Lydia wasn't sure if what Gregory said was true, but she wouldn't be surprised if it were. She didn't trust anybody right now.

"Greg, you got it all wrong. I'm not trying to use her man; you know that's not me. I didn't set out to take her from you, dude you didn't even really want her. You wanted to use her and you know it. I want to love her. As a matter of fact, I quit the escort service. I'm done with that." He looked at Lydia hoping to see some type of emotions for him in her eyes; he saw nothing.

"I don't care what the fuck either of you say, me and her are not related, at all. I swear if you go telling people that bullshit; I will get you. I promise!" Gregory flung the front door open so hard that the doorknob put a hole in the wall. Lydia flinched as she looked into Gregory's face…that's when she saw it. That same familiar scowl that she had seen so many times as a child. Gregory's face looked exactly like her father's. Alexis stood up and shook her head at the two of them. She was completely grossed out by the news she had heard. Gregory and Lydia were half brother and sister and had slept together. That was something straight off of Jerry Springer.

"By the way, tell your brother to watch his back, the next bullet may kill him." She slammed the door shut and left with Gregory.

THREE MONTHS LATER

Lydia was finally settled in. She decided to leave her collection job, Gregory, Alexis, and Brent behind and move to Virginia with her best friend Francesca. Francesca got her a job as the front desk secretary at the advertising firm where she worked. Lydia loved her responsibilities of answering the phone and directing calls to the proper people and departments. It was effortless. She took in deliveries and delivered them to the different ad executives. She was so happy that she had left all the chaos behind. She never found out who was after her and her brother or how she was even involved. She never found out what was in the bag. Two days after Anthony was released from the hospital, he was taken in for parole violation. She tried to visit him to find out what was going on but he had put her on the no visitation list. Typical Anthony, block out the people that care for you and embrace the ones that don't. She wanted to have a relationship with Brent but her trust issues wouldn't allow it. She knew she would be no good for him. He begged and pleaded for her to stay but she knew she needed to leave.

Lydia answered the phones and made small talk with some of the executives. It was a slow Monday and she was happy with that. She read her book and sipped her coffee. For the first time in quite some time, she felt at peace. The mailman dropped off a stack of mail, winked at her, and left. He was in his fifties and always made it a point to wink or flirt with her. He would have been a perfect match for her mother. After she had told her mother about Gregory and her relationship with him, it was too much for her mother to comprehend. Yet, another parent had totally rejected her. She stopped taking Lydia's phone calls. Lydia began to sort the mail and put it into the different mailboxes. She got halfway through the pile when she saw an envelope addressed to her. She was confused because no one, besides her mother knew where she had moved. There was no return address either. She took the letter and sat down at her desk. She glared at it, almost scared to open it. She finally picked it back up and opened it, "So you think moving to Virginia is going to solve your problems? Think again. No one steals from me and just walks away. See you soon." Lydia threw the letter down on the desk. She covered her face and started crying. She had no idea what was happening. What had Anthony gotten her involved in? It was becoming plain to her that she wasn't safe anywhere. She needed answers, and now.

Anthony laid in his cell rubbing the scars from the bullets on his chest. He couldn't believe he made it out alive. That definitely was not supposed to happen. It may have been a blessing that he was in jail now. Big K had gotten his property back, three hundred thousand dollars' worth of cocaine that he was supposed to deliver to Big K's girlfriend Cinnamon. Instead, he decided to try to sell the coke himself, get the cash, and get out of town. He didn't realize that Big K had over half the town in his pocket and word got back to him fast. He had his two boys killed and they were looking for him. He figured out that when he moved in with Lydia that Big K assumed she had something to do with it also, that's why he put her on the no visitation list. The less contact she had with him, the better. He would do his time and once he got out, he was leaving for good. He didn't get a chance to say good-bye to his sister or to thank Brent for trying to prevent him from being shot. He didn't have a chance to apologize to Alexis. He was truly remorseful for putting his hands on her. He was so messed up in the head. It was best if he stepped away and let her have her thing with that punk ass Gregory. He hoped that Lydia and Brent were happy together. He wiped away the lone tear that rolled down the side of his face.

Gregory sat in the booth beside Big K drinking his third glass of champagne. He was on top of the world. He had convinced Big K and Renee to let him come in on the partnership of the club. He had just recently found out the Renee was a dancer there several years ago. Gregory was glad that Big K decided to change the name from Papa Mack's to The K Lounge, a new name for a brand new club. Alexis was in charge of all of the dancers. She made sure they were on time and their outfits were on point. Alexis still danced on occasion just for fun but since she was paid a salary now she wasn't required to dance.

Big K sat blowing smoke rings from his cigar as he watched Renee fussing at the three bartenders at the bar.

"So G, you feeling this man? You ready?"

"Yeah I'm ready; I was made for this shit." Gregory sipped his champagne. He still didn't like being called G but he wasn't going to create unnecessary problems with his new business partner.

"Good to know. I need someone I know I can depend on. Loyalty is everything. I hope I can depend on you." He gave Gregory a frightening look. Gregory could tell he was sizing him up but he didn't show any fear.

"I got you Big K."

"Good. I have a couple of projects I need some help with. You down?"

Gregory sat his glass down and cleared his throat. He knew what kind of man he was. First of all, you don't say no when Big K asks for a favor, unless you didn't value your life. He was getting more nervous by the minute. He just wanted to help run the club and build his money, he didn't want to be recruited to do any side jobs for him.

"What kind of projects we talking about man?"

"Well," he sat his cigar in the ashtray and drank his shot of Patron, "I got a couple of people that I need to send a message to. They stole from me and I'm sure you know that's unforgivable."

Gregory nodded his head yes. "One person is local, locked up so that's going to be easy. The other person, it will require you and two of my boys to take a little road trip. I need this taken care of quickly and quietly. So, can you handle that?"

Shit, he thought to himself. Was Big K asking him to kill two people? Gregory wasn't a killer by any means and he didn't want to become one now. How the fuck was he going to get out of this?" Big K could see the concern on his face.

"Look man, you ain't getting your hands dirty, I just need you to oversee everything. Give direction and instruction. Got it?"

"Got it. I'm down." He was relieved. Big K slid him a piece of paper.

"Here's the two names and all the information you need."

Gregory took the paper and opened it. His eyes widened and he smiled ear to ear. It was too good to be true. He read the two names again to make sure his mind wasn't playing tricks on him, Lydia Marie Morrell and Anthony Jose Morrell.

THE END